The Sinclair Seven

ROYAL COWBOY

GEMMA SNOW

ENTWINED PUBLISHING

Royal Cowboy
ISBN # 978-1-80250-618-1
©Copyright Gemma Snow 2025
Cover Art by Erin Dameron-Hill ©Copyright November 2025
Interior text design by Entwined Publishing
Published by Entice, an Entwined Publishing imprint

Published in 2025 by Entwined Publishing, United Kingdom.

Entwined Publishing is a division of Totally Entwined Group Limited.

ROYAL COWBOY

Dedication

To Eunice and Sarina, who always pick up the
call.

Prologue

"With this reallocation of the discretionary fund, we'll be able to increase resource distribution to Title IV qualifying programs, without raising the taxes on citizens under the personal income threshold, as indicated in Article III."

Raffaello knew he was losing his audience. Around the room, glassy-eyed representatives were beginning to nod off, several doodling on their copies of his latest proposal, at least two openly sleeping in the House of Lords. He knew that tax allocations and distributions weren't the most exciting topic, but this was important work that would affect the day-to-day lives of their constituents, and it was worth sitting through a few boring House sessions to improve life in Contanari.

If nothing else, he *was* the Royal Prince, and generations of tradition dictated that he was deserving of respect for his title alone. Rafe might not agree, except for the fact that one of the representatives was now snoring three feet away from him.

He paused his presentation.

"I understand that the topic of tax exemptions and discretionary funds is lacking in its excitement. But each of you was elected to your position to represent the citizens of your district. There is no greater honor than speaking for your people."

Anger was rising in his chest now, and with it, a headache pulsed at his temples, beating hard against his skull. He had worked for a week straight to finalize the economic proposal and so had a team of government accountants. Hell, he had worked tirelessly for fifteen years straight, ever since he had been old enough to understand that the future of the nation rested on his shoulders, ever since his father had impressed upon him the importance of caring for his people.

"Now, if anyone before me feels they are no longer capable of performing the role to which they were democratically elected, I urge you to step forward and we will hold a special election for your replacement with all due haste. Otherwise, it is in your very best interest to *wake up*."

There was an assortment of murmured responses, but, to no one's surprise, not a single representative stepped forward. Instead, they all straightened and began flipping through the thick proposals before them.

Raffaello glanced at his top advisor, who stood beside the podium. Madison was older than Raffaello, nearing his fortieth birthday to hear some say it, fiftieth to hear others, sixtieth, still to a group who insisted he couldn't have achieved all that was said of him in such a short life. Madison had been by Raffaello's side since the day he had stepped into his first meeting in Lords, and Rafe trusted his advice above all else.

When Madison gave him a tight, nearly imperceptible nod, Rafe knew that his words, while harsh, were true. Perhaps the only person cared more about the political condition of Le Isole del Contanari than Rafe was Christoph Madison.

"As I explained before, we'll be relying on the remaining quarter three discretionary funds to increase distribution to…"

Rafe frowned. "To increase distribution to Article III."

No, that wasn't right. Article III was a section of the proposal in his hands. A proposal that had started to blur into harsh black lines on a very bright white page.

"Allocation to…citizens."

The words were right, he was sure of it, but they didn't *sound* right. They sounded as if they were coming through a tunnel or spoken under water, echoey and watery and difficult to make out, like he was climbing to the top of Monte Verde in the middle of a storm, like he was standing at the shore as the waves came bursting in with the tide, crashing and loud.

From far, far away, he could hear Madison calling his title, and then his name, again, and again.

Raffaello tried to respond, but he felt so *tired*, his limbs too weighted to hold up, his head a boulder on weakening shoulders, his eyelids so heavy he couldn't keep them open to see the House around him.

And then it didn't matter because he was falling, falling hard and fast, and completely without planning to, and blissfully, thankfully, before he hit the ground, everything went dark.

Chapter One

Raffaello pulled his horse to a stop and looked out over the vast Montana mountains. It didn't matter how many times he returned to Duchess, or how many months he had spent in these mountains the summer he had worked at Beau Sinclair's Ranch, they never failed to take his breath away.

Contanari was a string of small island nations, surrounded by aquamarine water, blossoming bougainvillea vines in rich purples and pinks, lemon and orange trees dotting the craggy mountainsides.

Montana was mountainous in an entirely different way, as if carved by old gods, ancient and grand, and completely...

Free.

It had been a month since he had passed out in the House of Lords, panicking the daylights out of a room of representatives, and pulling his own father from an important summit to meet him and the palace doctor in the private wing of the hospital.

Exhaustion, the doctor had explained. Overwork, lack of sleep, low iron, and good old-fashioned burnout. It should have come as a relief, but to Rafe, it was its own kind of dire diagnosis.

The path to recovery was rest.

Rafe hadn't taken a day off in over fifteen years, not when he had been at university, not when he'd done his Servizio term, the nation's required term of service, not when he'd spent the summer in these very mountains working as a ranch hand. He thrived on hard work, on solving impossible puzzles, on putting the final punctuation on difficult proposals or treaties.

And he'd been put on a strict work ban for at least six weeks.

Which was why he was meandering the trails of the Montana mountains. If he was back in the palace, with the private hallway to his office and access to his representatives and royal court, the temptation to work would be far too high. And what was the point of owning a ranch in Montana with six of his closest friends if he couldn't escape every time he passed out in the House of Lords?

Of course, The Ranch wasn't just a lodge for tourists wanting to enjoy the bursting fiery colors of the mountainside. It was also a secret club for people whose desires ran darker than most, a hidden oasis in the wilderness.

Besides his co-owners and their partners, no one knew of Rafe's involvement in the erotic club. It would be unbecoming of a Royal Prince to be connected to such a project, even if it was completely above board and they took every precaution to create a safe, welcoming environment.

But when Beau Sinclair had died and left The Sinclair Ranch to Rafe and the other six men he'd worked with that summer, the Sinclair Seven, they had been called, it had given them another gift altogether — the gift of connection. Even though Rafe lived thousands of kilometers away, even though Reece was more often than not found in the back country, and Gabriel in cities around the world, The Ranch and its secrets pulled them back to each other.

Of course, it had been a long time since Rafe had found *connections* of his own at The Ranch. His life was too busy, too complicated for relationships, too demanding for the kind of time and energy it took to give himself to another person.

Maybe his doctor had been a *little* bit correct in recommending time away from work.

Only a little.

Before Rafe could consider that damning thought much further, his phone rang, a shrill, cutting sound that broke the peaceful quiet of the mountain and made Rafe's horse whinny in protest.

Rafe reached for his phone. It was his private number, held only by close friends and family, and for a second, his stomach dropped.

Father.

Except it wasn't his father calling, or any of his father's aids who knew to reach out to him only in the case of true emergency. Instead, an old friend's name flashed across the screen.

"Anthony, to what do I owe the pleasure?"

Anthony chuckled. "Cut the bullshit, Your Highness. I know you're bored out of your wits."

Rafe grinned. Attending university as the prince of a nation had been challenging. But with Anthony Marchand, Prince of Fontaine, as his dormmate, they had almost been able to feel like kids off on their own for the first time, rather than royal sons. If anyone knew how difficult it was for Rafe to relax, it was the man who'd dragged him out of the library and to any party he could find, in a desperate attempt to help him enjoy his youth.

"You're right, of course," Rafe replied. "Though the riding is better here."

Riding had been his favorite sport since he had been old enough to stand on his own two feet. The summer he'd been in Montana had served many purposes, but it had opened Rafe's world to the possibilities of horseback explorations and open-sky adventures that had only made him fall more in love.

"Actually, Highness, that's why I'm calling."

Rafe frowned, and not because Anthony was using the same ridiculous nickname he'd used since their days at university. "What's going on?"

Anthony sighed. "Do you remember my sister, Charlotte?"

Rafe wracked his brain. Charlotte had been in primary and middle school when he'd been in university, but he did have some memories of a blonde-haired, pigtailed little girl trailing her big brother around. "Of course."

Anthony was quiet for a moment. "She took off, Raffello." That he didn't use Rafe's nickname was an indication of just how serious the situation was. "She's been gone over a week, Barcelona, I think, and Amsterdam. But by the time we show up, she disappears again."

"What's she running from, Anthony?" Rafe asked. He hadn't known Charlotte well, but she had always been bold and strong-willed, demanding to go sailing with them, or engaging in spirited debates at the dinner table when Rafe came to visit. Surely, she'd had a reason for the sudden departure.

"It's complicated," Anthony finally said. "But for now, we've tracked her down and she's in the United States."

People from Contanari always underestimated the size of the country. Rafe had done it himself the first time he'd traveled to Montana, asking how far a train ride it would be to visit New York City. The others had laughed at him, both for believing the East Coast was close enough to visit after a long shift, and for expecting there to be a train from the wilds of Montana. America was vast and ever-changing, he had learned in his time out West, and full of great, ancient beauties.

Still, he owed his old friend some grace, and it very much sounded as though Anthony was already at the edge. "Where in America?" he asked.

Anthony let out a dry laugh. "Give me some credit, Raffaello. I know your adopted home is a big place. I'm only calling because she's in Helena, at least as far as we know."

Helena *was* close, the nearest big city to Duchess, and it wasn't like Rafe had a lot else going on just at that moment.

Or for the next two weeks.

This was good. He needed a task, even if that task was playing babysitter to some lively princess who clearly didn't know what was good for her.

"You want me to bring her home." It wasn't a question.

Anthony made a sound of agreement. "She's been one step ahead of me all week, Rafe. I just... I just want to make sure she's okay. Charlotte has never been the type to take off like this."

That gave Rafe pause. "What changed?"

"I don't know," Anthony replied. "I honestly don't. But it feels like she's running from something, not picking up her phone, never staying in one place too long. I... I just need to make sure she's safe."

Rafe didn't want to admit it, but the favor Anthony was asking was exactly what he needed. Charlotte was obviously a challenge, a puzzle to be solved, and it wasn't going to be easy. He'd been wallowing in self-pity and frustration since the doctor had told him rest or he would make it bedrest, and Rafe's friends had threatened to take away his laptop and his tablet if he didn't *enjoy* his time away from the office.

But he would be *helping a friend*, nothing more. It was a simple drive to Helena and back. Surely no one could find fault with that.

"Not a problem," Rafe said into the phone. "Send me everything you can. I'll go pick her up tonight."

Chapter Two

Charli let the music carry her body, and all her worries. She had never expected to find a good dance club in the middle of nowhere, America — which it turned out made up a rather large part of the country — but with a few bats of her eyelashes, she'd been able to charm the information out of two skateboarders hanging around the bus station, who had told her about an abandoned warehouse known for its underground parties.

She didn't know much about the American party scene, but she had to admit that the arthouse DJ who'd set up his gear on some overturned milk crates was actually pretty good. The room was alive with the pulsing beat, and strobe lights had been hung from the ceiling, so it looked as though they were all moving together, just anonymous bodies undulating on instinct.

In Montana, she was most definitely anonymous. No doubt Anthony would search the major cities first, New York and Los Angeles, but she was getting wise to his games, and rather than blending into a big city, she'd picked the smallest town she could fly into without hanging around Schiphol Airport any longer than necessary.

Bozeman, Montana.

The airport was so small, she had exited at Gate One and had been able to see all seven of the available gates without straining her neck. But she had also seen the mountains rising in the background, glistening in purple and gold, and somehow, despite all that had happened in the last week, despite how her life had been turned completely upside down by the people she had trusted most in the world, she had felt...safe.

Montana was a refuge. A refuge of loud bass drops and flashes of neon light and the smell of cheap beer, but exactly what she needed. It would take Anthony weeks to find her in a place like this, and in that time, she'd be able to come up with a plan.

Yeah. A plan.

Like there was any way out of the situation that didn't include an estrangement, abdication, or suspicious circumstances.

Enjoy the music, Charli. Just enjoy the music.

Letting herself get carried away by the beat was a much better idea than letting herself get carried away by the worry and the fear and the anxiety. She deserved a night off, a night to let go, and maybe find some company that didn't refer to her by title.

Company like the man who was watching her from the bar with a dark look in his eyes. There was something deeply intimate about an affair with a stranger. She could let herself be free for a night, without having to worry about what was right or acceptable for a woman of her standing. She could confess, to herself as much as her partner, exactly what drove her to the edge, a world separate from the rules and responsibilities of the high society that normally dictated her life.

At least, she could have, if she had ever found a stranger in a dark club before.

The man at the bar wore a pair of dark, form-fitting jeans and a cropped T-shirt that rode up to expose the hint of a belly button ring. It flashed and twinkled in the bursting strobe lights, not so different from the man's eyes when he caught and held her gaze, a little dark and a little dangerous.

Perhaps she should have been more wary of meeting strangers in warehouse dance clubs, but so much of Charli's life was scripted and curated and strategized. She hadn't been able to enjoy wild years in university like other girls her age, or get her driver's license, or have social media profiles with pictures from concerts or camping trips. For tonight, for the moment, she was free, to be a regular person, to just be… Charli.

And a little tiny part of her had to admit, in the dark, in the anonymous, pulsing club, that she was drawn to the danger of it all, the spark of fear that accompanied the pleasure of being seen, the burst of adrenaline she got from doing the things she knew she shouldn't do. She *craved* it, in a deep and carnal kind of way, and nothing was going to stop her from going after what she wanted.

Nothing.

She moved toward the man at the bar, allowing the music and the crowd to carry her along. He was rather pretty, his hair long, his cheekbones high, a bar running through his ear, and rivers of ink running up both arms.

They didn't speak. Not with words, at least.

Instead, Charli reached out her hand, and he took it, following her to the dance floor. His fingers were rough, and when he placed his other hand at the small of her back to guide her through the crowd, it sent a thrill coursing through her body. She didn't know his name, didn't want to know his name, and he didn't know that she was the princess to a small island nation that no one had ever heard of.

For the night, for the moment, they spoke with their bodies, writhing to the electronic dance music that shook the warehouse walls, letting instinct take over when he pulled her close and pinned her hips with strong hands.

His tight pants did little to hide his arousal, and that only made Charli more aware of her own. She loved the pull, loved the idea of drawing out a hot, needy response from her partner, pushing them to the edge of their control until they were both drowning in the deep end.

The stranger leaned down and whispered in her ear, "Do you want to get out of here?"

Part of her did. Part of her wanted to take him by the hand and drag him through the back door into the alley, where they could unzip and unbutton just as much as was absolutely necessary. The other part of her wanted to see if he would try his luck with the hem of her skirt right there on the dancefloor.

Before she could respond though, a large figure stepped in front of them, blocking the strobe lights and causing Charli to stumble for the first time all night.

"She'll be leaving, but not with you."

The light flashed, illuminating the man in front of her and…

Charli gasped. She couldn't help it. Never in a million years could she have expected to see… Raffaello Chiaramonte at a random warehouse club in the middle of America.

The *fucking* Royal Prince.

You have got *to be kidding me.*

He stood out from the crowd, not just for his perfectly coiffed hair, unpierced ears, and skin free of ink of any kind. It was the way he held himself, in the sea of movement and looseness, ramrod straight, strong and imposing, accustomed to getting everything he wanted.

Because he usually did.

Because he was a *royal prince.*

And her brother's best friend from university, which was no doubt the real reason he was standing in front of her, interrupting what had otherwise promised to be a delightful night for everyone involved.

"Hey, man," the stranger at Charli's back said, pulling her in close, "this doesn't concern you."

"On the contrary, *man.*" Prince Raffaello's accent was barely perceptible over the beating music, but the mockery came through without question. "This concerns me a great deal. And it will concern you, as well, if you would like to avoid an international summons. I have the director of Interpol on speed dial."

The guy raised his hands. "I'm not looking for trouble, my guy."

Before Charli could get a word in edgewise, the stranger disappeared into the crowds, muttering under his breath about how *she's not hot enough to get my ass kicked over.*

Charli crossed her arms and glared at Prince Raffaello, the two of them the only people standing still on the busy, pulsing dancefloor. "What the hell?"

Raffaello barely raised an eyebrow at her question, only mirrored her pose, strong and unyielding against the tide of dancers all around them.

And then it was like the music and the lights and all the strangers faded into the background, like Charli was standing on the empty streets of some western town one hundred years in the past, staring down the sheriff, both of them a hairsbreadth from pulling the trigger. A standoff in a warehouse dance club in the middle of fuck-all America, and she wasn't going to be the one to back down first.

"He seemed like a *nice* guy, Charlotte," Raffaello said, breaking the heavy silence between them. "So glad to see that you're spending your time with such upstanding characters."

"It's *Charli*," she bit out. "And I don't remember it being any of your business who I spend time with, *Prince* Raffaello."

"It's my business when your brother, the Prince of Fontaine and my best friend, calls me in a panic because you've run away from home."

Charli scoffed. "I'm not a child. I can't *run away from home*. I'm a grown woman."

Too late, Charli remembered exactly what she was wearing, a micro leather skirt that rode up to mid-thigh with every movement, chunky boots that at least gave her a fighting chance at meeting Raffaello's gaze head on, though he still towered over her, and a mesh black tee over a lacy black bra. The glistening silver jewelry, a slip chain necklace and several chunky rings perfectly complemented the overall ensemble, but no doubt that wasn't what Raffaello was looking at now. Not a single piece of the outfit, from her leather jacket to her crimson lipstick would have ever been chosen by the palace stylist, and they both knew it.

Raffaello, for his part, looked as though he were a royal prince in the back country of Montana. He wore a perfectly fitted suit, expensive Italian loafers, and a designer pea coat made of fine wool.

What would it be like to have the advantage over a man like Prince Raffaello Chiaramonte rather than standing there like the child she insisted she wasn't, suddenly feeling exposed in an outfit she had so enjoyed picking out? This was supposed to be *her* space, her escape from all the chaos exploding back in Fontaine, and he had ruined it.

So, prince or not, he didn't get to come into her space and make her feel bad.

"Why didn't Anthony come get me himself?" She'd been rather enjoying outsmarting her brother. He thought he was clever, putting a tracker on her phone, but what he hadn't known was that she was tracking his phone in return. Every time she got the notification that he was on the way, she packed up and hauled out.

Except, of course, Charli couldn't have known that he'd send the *Royal Prince* of the country to come bring her home.

"He says you've been evading him," Raffaello said, raising his voice to be heard over the bass drop in the next song. "Why are you here, Charlotte?"

That made her see red, made her dig her nails into the flesh of her palms until the half-moons in her skin throbbed in pain. She was avoiding her brother because she didn't know if she could trust him, didn't know how much he knew about their father's insane decision, a decision over which she had no sway, even if it would affect the rest of *her* life.

As for the rest of it. "I said, my name is *Charli*."

She turned, ready to make for the exit, to find some way back to the hotel and out of Montana before Anthony showed up.

But she didn't get very far before Raffaello grabbed her wrist, his much stronger hand pausing her escape. She tried to focus on the anger, on the righteous indignation of being treated like a child, and not like the grown woman she was, but the white-hot fury was ebbing away, frustration blurring at the edges into something else altogether, a need she had tried so hard to suppress, but which never seemed to go away for long.

Other women didn't want to be bound by strong hands across their wrists, or pinned at the hips, or pushed against the wall until there was no escape. She was sure of that. But Charli *ached* for it, and in the dead of night, fantasized about finding the relief she craved in anonymous strangers in hidden clubs.

Prince Raffaello was *not* an anonymous stranger.

She tugged at her wrist trying to break his hold, but he held firm. "Charlotte. We are leaving," he said firmly, the voice of a true political leader, not someone accustomed to being denied.

"You can leave," she replied. "I'm staying here. And unless you want to drag me out of here like some royal caveman, there's not a damn thing you can do about it."

She had expected him to leave. Or maybe to make some dry cutting remark about the propriety she always failed to live up to, or even to call her brother right there on the dancefloor.

What she hadn't expected was for Raffaello Chiaramonte, Royal Prince of Le Isole del Contanari, to pick her up and throw her over his shoulder.

The room tilted, and it took Charli a moment to realize she was seeing everything upside down. A few people gave them funny looks, but the party was too loud and the room too dark for anyone to see much more than the strange figure of Raffaello literally carrying her out of the club.

She beat her fists against his back, the blows landing on soft wool, and barely seeming to register at all.

"I'm going to tell the press about this," Charli shouted. "I'm going to tell the whole country that you're a bully…"

"No, you're not," Raffaello replied. "Because then you'd have to explain the situation in which you were at a…dance club in the first place. And I'm certain you wouldn't want to put your family in any kind of uncomfortable position."

Actually, after the last week, Charli didn't much give a shit about what her family's standing in society was. But she had no intention of telling the prince that. No doubt the royals were perfectly familiar with what went on in the halls of their lands. Hell, Raffaello might even be responsible for suggesting it in the first place.

"Your *Highness*, put me down," Charli demanded, beating on his back again. Even through the wool, she could feel the strong cords of back muscles there, likely from holding himself so ramrod straight all these years.

"No," Raffaello said simply. "If I put you down, you'll run, and I have no intention of chasing you."

At that moment, he stepped out of the club's basement stairwell, bringing them into the biting cold of the Montana fall night. It hadn't been nearly so frigid when she had arrived at the club, and in her upside-down state, she caught sight of snowflakes landing on an already thickening layer of fresh snow. A few fell on her exposed legs, the microskirt no longer looking like the brilliant option it had been back at the hotel, and she shivered despite herself.

"We're almost to the car," Raffaello said.

"I'm not going anywhere with you," Charli bit back, though nothing sounded better than being inside of a warm car right at that moment. She was born and raised on a Mediterranean island, for goodness' sake. She was neither experienced with or properly dressed for a cold and snowy night in the mountains.

"You are going directly to the airport with me," he replied. "And then we'll be boarding a plane back home, from which you cannot and will not escape."

Like she was going to jump out of a plane to avoid returning to Fontaine.

Actually, worth it.

Anything would be worth it, to avoid doing her father's bidding, to stay true to herself, no matter what.

She struggled against Raffaello's hold. If she was contemplating jumping out of plane to avoid going home, certainly she couldn't be afraid about fighting one, unarmed prince.

But wiggle as she did, Charli still couldn't get free of his grip. He was so much bigger than her, and he pinned her against his back and shoulders with such a strong, firm hand, and maybe just a tiny part of her was leaning into him for the warmth, because she might not have to worry about going home after all, since she was about to freeze to death.

"Stop moving," Raffaello instructed, and there was that odd pull again, that need to fight against an instruction just because she didn't want to do as she was told, that ache that made her feel like a fraud in a doll house, the princess at the palace with sinful and dangerous desires.

"No," she said, thrashing again.

"Charlotte, stop moving." When Raffaello spoke, his voice was no longer the controlled tenor of the lifelong politician. It wasn't polished or diplomatic, or the articulated syllables of a high-class education. No, it was the tone of a man demanding, promising something so dark and wicked in the unspoken.

Do as I say or you won't like the consequences.

All once, Charli saw the veil fall, for a second, for the briefest second, and she saw the man behind the prince. Perhaps a man who asked for more the way she had never let herself, perhaps a man who wielded his power in practices that had nothing to do with politics or nation states.

And it was so disarming, so deep in her psyche to respond to that tone that Charli couldn't help herself.

She stopped moving.

They had arrived at his car. She hadn't realized how far away from the club they were, focused as she had been on not getting sick from having her head upside down for too long, but Raffaello was opening the door to a large SUV and, without the ceremony she might have expected from a prince of his reputation, tossing her into the back seat like a load of laundry.

She yelped as she landed on the leather bench, but to Charli's surprise, it was already warm and toasty in the cabin of the SUV. He had apparently started the heater sometime in their eventful walk over from the club.

Which would not endear him to her. It would not.

When Rafe climbed into the driver's seat, Charli poked him on the shoulder. "Drop me off at the hotel," she said. "My stuff is there."

"I'll send someone to collect it later," he replied. "We're going to the airport."

Except the sky was growing lighter, a steel gray that she was quickly coming to understand meant a snowstorm was on the horizon. It was only mid-October, and back home they'd still be swimming and sailing in the sunshine, but apparently the American West got winter early, and fat snowflakes were falling fast and hard, spotting the windshield and covering the road as Raffaello pulled away from the curb.

He peered out of the windshield and up at the sky. Then he made a quick call on the SUV's audio system. "Madison, any chance we can fly out of Bozeman tonight?"

On the other end of the phone, Raffaello's top advisor responded, crackly and difficult to hear, but Charli could make out the most important parts. "Air traffic is grounding flights out tonight. There's a major blizzard headed your way."

Charli couldn't help herself. She turned away from Raffaello and looked out of the window to the snowstorm around them. She'd been in New York City for New Year's Eve once, but the snow had been gray and slushy, piling up at the edges of the crosswalks and making it difficult to walk without tracking muddy salt that stuck to the bottom of her boots.

This, this was something else altogether, bright, sparkly flakes falling quickly and piling up as Raffaello navigated them out of the small corner of town and through the streets of Helena, which were already quiet for the night.

She tuned back into Raffaello's conversation, only to hear the very last thing he said. "Tell Anthony we'll be in Montana a little longer. We'll leave for home when the storm clears."

When he ended the call, the cabin of the SUV fell quiet, and Charli couldn't help but marvel at the fact that Prince Raffaello was actually driving them, no driver in sight. She could only imagine the kind of freedom that would give her.

And speaking of freedom…

"So, we're not going to the airport?" she asked, like there was any way she hadn't heard the end of the conversation.

"No," Raffaello replied. "We're not going to the airport."

Charli bristled. For a man of diplomacy and politics, he seemed to have an incredible ability to rub her in all the wrong ways. "Then exactly where *are* we going?"

Raffaello briefly caught her gaze in the rearview mirror, piercing blue eyes turned nearly to steel in the bright light of the snowstorm around them. "We're going to The Ranch."

Chapter Three

Charli stirred to life slowly. She was warm and cozy, which meant she couldn't possibly be back home in Contanari, where they slept with the windows open all year long and made their comforters from linen and fine cotton.

No, for the moment she was wrapped in a thick, heavy blanket, pulled up to her nose. She should open her eyes, figure out exactly where she had ended up after going to a sketchy warehouse club in an anonymous city and...

All at once, memories of the night before came flooding back to her — the club, the *prince* showing up and all but kidnapping her, throwing her into the back of his SUV before bringing her to...

Where the hell am I?

That finally prompted her to look around, and Charli opened her eyes with some reluctance, as sleep and warmth threatened to drag her down again. But she had to keep her wits about her, had to find a way to keep from going back to her father and everything he threatened.

I could appeal to the prince.

She could. Assuming that he wasn't the mountain on high from which the directive had come down. More importantly, she hadn't exactly given him the sweet, deferential treatment a prince of the realm was accustomed to. And he had *thrown her over his shoulder and carried her out of the club like a sack of potatoes.*

Charli pushed up to sit, wanting to take any advantage she could in this strange room in this strange situation. At once, she realized she wasn't wearing the same clothes she had worn to the club. Instead of mesh and leather, she had on a pair of cozy flannel PJs in a red and black check.

"It's early. You should go back to sleep."

Charli turned to see Raffaello sitting at the desk in the corner of the room. Unlike her, he wasn't covered head to toe. Instead, he wore only low-slung flannel pajama bottoms and a pair of round, wire-rimmed glasses he was using to read the page in front of him.

"I didn't know you wore glasses." Charli had no idea why that was the thought that managed to free itself from her confused and sleep-addled brain, but it was possible she had shorted out at the sight of the prince looking so much…

Like a man.

Now there was a dangerous thought to have. Especially now, when her future was balanced so precariously on the knife's edge.

"There is quite a lot you don't know about me, Charlotte."

She gritted her teeth. "Charli."

Raffaello raised a brow. "Since when?"

Charli shrugged. "Since I realized that I was never going to be able to pick out my own clothes or my own future, so I thought I'd change what I could."

Raffaello studied her intently. "Speaking of clothes," he said, "yours are in the dryer." He turned back to the papers before him.

"I don't remember removing them last night," Charli muttered.

Raffaello shot her a look of admonishment. "You were completely passed out by the time we arrived. I figured you would want to sleep in something more comfortable than"—he gestured toward the door, and presumably the laundry room—"whatever you would call that."

He couldn't understand what it had meant to her to pick out clothes of her own the first time she had done it, to wear red lipstick, only to wipe it off with a dozen tissues, to slide on thick, weighty rings because she liked them, not because they belonged to some long-dead royal. He couldn't possibly see the importance of a mesh T-shirt and combat boots for a girl like her.

"And I assume you wiggled me in these…"

"No," Raffaello replied. "Saint and Rhylee helped."

She had no idea who Saint and Rhylee were, but Charli knew she should have been relieved that Raffaello had lived up to his honorable, gentlemanly reputation. And she absolutely shouldn't have been disappointed at all.

Not. At. All.

Instead of pushing further, Charli looked around the room. It was nothing like her family's palace, with its opulence and circumstance. In fact, she would never have known that the room housed a royal prince, if not for the details in royal blue that seemed to bring all the pieces of the room together, elegant and refined, much like Raffaello himself. The rest of the room seemed to mirror an old hunting lodge or mountain cabin, a large fire roaring in the fireplace, a wall of windows looking out over the mountains, where the snow spilled fast and hard from the sky.

Charli couldn't help herself. She jumped up from the bed and ran to the windows, aware of Raffaello's dark gaze upon her, and not caring one bit as she pressed her hands to the glass. She had expected it to be cool, but no doubt he had some kind of heater installed, so she imagined the cold, imagined what it would be like to roll down the hill in the fluffy snowbanks, just as she had seen in the movies.

She turned to Raffaello. "Can we go out in it?"

Raffaello shook his head. "No."

Charli pursed her lips. "I've just never seen snow like this," she said. "I promise, I won't go anywhere." It was jarring how she still had to *behave*, still had to stay within her keeper's reach, but the promise of the bright, fresh snow overshadowed that dark thought.

"No one is going anywhere right now," Raffaello replied. "We're grounded here for at least a few days with this storm."

Which mean she had a brief stay of execution.

Thank God for some small favors, at least.

After a moment, full understanding dawned, and Charli turned away from the window to look at him, though it was a bit of effort to keep her eyes trained on his face, not straying to his strong, muscled chest.

"Where is *here* exactly, Highness?"

Raffaello groaned. "You Marchands are going to the best the death of me. This is The Sinclair Ranch."

It was Charli's turn to groan. "You don't have to pay per word," she muttered.

The corner of Raffaello's mouth lifted in the smallest hint of a smile. It was only then that she realized just how tired the prince looked. Under the rim of his glasses were dark circles that came from so much more than one late night. His dark blond hair was ruffled and mussed, as if he had been pulling at it, and his fingers seemed to tremble ever so slightly, making the pen in his hand bounce against the surface of the desk.

"Very well," Raffaello finally replied. "You recall that my father sent me to America the summer before university."

Charli nodded. It had been a big deal for the young prince to go off and labor on an American farm, part of his Servizio, and the image of Raffaello in a cowboy hat waving good-bye from the steps of the royal plane still circulated on slow news days.

Raffaello continued, "I worked this ranch with six other boys, about my age. We became very close friends. They…treated me like a normal person."

She could appreciate that more than he knew, the need to be seen for something other than the title. Perhaps there was common ground to be found between her and the prince after all.

"The owner, Beau Sinclair, he treated us like we were his own boys. Kept a bunch of wild, rowdy kids in line that summer. They called us the Sinclair Seven."

Charli couldn't quite picture the prince as rowdy or wild, but it was difficult to forget the tone in his voice the night before, the one that had caught her by the middle and dragged her down, that had made her wonder if maybe there was something more to Raffaello's strong and stern exterior.

"That was over a decade ago," she replied. "Do you come back to visit?"

Raffaello shook his head. "Beau passed some years ago. But he left the ranch to us. All of us, and made certain we couldn't sell it. "

"He kept his family together," Charli said without thinking. But the spark in Raffaello's eyes told her she had hit the nail on the head. This was his sanctuary, his home away from home, and he had brought her to it.

"No one knew where you were recovering," Charli said quietly. "But you've been in America the whole time."

Raffaello nodded. "I have. And your brother knew. That's why he asked for my help."

At the mention of her brother, Charli's stomach soured. "I don't want to talk about him right now."

Raffaello shrugged. "Would you prefer to discuss what you've done with your hair?"

Charli couldn't help but grin. She fingered the blunt, short edges of what had been long, blonde curls only the day before. "Do you like it?"

Raffaello was clearly trying his best not to laugh. "I'm assuming you cut it yourself in the hotel room right before you walked out of the door."

That was *exactly* what she had done, a moment of total freedom as Charli had made a decision for herself she'd been wanting to make for over a decade. But she wasn't about to tell him any of that, not while he had that know-it-all expression on his face.

"What's wrong with it?" she asked, suddenly feeling uncertain about the decision she'd been so sure of the night before. Her hair was always talked about in the society papers, and some stylist or photographer was always messing with, tugging or pulling her this way or that, and she had just wanted to be free of it.

"Nothing is wrong," Raffaello said indulgently. "You look…" He paused, as if the words were difficult for him to get out. "It's actually a good look for you, Charlotte. But Anthony is going to have...words."

"I don't care," she practically yelled. It was difficult not to yell when discussing her brother. "I don't care what Anthony thinks or what my father thinks or the newspapers or any of them. And—" Charli walked up to Raffaello, close enough that she could see the spiral of curls that fell over his forehead, that she could see the crinkle of lines at the corners of his eyes. "And I don't care what *you* think, Highness."

Raffaello stood, and only then, without her combat boots or the armor of leather, did Charli realize how much *bigger* he was than her. He was tall and strong, lithe from years of riding and swimming and polo, and he towered over her small frame, looking down upon her in so many more ways than one. In the normal order of course, Charli wore heels as part of her princess uniform, but at the moment, she was barefoot, standing just a few breaths away from the shirtless prince, and the storm was swirling outside and...

It was just them. No palaces, no lands, no titles. Just Rafe and Charli.

Rafe stepped back, before making his way into the bathroom. He closed the door most of the way, just enough so that she could hear him through the crack.

"Don't go anywhere without my say so, Charlotte. I want you to stay in this room until I return."

She wanted to stick her tongue out at him, but managed to rely on years of formal training to resist at the last moment. "I'm not your prisoner, Prince Raffaello. You can't just hold me hostage here."

He stepped out of the bathroom, dressed, once more, for the real world. On a cozy, snowy day, it felt wrong to see him in a full suit, hair coiffed and smelling of expensive cologne. But that was the prince, always one for formality and dignity.

She, on the other hand…

Raffaello sighed in response to her outburst. "You're not a hostage, Charlotte. But you haven't exactly been acting trustworthy, you must admit. Show me you're not about to start trekking the wilderness and we'll revisit the issue."

He was so…controlled. Like nothing in life seemed to throw him off balance, except maybe Charli herself. And that meant she *very* much wanted to throw him off balance.

He seemed to sense her instinct to fight and stepped toward the door. "I'll send breakfast up. Do you still like pineapple juice in the morning?"

Charli faltered. She hadn't realized he had been paying attention all those times he had visited on school breaks. "Um, yes."

With a tight nod, Raffaello walked out into the hallway, closing the door behind him.

And Charli was alone again.

Chapter Four

If there was one thing Raffaello Chiaramonte had learned early on in life, it was that gossip was currency. The greenest house maid could learn of an illicit affair after finding pink undergarments hidden under the bed, and become the de facto leader of the household staff until the next tantalizing tidbit came along. A veteran gardener, a grade-school teacher, a fencing instructor, no one was immune to the power of gossip, and more often than not, that gossip centered on Raffaello and his family.

Which was why he shouldn't have been surprised when he walked into the back kitchen at The Ranch to find his best and oldest friends immediately quieting upon his entry, and looking extremely guilty.

Of the Sinclair Seven, only Bastion was missing, out on tour, no doubt. The other five of his brothers, and their respective partners, Skylar, Morgan, Emerson, and Saint, were all doing their damnedest not to make eye contact when Rafe finally closed the door behind him.

Rhylee Cash, who was seated on one of the kitchen counters, leaned forward with a devilish grin on her face. She was Caleb's sister, but in the years since they had opened The Ranch together, she had become a de facto sister to all of them, driven, bright, and always sticking her nose where it didn't belong.

Raffaello glanced behind Rhylee, where Van stood glowering.

Perhaps not like a sister to *all* of them.

But he didn't have a moment to think on it because Rhylee raised a brow. "So."

Raffaello sighed. "So."

She shook her head. "So, you kidnapped a princess and brought her to your tower. Like. An *actual* princess."

Raffaello scoffed despite himself. "I happen to be an *actual* prince."

Rhylee shrugged. "The novelty has worn off. But you kidnapping someone is a whole new thing."

Raffaello shook his head. "I didn't kidnap her. I'm returning her to her family as soon as the snow clears."

Saint cleared her throat. She was one of the quieter of his friends' women, but he had first met her in the hospital after Dante had been injured by his criminal father, and Saint's resilience, strength, and quiet fortitude never failed to impress. "At the risk of overstepping, are we sure she wants to go back to her family? She must have a reason for…running away."

Raffaello knew only pieces of what had first brought Saint to Montana the previous year, but she had been on the run from forces outside of her control. He considered her words carefully, and the way that

Charlotte had reacted when he'd first arrived at the club in Helena the night before. She had always been strong-willed, but if he hadn't picked her up and thrown her over his shoulder, Raffaello had little doubt she would have run for the hills.

Why? Why is she here?

"Maybe you can find out for me?" he asked Saint. "Charlotte...it's my understanding she's on a bit of rebellion at the moment. And that included an impromptu haircut."

Saint shook her head, but there was a smile on her face. "I used to cut my grandmother's hair when she could no longer leave the house. I'm sure we can manage something."

Raffaello nodded. "I appreciate it. And I would appreciate it if you all kept this to yourself. Charlotte may be out of sorts at the moment, but she is a ranking royal."

Skylar spoke up, then, "Maybe I dropped out of high school before we covered Contanari, but how exactly is Charlotte related to you?"

For some reason, that thought made Rafe's stomach squeeze. Anthony may have been one of his closest confidants at university, but in no, way, shape, or form was Raffaello related to Charlotte Marchand.

"We're not," he explained. "Contanari is made up of five islands, Le Isole, each with their own royal, governing family. My island, Cielo, is the largest, a position which grants my family rule over the entire nation. My father is the King and I'm the Royal Prince. Charlotte and her brother Anthony are from the island of Fontaine. Their father is a sovereign prince."

"So not in line for the throne?" Skylar prompted.

Rafe shook his head. "Not by blood. If I fail to produce an heir, an election will be held as to who ascends to the throne from the remaining sovereigns, and he or she will rule."

"Ooh, *she*," Emerson pointed out. "That *is* within keeping with the times, isn't it?"

Raffaello grinned despite himself. At home, he was the prince of the nation. Here in Montana, with friends who worked the land and made art and followed their dreams, he was just Rafe.

It was…refreshing.

Perhaps Charlotte is running from responsibility too.

Except he wasn't running from his responsibilities. He was taking some forced rest and relaxation at the threat of having another episode. Forced rest and relaxation from the intense pressure of keeping his country running smoothly.

And what would a girl like Charlotte know about something like that?

"Contanari is still young," Raffaello explained. "Women have been allowed to inherit since we first became a sovereign nation."

And he was proud of it. He was proud of so many things about his home, of the Servizi program and the extensive education and its high quality of life, and fair wages and a million and two other matters he advocated for endlessly on the House floor. There was still much yet to be achieved, and there would always be losses with the wins, but the crown had never felt heavy, not when he had seen each and every day the importance of his work.

"I have a question that might be a little more relevant to today," Caleb said. "Do your…people, do they know you're a part owner of a sex club?"

Rafe grimaced. "They do not." He nodded at Gabriel. "We made sure to carefully hide the details of my involvement here. *Not* because I have any shame regarding what we have built."

"We understand that," Reece put in. "We all have our reasons for keeping this secret. But *how* exactly are you planning on keeping it a secret?" He looked around the room. "Not a single one of us managed to do that."

Morgan muttered to Saint at her side. "And once again, I *am* sorry for spilling the down and dirty…"

Saint laughed. "Do you hear me complaining? Not a chance."

Raffaello looked at the group of them. Skylar, he knew, had come to the club with eyes wide open, and she had become a staple in the years since she'd met Caleb. Emerson had agreed to a short-term fling with Gabriel, who had been her political rival. But Morgan had been injured by a corrupt politician and Reece had brought her to the club for sanctuary and recovery, and Saint had been on the run and working and living at Dante's shop. If Dante couldn't even keep the secret with miles between there and the club, how on earth was Raffaello going to do so with Charlotte literally living in his private quarters? If she so much as glanced in one of the drawers, she'd no doubt be scarred for life.

Although.

Although…there had been something in her eyes the previous night, something Raffaello barely recognized, so long he had been away from the play of the place, but familiar and deep and innate. She hadn't been completely horrified when he'd carried her out of the club and demanded she stop moving in his arms.

She had pushed right back, refusing to give him a centimeter, and with each refusal, that brightness in her eyes had gotten a little more wild, a little more intense, *promising*. He had been so intent on getting her in the car and to the airport, and then eventually on navigating the winter storm, that he hadn't allowed himself a moment to think about it. But all at once, it was the only thing on his mind, her refusal to bend to his direction, the obvious delight she had taken in pushing his buttons...

What would push Charlotte over the edge? What would make her finally submit?

Rafe didn't want to know. He didn't. She was his best friend's younger sister, the princess to his neighboring island, almost a decade younger than him and, most of all, an unrelenting pain in his ass.

But that's just your type, isn't it? The kind who needs to be taught a lesson, who fights for control until the very last? You've always loved a challenge.

"Earth to Prince Raffaello," Dante said, tossing a napkin at his head. "If you're going to have kinky fantasies in the kitchen, you are legally required to share."

Saint nudged his hip and whispered, not quite quietly for it to be a secret, "I thought you said we only *shared* on special occasions..."

Raffaello cleared his throat. "I...apologize. It's been a trying day."

Caleb grinned and elbowed Reece. "He's reverting back to his fancy diplomat talk. You know what that means."

Reece held up his hand in a terrible approximation of a queen's wave. "The Lord hath fallen under the spell of embarrassment, I doth declare." He couldn't continue because he was laughing too hard to lift his head up from between his knees. Caleb and Dante were both wiping tears from the corners of their eyes, and even Gabriel had a shit-eating grin on his face. Raffaello glanced at Van in the back, who hadn't spoken since they'd arrived.

When Raffaello caught his eye, however, Van gave a tight nod. It was a reassuring gesture, coming from the normally taciturn veteran, and told Raffaello that Van had his back, and the distance was his own.

"Amazing accent," Rhylee replied to Reece. "No notes." She turned back Raffaello. "While you're stuck here, how can we help with the princess?" When Raffaello raised a brow, she held her hands up in surrender. "Think of it as my penance for sending the glee club into a tizzy here."

That, of course, only made Raffaello's friends laugh harder, until even Rafe felt the edges of his lips lift up. Despite their claims that he turned on his fancy talk when he was embarrassed—and he'd never admit to the truth of it—it *had* been a trying day. He missed his work, and he *had* all but kidnapped a fellow royal at the behest of her brother.

And with all that, the thing that seemed to be weighing heaviest on Rafe's mind was the inexplicable…*ache*. He had seen something in Charlotte's eyes last night, and it was stirring some dormant, sleeping monster back to life, a version of himself he hadn't embraced in quite some time, and he wasn't entirely sure he wanted to open the door to welcome in.

"I appreciate it," he said, finally responding to Rhylee's offer. "If you don't mind checking in on her, maybe…the hair? I think Charlotte will respond more favorably to your presence than my own at the moment."

Rhylee hopped off the counter, nearly colliding with Van, who had stepped forward out of his corner in the back of the room. He steadied her around the waist, his fingers lingering a second too long before he stepped further back than necessary, muttering apologies under his breath.

Rhylee tried to shrug it off, but her cheeks were tinged with pink, and she couldn't seem to look away from Van for more than a second, her eyes returning back to him with every passing beat.

With everything going on in his own life, it was the very last thing in the world Rafe should be paying attention to. But worrying about his friends' complicated and antagonistic *situation* was far preferable to thinking about his own complicated and antagonistic situation.

He turned toward the door. He needed something to focus on, something to clear his head from the sudden tangle of possibilities he had no right to entertain.

"And where are you headed?" Dante teased.

Rafe disappeared into the hallway, calling back only when he was too far away for them to stop him. "I'm going to do some work."

Chapter Five

Charli opened the door on the second knock, righteous fury propelling her toward the door. "I cannot *believe* you left me all morning. I'm not your prisoner. You can't just order me around and tell me where I can and cannot go. My brother may be your best friend, but you are *not* my keeper... Oh."

She finally stopped her tirade when she realized it was not Raffaello Chiaramonte, Royal Prince of Contanari, on the other side of the door, but two stunning women staring at her with a mixture of amusement and reverence.

"Princess Charlotte?" the petite blonde one asked.

Charli stared for a moment, before finally recovering her manners. "Charli is fine. You are not Raffaello."

She laughed, and it was a light, fairy-like sound. Charli wasn't certain she'd even been so elegant or delicate in her life, and she had been raised to it from youth.

"Rafe thought he'd give you both a reprieve, so he sent us instead. I'm Saint and this is Rhylee."

Charli grimaced. "You two undressed me last night."

Rhylee laughed. "Better us than the prince of the realm, right? We come bearing gifts." She held up a tray laden with breakfast, coffee and a small pitcher of pineapple juice. Charli very much wanted to hate the prince in that moment, but she wasn't sure she could. He was a man of principle, to his very core.

Charli moved away from the door, allowing the women to enter, and a moment later the three of them were settled at the table sharing breakfast.

"So, what's it really like?" Rhylee asked, "being a princess?"

It was all she had ever known. From the time Charli had been old enough to see over her mother's knee, she'd been in training of some kind of another, diplomatic training, etiquette training, training, training, training… She could count on one hand the number of times she'd actually truly felt like she'd made a decision for herself, one that didn't involve a royal decree.

"It's a job," she said finally. "I love my country, and I will always fight for my people, but I wish… I wish I'd had a measure of freedom to be…me, I suppose." She hardly knew these women, and yet she was spilling her inner most thoughts to them. Maybe it was the overwhelm of feeling like she had been on her own for so long, even with a life surrounded by people. Maybe it was the absolute absurdity of sleeping in the prince's bed after he'd kidnapped her from an underground warehouse club in an anonymous city. Maybe it was the snowstorm whirling around outside.

Or maybe it was just them, these sweet, gentle women who had taken care of her, who offered her a sympathetic ear, who'd made her feel, if for a moment, what it might have been like to have real friends.

"I understand that," Saint shared quietly. "My...my grandma got sick during my first year of college. It was the most important thing in the world for me to take care of her, and I did, of course. But it did feel like my choices were made for me."

Charli nodded. "And now?"

Saint smiled. "I started art school again last year, and Dante's training me as an apprentice. It took time, but I got to start building my own life again. And..." She paused, her eyes shimmering slightly in the brightness of the storm outside. "And I know my gram would be proud of me."

Rhylee reached over and squeezed Saint's hands. "We're *all* proud of you."

Saint nodded, swallowing back her tears. "I don't mean to get so emotional," she said to Charli on a laugh. "I just feel so incredibly grateful for Dante's family. They saved me, in more ways than one."

Rhylee shook her head. "You saved yourself."

She turned back to Charli. "We're a bunch of misfits here. Even Rafe."

"The Sinclair Seven," Charli murmured.

Rhylee watched her, and Charli got the impression that there was much more below the surface of the vivacious, outgoing woman than people gave her credit for. "He told you?" Rhylee asked after a moment, "about the summer they all spent on The Sinclair Ranch?"

Charli nodded. "Bits and pieces. Prince Raffaello was lucky for it. There's a...bubble around royal life, you understand. We don't get to exist as real people in the real world. It sounds like he learned a lot that summer."

"What would you want to do?" Saint asked. "If you could do anything?"

Charli didn't have to think twice. The answer was deep in her heart and soul, and had been for the better part of a decade. Not that her father would ever allow it. Not that it could even be possible, a circumstance of birth and all that. "I want to teach."

That surprised the two women, and Charli couldn't help but laugh. "In Contanari we have Servizi. The year after you finish secondary school and before you start university, you have to serve the country."

Rhylee leaned forward. "That sounds amazing," she said. "Can you do any kind of service?"

"There are a few different options," Charli explained. "Medical training is a common path for students who want to become doctors. And some people build houses or help work community farms. Raffaello's summer here in Montana was part of his Servizi training."

"And you taught?" Saint asked.

Charli nodded. "My father offered to get me an exemption, more for himself than me, I think. But the whole point of Servizi is that we *all* give back. We all build a better country, together. I went to a village where the school had been destroyed by coastal storms and helped them rebuild."

She thought back to that year, of challenging physical labor, of early mornings and late nights spent solving problems, stretching resources, working together to create something lasting. She had thought of that summer so many times, it was a well-worn photograph in her mind, a talisman for when the road ahead felt rough and jagged.

"How do we help?" Rhylee asked, her back straight and a look of determination in her eyes.

Charli let out a startled chuckle. "What?"

Rhylee shrugged. "I'm a scientist. I see a problem and I try to find a solution. How do we get you back into a classroom?"

The truth was that Charli had considered the possibilities from every direction. It simply wasn't feasible. She was a princess, and that meant she would always been destined for something larger than herself.

"It's out of my control," she admitted. "My father, he...he has plans for my future. I don't get much of a say in them."

Saint cocked her head to the side. "What do you have control over?" she asked.

Charli reached for her phone, turning it on for the first time since she'd left for the nightclub the night before. "I'm trying to modernize the strategy for education funding." She quickly pulled up the proposal, showcasing just the abstract of the hundred-page document. "Right now, the funding is distributed by island state. If we could create a comprehensive, federal top-down approach, we wouldn't have to worry about schools going without. No one deserves a better education than anyone else."

Rhylee glanced at the proposal and then back at Charli. "Does Rafe know about this?"

Charli shook her head. "Raffaello is too close to my brother. I can't... I don't know that I can really trust him."

It was Saint's turn to look at Charli with too much insight and awareness in her pretty blue eyes. "It takes one to know one," she said quietly. "What are you running from, Charli?"

How could she tell them the truth? It was one thing to share her hopes and dreams, trivial and impossible as they seemed compared to running a nation. But the truth of what her father was trying to do was too raw. She had run in a state of adrenaline and survival, but now that was all wearing off, and she was left with the very harsh reality of what her future might hold, and how willing her family was to throw her to the wolves at the earliest convenience.

"It's not important," she murmured quietly. "I..."

Saint put her hand on Charli's. "You don't have to tell us anything unless you want to. But if you do, just know you have help here." She flicked her eyes to Rhylee. "This is a safe place to put down your burdens."

Charli tried to respond, but her throat felt tight and swollen, and she simply nodded. Saint, who was very much starting to live up to her name, held up a small cosmetics bag. "Now, I know a thing or two about fixing bangs. What do you say to a little touch up?"

Charli peeked at her hair in the mirror. She had done her best after a shower, but it was still sticking up in all directions.

Because you don't have a stylist or a maid.

When she had worked at the school, she'd pinned her hair up every day and braided it at night to keep the curls from the coastal humidity at bay. But it had been long then, before she'd taken a hacksaw to it, and now she had no idea how to deal with the mess.

"Please?" she begged Saint. "Fix what you can."

Saint guided her to the bathroom, before wrapping a cape around her shoulders. "You should see what I did with my hair in high school. I *attempted* a wolf cut."

Rhylee laughed and Saint glared at her. "I wanted to look edgy!" She caught Charli's eye in the mirror. "It looked like a mullet. And not a cool, alt one either. Just a Billy Bob mullet."

"I tried to dye my hair blue without bleaching it first," Rhylee put in. "It was mossy green all summer long. Looked like the swamp monster."

And for the next few minutes, as Saint snipped and trimmed, the two of them regaled her with stories of their youth, failed experiments in hairstyling, home ear piercings, a joyride in a stolen classic car. It was like looking at a memory book of what her life could have been, if she'd been allowed even the freedom Anthony had been given growing up.

You're a princess. Girls around the world would kill for that.

Except she was like the princesses in the old storybooks, trapped in a tower, needing to be rescued. She hardly even had the skills to cut her own hair, let alone start a life without the trappings of royalty. She had gotten as far as running away, and hadn't considered where she would go or what she would do after. The fact that Raffaello had found her in an anonymous club in the middle of nowhere meant Charli would never be able to fully escape her father's reach or build a new life for herself.

I wouldn't know how.

She had a lifetime of education and etiquette training. She knew which fork to use for fish and which to use for chicken, and the formal methods of address for dozens of countries. But she couldn't cut her own hair or buy groceries or even order a car using her own phone.

"Almost done," Saint said, before making a few final snips. "Now this *is* edgy. You just tell me when I can give you your first tattoo."

Do princesses get tattoos? Charli was starting to get very tired of wondering what princesses did and did not do. A tattoo might be a bit much but...

"Hey, what are you guys doing after this?" she asked, using all her self-control not to blow hair out of her face.

"Storm has us stuck up here," Saint said. "We couldn't get back to the shop in this even if we had to. So not much. Why do you ask?"

"Well," Charli admitted. "It never snows in Contanari."

Rhylee gasped. "Please say you want to have a snowball fight."

Charli grinned. "I was kind of hoping to have a snowball fight."

Rhylee clapped her hands together. "Okay, you're going to need warm clothes. I think you'll fit into some of Skylar's stuff, and since she's officially my sister now, it's my stuff. I'll be right back."

"Wait," Saint called to Rhylee, who was already halfway out the door. "First tell her she looks hot."

Rhylee stopped mid-step and gave Charli a once-over. "Better than hot." She kissed her fingertips. "It's a whole new you."

She darted out of the door, and Saint turned the chair back toward the mirror. "Okay, close your eyes — now, open!"

Charli opened her eyes. The woman staring back at her was at once familiar and entirely new. It was an edgy cut, sharp and short, but with the waves and softness that spoke to her feminine side. She felt grown up and sophisticated and cool all at once, the emotions caught and clogged, until all she could do was wrap her arms around Saint.

"I take it you like it, then?" Saint asked, squeezing her back.

"It's amazing," Charli replied, running her fingers through the thick waves. It *was* amazing, healthy, full, a whole new look for her whole new chapter—wherever it might lead.

Saint caught her eye in the mirror. "I don't know your story, Charli. But the girls here, they didn't know mine before they took me in, before they gave me what I needed to make my own way. I guess what I'm trying to say is, we've got your back. You're not alone. Not anymore."

And that might have been the most amazing thing of all.

Chapter Six

Charli stepped through the kitchen door after the other women, face red, nose cold, fingers burning with the blast of sudden warmth, and a smile on her face she knew would never leave. She was soaked to the bone, freezing cold beneath layers of winter clothes, and dripping wet from the many, many snowballs she had taken to the chest, back, and face.

Snow. Real snow. Like in the movies.

Montana was nothing like Le Isole del Contanari and there was something so freeing about escaping all that she had ever known, diving with both feet into a whole new world, if only for a moment.

"How was your first snowball fight?" Rhylee asked, pulling off her own soaking outer layers. They plopped to the kitchen floor in a pile of melting snow.

"Freezing," Charli replied. "But perfect."

"Next we're building snow people," Skylar said, as she carefully laid her clothes on the radiator. Skylar wasn't much older than Charli, but she had a worldliness about her, like she'd managed to survive and taken the lessons to heart.

"But first," Morgan said, as she and Emerson pushed through the door, each covered in snow, the tips of Morgan's braid white with powder, "hot cocoa!"

The others cheered, and Skylar started up the kettle on the stove, pulling ingredients from the cabinets as they all continued to undress.

Charli was accustomed to being dressed by stylists and ladies' maids, but there was a comfort among the friends that spoke to something deeper and more intimate, and she wondered, again, at exactly what kind of world Raffaello had created with his friends in the mountains.

She wondered, too, at the dark look that had been in his eyes when he'd thrown her into the car the night before, at the way he had seemed so innately to rise to the challenge of her refusal, like there was no winning in a game of tug-of-war, but the game itself was the prize.

What would it take to push him to that point again?

And better yet, why did she want to?

"You can make your escape." Saint leaned down to whisper conspiratorially. "If it's too much. No one here would mind."

Charli nodded, and draped her own wet jacket over the radiator, before plopping her gloves to the floor beside the others. It had been a very trying few days, between arriving in the United States and finding herself staring down the leader of her country while he scared away her potential suitor, to ending up snowed in at the top of a mountain. Perhaps she did need to clear her head and figure out what came next.

Maybe I need to clear my head before I see Raffaello again.

Maybe she did, but it was a dangerous thing to consider, that he might already be under her skin. The moment the roads and skies cleared, he would be dragging her back to her father's home, and she would have no say in the matter. It was important to remember that Raffaello was not her ally. Even if her mind kept returning to the image of him in his sleep pants from early in the morning, with his wire-rimmed glasses and strong, powerful shoulders and rippling muscles and…

Despite the cold stinging her fingers and ears, Charli's face grew uncomfortably warm. She didn't need the others guessing what kind of damning thoughts might be floating through her head just at that moment, so she waved to Saint and slipped through the kitchen door and back out into the main lodge.

Raffaello's room had to be around somewhere, and she wandered down the hall looking for familiar sights. It was a beautiful lodge, the rooms no doubt in great demand by the tourists who traveled far and wide to stay in the Montana mountains. Everything was edged in elegant woods, with an authentic, historical feel that was all at once still modern, cozy, and inviting. The scent of rich pine, crackling wood, and leather lit the air, and drew Charli along, even if she had no idea where exactly she was going.

To her right was a door that looked vaguely familiar, but when she tried the handle, she found the room locked. To her surprise, however, there was a small window just beside the door, and she peeked through it, expecting to perhaps catch a glimpse of a far-off mountain ridge or lake.

What she saw instead sent her stumbling back on her feet.

Surely, *surely* she was not seeing what she thought she was seeing. She was tired, and no doubt her eyes were beginning to play tricks on her, making her see things that would under no circumstances be found in a respectable mountain lodge.

One of the owners was a *prince,* for God's sake, and the room held a...

She looked through the window just to be sure, just to verify what deep in her heart she had known to be true from the first glance.

It was a *sex dungeon.*

A tasteful sex dungeon, she had to imagine. There hadn't been much opportunity for her to explore sex dungeons in her experience as a member of a royal family.

But Charli couldn't tear her eyes away from the secret room. An enormous bed took up most of it, covered in a deep red bedspread with a black headboard, which was lined with rings. A large, free-standing cross was off to the side, beside a complicated-looking leather swing, and the far wall covered in an array of what Charli could only consider...*tools.* At a distance, it was difficult to make out their specific uses and functions, but the general tapestry was undeniable.

And she...

Wasn't as horrified as she should have been.

In her gut, Charli knew that the whole reveal should have been scandalous and overwhelming. She was supposed to be a reserved member of the aristocracy. But she was also twenty-five years old, and despite all that her father had always done to hide it, push it down, and terrify it out of her, she'd always had a wild streak deep in her heart and soul, a part of herself aching to jump off the cliff and into the deep end, to dance through the night, throw snowballs with strangers, hack off all her hair, and maybe, just maybe…see what was behind door number two.

She stepped away from the room and moved farther down the hallway, the cozy, enticing lodge suddenly taking on a whole new vibe in light of what she had just learned. Now it made sense to see the small groupings of plush chairs hidden in dark corners. Now the leather and wood and rich masculinity of the space meant something new and different and…

Promising.

Despite herself, and the complete and utter madness of the last few days, Charli found her body suddenly and unavoidably responding to all that that was revealed to her. The sight of the straps on the bed in the hidden room was awakening something as if from some long-cursed magical sleep, like she could admit, only in this dark hallway with herself for company, that she was…

Curious.

That curiosity drove her to peek through the window to the next room on the floor, which looked entirely different from the first. It was softer, more feminine, done up in shades of pink and white. At a glance, it could almost have been a ballet studio of some kind, with the barre and the large mirror on the far wall, but when she looked closer, Charli could see the silk ropes suspended from the ceiling and leather braces locked into the floor.

Not all the rooms had windows, and not all that she could see into were entirely to Charli's taste. She passed a medical-themed room, which gave more horror vibes than erotic ones to Charli's mind, and a room filled with latex masks that were most definitely going to haunt her.

But most of the spaces, the common areas and the dark, hidden rooms, only heightened her curiosity, only made her want to explore more, not only within the club...but also within herself.

At the far end of one distant hallway — she'd been wandering so much she had surely lost her way in the maze — Charli tried a door and found that unlike the others, it wasn't locked. It opened easily, and even knowing she shouldn't, Charli stepped inside, closing the door quietly behind her.

There was no window into this space, and Charli understood why. It wasn't a room for voyeurism or exhibitionism, not this one. This was intimate, erotic and sensual in the truest, most instinctive way, like an altar set for sacrifice.

She had no doubt of Raffaello's hand in the creation of the room. It was like stepping through a door in Montana and back out onto the beaches of Le Isole del Contanari with its ancient ruins and aquamarine waters and purple night sky. In the center of the room was a small pool, each tile with a unique geometric design in shades of blue, half-hidden under the spray of a gentle waterfall. The room was warm and steamy, like the summer days back home, and it added an extra touch of the sensual and erotic to the space, though there were no toys or tools on the walls, no obvious brackets to loop around a person's wrist or restraints to keep them pinned to the bed.

For a moment, Charli wondered if maybe Raffaello didn't know about what went on in his establishment, but the thought evaporated in the hazy, lavender-scented mist of the room. He was too insightful, too smart not to know.

There was a stronger possibility that perhaps he was the one of his friends who didn't indulge in the lifestyle, that he was too refined to partake in the deep, desperate urgings of the average man. That seemed more likely, as staid and controlled as he was.

And the possibility sent a distinct twinge of disappointment right to Charli's gut.

She didn't want to *play*, not with him, not at all.

Right.

Before she could tell herself any more lies, the door to the stone bathhouse flung open, and Raffaello himself stepped inside, slamming it behind him.

"I thought I told you to wait in the bedroom," he said, his voice harsh, right at the edges of tearing, and Charli instinctively stepped back, further into the room.

"That was hours ago," she replied. "I told you, I'm not some whimpering sycophant waiting around to do your bidding."

"You are..." Rafe groaned, as if trying to get ahold of himself. "Charlotte, you are under my care, and I cannot have you running hither and yon before I bring you home."

"You cannot have me running." She stood her ground, feeling the warm mosaic tile under her bare feet, the steam curling her new hair at the edges, the strength of their ancestors in the room Raffaello had clearly brought with him from home. "You cannot have me running, or you cannot have me finding out the truth of exactly what it is you do here in America?"

Charli gestured to the room. "You think I'm so sheltered I can't figure out what this place is, Your Highness? What, are you afraid I'll go running to the press to spill your dirty little secret?"

Even though it didn't quite feel like a dirty secret. She had looked into so many rooms, stood in the very center of the bathhouse, and it didn't feel dirty or depraved at all. It felt...like freedom, like possibility, like the chance to find out a dark, hidden piece of herself and to nurture it and bring it into the light. There was artistry within the walls of the club, and an invitation Charli could never have expected to find herself wanting.

"Charlotte," Raffaello said very, very quietly. He took a step forward, and then another, his perfectly polished and tailored suit bending to the humidity of the room. "This is not for you."

They were too close now, too close for the conversation, for the lines in between what was said and what was meant. The air was thick and steamy around them, cloaking them, drawing them closer through the haze.

And despite the fury she felt at the man who had dragged her from the club the night before, the man who was meant to be her ruler, but instead had become her jailer, Charli couldn't pull back from the draw. The string around her belly pulling her toward him was invisible and unbreakable, her wild streak, the call to danger that had always meant she could never be the perfect princess.

"Why is it for you and not for me?" she found herself asking. "Why can't I know what goes on behind these closed doors? I have lived a life too, *Highness*, thought quite clearly not one as colorful as your own."

Raffaello leaned his head back and drew in a deep breath, as if her very words were pushing him to the edge. "I cannot understand how you manage to try my patience with such few words," he said. Growled. The words tinged at the corners with blood. "You make me…so…"

"Good," she replied, not allowing him to finish. "Good. The prince feels human emotions like the rest of us. Perhaps, one day, you might even let go of all that fucking control and let yourself be a person."

He was in her space then, trapping her under the curved ceiling of the shower wall, locking them both into a heated, frozen moment of battle. Then he leaned down, whispering words that could only barely be heard over the stream of the waterfall. "You do not want to see what happens when I lose control, Charlotte."

She should have let the words stand. Charli knew that. She knew how a man like Raffaello used his power as if it were a sword, rapier thin and razor sharp, the entire world perched right at the edge of his demand and call.

But she was so *fucking* tired of constantly responding to someone's else's demand. These were not the commands of her ruler. They were the commands of a man who had never been told no.

"I said," she bit out, salt on her tongue from the shower, lavender on her lips from the hot steam, fury in her words, "my name is Charli."

Raffaello stepped back, and despite the steam of the room, Charli felt at all once like she could breathe again, his presence no longer choking her, clouding her vision, no longer making her forget what was most important.

"Your name is Charlotte Marchand of the royal family of Fontaine. And it is my responsibility to return you home."

"Maybe I will tell the world about your club," she taunted. "Your den of iniquity and vice. I'm certain the press would love the sordid details."

He whirled on her. "And what would you know of iniquity and vice, Charlotte? What would you know of sin? Of desire?"

She almost choked on her response, the thick, molten need of his words making it difficult to remember her argument, to remember anything that had come before that very moment. She had seen things that afternoon that had cracked open a whole new world and left her spinning, and she wasn't about the shut the door now that she had glimpsed all the possibilities.

"You may see me as Anthony's little sister, but I am a woman now, Highness, and I know what I want out of my life more than ever. What makes it acceptable for you to run this club, but not for me to stand within its walls?"

"You are a lady."

"And you a gentleman."

It was as if their words were weapons, aimed at each other's vital organs, pressed to the spleen, to the heart, to the throat.

"Or perhaps," Charlotte circled, "you are not the gentleman you wish the world to see. Perhaps you are the masked buccaneer of the stories, the marauder, the *scoundrel*. Who is the prince behind closed doors?"

"What I do behind closed doors of is of little consequence to you, Princess Charlotte, and you would do well to remember it."

"Then what I do should be of little consequence to you, *Prince*."

If Raffaello had been a different man, he would have thrown his arms up in frustration, she was certain of it. As it was, he let out a low growl that truly meant she was getting under his skin.

"This is not for you," he tried again. "You are untouched, Charlotte, innocent of this world. You don't need to know of these matters."

It was her turn to huff. "Don't patronize me. I know of worldly matters. And though it may shock you to hear, Raffaello, I know of pleasure, too."

"No." He shook his head. "No, you are under my care and too...young for all this."

And that was too much, the straw on the proverbial back, the world of possibility fading away, her future turning to the rivulets of water spilling down the drains.

Charli put down her swords, sudden tiredness overwhelming her. "Too young for sex," she managed. "But not too young to be married against my will to a man my father's age for political gain. Not too young for that."

Chapter Seven

Rafe stepped back, as if Charlotte's words had physically moved him away from her, a sudden chasm in the truths they both knew and understood.

But not too young to be married against my will to a man my father's age for political gain. Not too young for that.

Rafe *knew* Charlotte's family, had sat around the dining table at holidays and spent summer vacations in their home. Anthony had been near as a brother to him since the days of university. It was unthinkable, unimaginable that they would resort to such antiquated tactics as to marry their daughter off, as if the world they lived in had never evolved from its ancient and tired traditions.

Surely, surely the King, Raffaello's own father, would never allow for such an act of coercion.

If father knew.

Which was hardly a guarantee in recent months.

Still, Raffaello had one problem to address at a time. "What did you say?"

Perhaps he had simply heard wrong. Perhaps he had misunderstood her fear and panic and anger and seen something that wasn't there.

Except why else would a princess run halfway across the world and refuse to return home? What awaited her back home that would make her cut her hair off and start dancing in underground clubs, as if in desperation for escape?

"It's nothing," Charlotte replied, shaking her head. The steam in the room all around them was curling her hair at the edges, making her look ethereal and elegant, her rich brown eyes glowing, like the gold of the seaside sunset outside his childhood window, and in them, Raffaello saw pain, of betrayal, perhaps, of uncertainty. But he also saw the fight he had quickly come to associate with Charlotte, the refusal to back down, to give in.

And that terrified him most of all.

"Charlotte."

She let out a hollow laugh, the sound echoing off the stone walls of the steam room. "You just don't get it, Highness."

"What don't I get?" Raffaello asked, his frustration mounting as he finally stepped toward her. Even with the closing distance between them, it was as if they were separated by whole worlds, by lives Raffaello would never live. "Charlotte, please, tell me."

She threw her hands up in the air. "Any of it," she practically shouted. "You're this brilliant strategist, to hear tell of it. You know all these...these languages and you have your law degree and your doctorate and all of it, and you still don't understand."

Raffaello resisted the urge to grab her arms and shake her. Barely. "Then tell me. Tell me what I'm missing so I can fix it."

Charlotte brushed past him, the contact leaving him feeling bruised and battered where their bodies touched. She walked toward the door, but Raffaello grabbed her wrist to keep her from leaving.

Which was a tactical error of the highest order.

She had slim, delicate wrists, wrists that would have normally been adorned in dripping gold jewelry or diamonds. Wrists that he wanted to bind with his own jewelry, that he wanted to pin and cuff until the bold, powerful woman below finally gave him into him, finally stopped fighting him.

He dropped her hand immediately. It was physical attraction, nothing more, the familiarity of a face from home, exhaustion from his recent fainting spell in Lords. It had nothing to do with Charlotte Marchand, Princess of Fontaine, whose sole purpose in life seemed to be driving him to the very edge of his control.

Charlotte shook her wrist out, as if trying to get away from his touch, and moved toward the door, pushing it open. The cool air from the hallway filtered in, sending a chill racing down Rafe's back.

"Where are you going?" he asked, the need to protect her like a gnawing sickness in his gut, the need to keep her from getting into any more trouble seemingly the only thing he could focus on.

"Wherever I damn well please," Charlotte replied, walking out, and letting the door slam behind her.

Raffaello stood in the steam room for a moment, watching the door as if Charlotte would decide to walk back in on her own volition.

She didn't.

Of course.

No doubt, she saw Raffaello as an extension of her own family, as if he was just another brother deciding her future for her.

Right. Brother.

And he felt a strange sense of alarm at the idea that Charlotte might think of him as a brother, well, that was neither here nor there. It did give him a course of action, however, and he walked into the hall and back toward his office, dialing Anthony's number as he did.

By the time Anthony picked up, Raffaello was settled back in his office, door closed and locked behind him. It felt imperative that he get to the bottom of the situation as soon as possible, and just as important that he keep the situation well hidden from prying eyes. If Charlotte told the truth, there would be significant consequences for the future of the nation. If she had lied to him, that meant she didn't trust Raffaello enough to share the truth, or the real reason for her adventure.

"Are you able to fly out?" Anthony asked his voice eager.

Raffaello sighed deeply. "We're still snowed in, land and sky for the time being. But your sister is safe here, I can assure you of that."

Anthony made a noise of acknowledgement. "I know, Highness, I know."

The urge, ancient as boyhood bonds, surged to calm Anthony's nerves, to remind him that Charlotte was a grown woman, capable of making her own decisions, and Raffaello would never allow harm to come her, as a princess of his country and his best friend's sister, but also as his citizen. He had dedicated his life to protecting the people of Contanari and that included each and every one of his constituents.

But Charlotte's words in the steam room, and the resignation in her eyes when Raffaello had pressed for more information, it had rung an alarm bell deep in Rafe's gut. That was why he was calling, after all, to make sure he knew all the information before deciding how best to move forward.

"Listen, Anthony," Raffaello began, leaning hard on the many years of diplomatic training he'd been given to avoid offending his best friend and one of the crown's closest allies. "Your sister...she mentioned something about a potential marriage contract." He channeled a neutrality he hadn't felt at seeing Charlotte's face into his words. It wouldn't help anyone if he went into the conversation guns ablaze, to borrow an American turn of phrase. "Now, I know your family well, Anthony, and I'm certain Charlotte is feeling overwhelmed by all that's transpired these past few days, so I thought it best to ask you directly. Is your father marrying Charlotte off for political gain?"

Silence stretched for long seconds on the other end of the phone, and Rafe had to resist the urge to fill it, which he'd never felt inclined to do with Anthony before. Theirs was an easy friendship, and before that very day, Rafe would never have believed Anthony capable of anything but honesty and directness. He was always the charismatic one, the center of attention in every room, the man everyone wanted to be friends with.

But the image of Charlotte in the steam room, her voice cracking, it had unsettled him, and Raffaello was not a man who liked to be unsettled.

"Are you asking if we're forcing my sister into marriage?" Anthony finally responded, his voice as neutral as Raffaello's, as if they were playing chess with their faces covered. It was nothing like the heated sparring match Raffaello had shared with Charlotte, all the strategy, but with passion and fire and intensity simmering with every stroke of the blade.

"I cannot believe you would," Raffaello said, "but her words were troubling."

"I should say so," Anthony's façade broke, and anger burst through with his words. "If Charlotte is to be wed against her will, this would be the very first I am hearing of it, and you know I'd never stand for it, Raffaello."

That Anthony called him by his name, and not the teasing nickname he usually used, showed just how serious Rafe's old friend was about the situation. Still, Charlotte seemed intelligent, capable and self-possessed, and Rafe had yet to understand why she had shown up at an underground club in the middle of nowhere, running from the life she had always known.

"Why is she here then?" he asked carefully, aware of just how loaded the question was. Princesses ran away all the time in movies and fairytales, but this was real life, Contanari was modern and progressive, and the pieces just didn't quite seem to be falling into place.

Anthony took a moment to respond. "I just... I just don't know, Rafe. That's the most troubling thing. Charlotte is headstrong, I'll be the first to admit, but she's never done anything like this before."

Which left them both in the same place they had started, Raffaello playing babysitter to his old friend's sister for reasons he had yet to understand. Even worse, if she had lied about a forced marriage, she had done it to cover up some other truth, which left him with even more questions.

"Will you look into it?" he asked Anthony finally. "Just to make sure... Just to see if there's something happening you're not aware of?"

Anthony, thankfully, took the words on their face. "Of course. I want Charlotte to come home safe and sound. I'll do whatever it takes."

They exchanged final words, before Raffaello ended the call. With Anthony's voice a million kilometers away, and his office soundproofed, the room was eerily quiet. Outside the enormous picture window, the snow continued to fall in thick, heavy blankets, which meant his plans for escape were going to have to wait. Until the snow let up, he was trapped in the mountains with a runaway princess.

So much for a relaxing sabbatical.

Except when Raffaello pictured Charlotte's broad smile, her bright eyes, the way her new hair cut made her look chic and counterculture all at the same time, when he thought about how she had fought him leaving the dance club, and how she had stood toe to toe in the steam room and challenged him like few ever dared to challenge a prince, Raffaello found that he didn't much mind.

He didn't much mind at all.

Chapter Eight

Raffaello was already in his suite by the time Charli returned for the night. After leaving him in the steamy island room, she'd gone wandering, planning to explore more of what the club had to offer. Before she'd gotten the chance, however, she had run back into Rhylee and Saint, who had invited her to a movie night in the lounge.

Her and Raffaello.

Charli wasn't entirely sure what the others thought of her relationship with the prince. It was clear that the sleepy Montana town had quite a reputation for love stories, but she wasn't going to be one of them.

She didn't think Raffaello *could* be one of them.

And if that made her a little…sad, well, it was to be expected. They were royals. They had their titles and their heavy crowns and the responsibility of generations sitting on their shoulders. Surely Rafe wouldn't be the first to prioritize duty over personal desire, and Charli wouldn't be the last sacrificial lamb led to the aristocratic altar.

It had *hurt*, though. That he hadn't believed her. She hadn't truly given him any reason *to* believe her, but something in Charli's heart and soul had told her that Prince Raffaello was different, that he was a good-hearted and intelligent man, someone who could see though the bullshit and get to the truth on the other side.

Apparently, she had read him wrong.

Then again, she had also never expected to find out that he ran some kind of kinky club in the mountains with his friends from his time abroad, so maybe she wasn't really as good at reading people as she had believed.

And at that thought, all the memories of their fight in the steam room came flooding back, the thick tension in the thick air, the way he stood so close, how he towered over her, how he made her want to spit and fight and…

Beg.

And that's enough of that, Charli Marchand.

"There's a movie party tonight," she said, instead of offering him a greeting. The frustration from their previous fight, mixing with the strange, unnamed need she'd been battling all afternoon, was making it difficult for her to look at him, let alone treat him with the respect deserving of the second highest seat in the kingdom.

"Dante informed me," he replied, barely looking up from his desk. Wasn't he supposed to be resting? Her arrival, or *kidnapping* notwithstanding, he had been in the mountains for recovery. Based on the stack of papers before him, he was working even harder than usual.

"Are you going?" God, sometimes it felt like she was trying to squeeze conversation out of a stone king, the last to fall on the chessboard.

"Do you want me to go, Charlotte?" Raffaello asked, and when he finally turned to face her again, he was wearing those damned glasses, the ones that made her think of professors and dark classrooms, and extra credit...

Except her professors had never looked quite like *that*. Certainly, she would have enjoyed comparative histographies and medieval literature much more if they had. Or perhaps she would have learned even less about the great kings if she'd had to watch the flex of Raffaello's muscles straining against a tweed waistcoat, the tapered vee of his strong chest into lithe, powerful hips, the way he leaned the pen against full, pink lips in concentration...

"Charlotte?" he prompted, pulling her from the increasingly scandalous thoughts swirling faster and faster. It wasn't about him, certainly. It was the place, the eroticism of a secret club that made her curious and all that came with it, the desire to learn more. Raffaello just happened to be close by.

Right.

"Raffaello," she responded, hoping he couldn't hear the high tone of her voice, as if she had been caught with her hand in the cookie jar.

"I asked if you want me to go tonight," he continued. "We're closed down with the weather, it would only be the owners."

She knew what he meant with those words the way only another royal could. For the night, they could be anonymous, the same kind of anonymity she had been chasing in the club in Helena. For the night, they could be regular, normal people who didn't have to hold the fate of a nation in their hands.

And that was a gift.

"Yes. You should come." Because who was she to deny him the same escape she had been searching for so desperately? Hell, Raffaello could use freedom nearly as much as she could, although for very different reasons. And she knew if she asked, he would stay in the room and away from his friends, locked up in a tower of his own making with his proposals and amendments.

And you want him to come.

Only the tiniest, smallest, most unhinged part of Charli wanted to see what Prince Raffaello could be like when he put down the crown. What was the man behind the suits and the glasses? Who was he in the dark?

Watching a movie, of course.

"Then I'll come," Raffaello replied, turning back to his papers.

Charli sucked on her teeth. "One thing," she forced out. "Just because Rhylee and Saint were *very* insistent... It *is* a pajama party."

* * * *

Raffaello had faced down dignitaries, ambassadors, heads of state, and his own House of Lords. But nothing could have prepared him for the moment Charlotte stepped out of the closet wearing a pair of his pajamas. Her belongings had been held up in the city with the storm, and he hadn't thought much of it when she'd asked to borrow a pair of sweatpants, but princes didn't *wear* sweatpants. Princes didn't *own* sweatpants.

They owned silken sleep sets with monogrammed pockets that sat in the bottom of their suitcases because most nights they fell asleep at their desks...

Or maybe that was just him...

But whether he had worn the kit or not, Raffaello was admittedly glad he'd brought it. Because Charlotte looked...

Like a fucking fantasy in his clothes. A fantasy Raffaello had never had until the moment she'd walked out. The pants had been way too long, but she'd snatched the monogrammed shirt out of his hands and dug around in his side of the closet, only to emerge wearing his silken pajama top as a dress, with a pair of socks pulled up to her knees, and a devilish grin on her face.

"I've never been to an American pajama party before," she said, spinning around, which made the very high hem of the shirt ride up her thighs. Tanned, golden thighs, from a life spent in the sun, strong from sailing and climbing ancient stone steps to mountain tops... "How do I look?"

Raffaello coughed, because *fuck* he was supposed to be keeping this girl out of trouble, not dragging her into the very depths of hell and depravity, as much as his mind kept returning to their fight in the steam room, to her boldness and vigor...

"Looks good," he managed to get out. "You might be a bit...cold."

She shrugged. "Rhylee said they'd turn on the firepit in the lodge." She walked up close to him, no doubt to see just how hard his buttons could be pushed.

Hard. The answer was very, very hard.

"Besides," Charlotte continued, as if Raffaello's own pair of silken pajama bottoms held any secrets. "We could always cuddle for warmth."

"Charlotte."

She threw her head back and laughed, tossing her new light waves bouncing around her face. "So easy, it's so easy, Highness." She poked him in the chest. "You need to learn how to let go of all that control."

That was the last thing he needed to do. Control kept him focused, kept him balanced, kept him from grabbing her around the waist and pinning her against the wall, and showing her exactly how he managed misbehaving little subs.

Instead, he wrapped his hand slowly around her wrist, and held her gaze. "You don't want to see what happens when I lose control, Charlotte," he said for the second time that day.

She tried to tug free, but didn't break eye contact for a second. "Or what, *Prince*, you'll take me to your big, bad dungeon and spank me?"

He didn't respond for a moment, simply let her words sit in the thickening air, the tension between them somehow even stronger than it had been in the steam room, the intensity in Charlotte's eyes fading from brash confidence to understanding, and she parted her full lips.

"You would." She stopped trying to tug her arm free. "You do..."

"Charlotte..."

They were so close now, bodies separated by thin layers of silk, the winter storm outside narrowing the whole world down to just them, breathing the same breath, never breaking contact.

"Raffaello."

Her name on his lips had been a warning.

His name on her lips had been a challenge.

"Don't..."

But before he got the words out, a knock sounded on the door to the apartment.

"Movie time," Rhylee's bright voice sang out. "We have snacks!"

"Coming." Charlotte shook her head, as if trying to bring herself back to rights. "Be right there." She glanced at him one more time, before stepping back.

It was as if all the cold from the storm outside spilled into the growing space between them, as if their proximity, the growing promises in shared, unspoken moments, had been the heat at the very core of the world, and now they would both be burned by the ice instead.

But Rafe couldn't say any of that. He was a prince. She was the sister of his best friend, on some kind of personal journey he couldn't quite understand. More than that, they were all wrong for each other, puzzle pieces that would never fit, combustion in a bottle sure to burst. One day, Raffaello would have to marry, but his future bride would be demure, stately, diplomatic. Charlotte was...wild and bold and impossible to pin down.

"Let's go," he said. When he opened the door, Rhylee, Saint, and Dante were standing on the other side, Dante's arms wrapped around Saint's shoulders, and a dangerous grin on his face. Perhaps it was because Dante was a bartender or a tattoo artist, but he always seemed to be able to read people, to tease out the secrets no one wanted to share, until they were confessing and he was absolving in the way only a tattooed, pierced, motorcycle-riding artist could.

Raffaello could admit he envied his friend's way with people. For most of his life, he'd known the hierarchy, been locked into his level, equals with the few allowed through the gilded doors. It was a paltry thing to complain about being a prince, but when was the last time he had enjoyed a movie night with friends?

"*Come sta la tua principessa?*" Dante asked.

"*Non è la* mia *principessa,*" Raffaello replied.

With their proximity to Italy and Greece, he'd grown up learning most of the Mediterranean languages. Along with their shared connection of Renaissance artist names, he and Dante had bonded in two languages, over food and a longing to return to the homeland.

"*Per adesso,*" Dante teased. *For now.*

"*Vai fanculo,*" Raffaello replied, which made Dante crack up, and he leaned down to whisper in Saint's ear.

"The prince just told me to go fuck myself."

"*Questa principessa vorrebbe guaradare un film,*" Charlotte said from behind them. "*Per favore.*"

"*Si, principessa, si,*" Dante teased, leading the small party of them down the hall.

"I didn't realize your friends spoke Italian," Charlotte murmured, as she and Raffaello followed them. "It's refreshing."

"Dante and his brother were born here," Rafe explained. "But their mother was from Firenze. He can cook quite well, too." He raised a brow at her. "But don't tell him I said that."

Charlotte mimicked locking her lips and throwing away the key. "Secret's safe with me, Highness."

But as they neared the lodge, which had been turned into a makeshift theater, Raffaello couldn't help but wonder exactly which of his secrets she was talking about.

Chapter Nine

Charli had been ever so slightly worried that a pajama shirt was on the risqué side for a movie night with friends. But, of course, Raffaello's friends ran a kink club, so shouldn't have been too surprised when Saint showed up in a cute matching silk set, and Rhylee in a pair of loose yoga pants and the smallest tank top Charli had ever seen.

Apparently, she wasn't the only one who thought so, because when they walked into the main lounge to greet Rafe's friends, one of the men practically growled from across the room.

"Rhylee, what on earth are you wearing?" His arms were folded across his chest, and he had the look of a warrior about him.

"Donavan."

"Caleb, tell your sister to put on a sweater."

Caleb, Skylar's husband, walked through the door with Skylar at his side. "She's almost thirty, Van." His exasperated tone indicated that this was an all-too-common occurrence. "And I couldn't tell her what to do when she was sixteen either. You're welcome to try, though."

The man named Van glared at Rhylee, but she held her ground, folding her arms as if to imitate his pose.

"Don't even think about it," Rhylee said, before he got the chance. "Unless you want me to return the favor."

Van growled again. "You're going to get cold."

She flipped her long braid over her shoulder and turned her back to him. "I think I'll live."

Van clearly had a response in mind, but practically turned purple when he read the back of Rhylee's skimpy tank. "Does your shirt say Future DILF? Rhylee."

Instead of responding, Rhylee just settled into the large chair at Charli and Raffaello's side.

"All good?" Charli asked, though her curiosity was burning. It was clear that the history between Van and Rhylee was deep and complicated, and the rest of them seemed completely used to it.

"All good," Rhylee said, though her voice was tight. "Van just has a hard time remembering I grew up."

Charli turned to look at Raffaello, who was looking anywhere but her. "Can't even imagine what that feels like," she muttered.

"It's not the same," Raffaello bit out. "You are my responsibility until we get back home."

"Or," Charli replied, "Rhylee and I could run off together and leave the whole sorry lot of you behind."

"I'm in," Rhylee replied.

"You'll have to wait for the snow to stop," Saint put in helpfully. "If you're off on some sapphic girl crusade, it wouldn't do you any good to freeze to death."

"Especially when you look so damned cute." This came from the Morgan, as the last two couples entered the lodge. "This is Reece." She indicated to the blond man at her side, whose powerful arms seemed to be straining at the seams of his cotton shirt. "And let's be honest, we're the ones most likely to get caught in a mountain snowstorm."

"The adventurers," Rhylee put in helpfully. "Met on a mountaintop in a rainstorm."

"We met in a rainstorm too," Saint added. "But in a bar."

"Airport," Emerson said. Out of her winter coat and boots, she was tall and slender, elegant in a city way, and the man she was snuggled up with looked awfully familiar.

"Gabriel North," Raffaello said, leaning low into Charli's ear to whisper. Too low, too close, too warm and enticing and intimate in a room full of near strangers. Until his words finally cracked the surface.

"The billionaire?"

"Not anymore," Rhylee whispered, leaning in conspiratorially. "Gave it all up for her."

"We can hear you," Gabriel replied. "But yes, I did, and I'd do it again." He leaned down and murmured something into Emerson's ear, and she laughed, until the laugh turned into a deep moan as he licked and kissed down the length of her throat.

"Can't you to control yourselves?" Dante asked. "There are royals here."

"Such a hypocrite," Morgan responded. "We had an appointment last week and you'd closed the shop and the blinds for the whole afternoon."

"And for a very good reason," Dante replied.

"Are they just...like this?" Charli asked. She had been playing the wild child for exactly two days. It had felt right, cutting her hair and smearing her eyeliner and wearing leather boots to dance in underground clubs, but it was still so new and exciting, and years of training and etiquette held strong below the surface. What would it be like to be so carefree and cool, to enjoy the casual intimacy of romance and eroticism and friendship all at once, no reservations, no fear.

"I can tell them to stop," Raffaello offered, his tone strong and unyielding.

"No," Charli replied quickly. Too quickly. "I just mean, it's nice. To be this...open."

She had expected him to make some kind of comment, to wrap her words around his palm and use them to drag her closer, but instead Raffaello just held her gaze. "Yes," he murmured after a while. "It's nice."

"Okay, newbie picks the movie!" Rhylee said, clapping her hands together. "So, Princess, rom com or action?"

Charli smiled sheepishly. "I don't...know that many movies."

Rhylee grinned. "Classic rom coms it is!"

The men groaned, but wasn't long before they were all settled into the big chairs before the dropdown screen, cozied up under blankets, passing around big bowls of popcorn and boxes of candy. At both sides of the large lodge, fires crackled in the fireplaces, and the grand picture windows added a glow of winter brightness to the gathering.

It was so normal, watching movies with friends, but Charli could count on one hand the number of times she had done it in her life. Unlike Anthony, her university experience had been strictly monitored, and the only time she'd truly been off on her own had been during her year of Servizi, at which time they'd been too busy to do much but fall into their beds at the end of long, long days.

"Do you envy them?" she whispered to Raffaello. In the dark, with the movie large and exciting before them, and the distraction of hidden corners and sweet treats, there was an intimacy and a freedom that allowed Charli to ask the questions she might never have otherwise asked. "Your friends."

He leaned his head back against the large chair and sighed. "Sometimes," he admitted. "Sometimes I wish I could be here with them all the time. But I love running my country. I... I feel like it's what I was always meant to do, and not simply because I was born to the right family."

She smiled at him in the dark, but Charli knew it didn't reach her eyes. Girls all around the world dreamed of being princesses. But she just wanted to be free.

"Charlotte." Raffaello leaned close, causing the couch to dip until their thighs were very nearly touching. Not that Charli noticed. "What would you have been? If you weren't born a daughter of Contanari?"

His tone was so genuine, as if he cared in his heart and soul to know the answer, and she understood how true rumors about the prince really were. He was a man who cared about his country and his people, no matter who they were.

"A teacher," she whispered back, feeling bold in the dark. The cloak of the storm gave them cover, and the presence of his friends somehow made the shared intimacy all the more dangerous. It was as if she wanted him to touch her where they could so easily be heard and seen.

"You're not like any of the teachers I had in school," Raffaello said quietly. Charli rolled her eyes, but before she could turn on the flamethrowers, he chuckled. "It's a good thing, Charlotte. You would be an amazing teacher."

She knew he meant it, and that only made the pressure in her chest grow tighter. Her madcap runaway scheme had never had a happy ending. She had always known it would lead to her return back home eventually, but for a brief second, for a hesitation in the timeline of the universe, she lived life on her terms.

And she was going to make every second of it count.

"Thank you, Prince," she murmured, settling back into the couch, a little closer to him, a little closer than was safe for two friends, if they could even be called that. But Charli couldn't deny the pull to him, or the way he made her want to melt the hard exterior and make him lose control. He had said she wouldn't want to see what happened when he lost control, but Charli *did*. Who was the man behind the crown and scepter?

"Charlotte, I suggest you find a comfortable position and stay there," Rafe bit out, his tone altogether changed from the supportive, amused tenor of a moment before. No, this was the Rafe she knew, tight and unyielding, demanding.

And in the next instant, Charli understood why. Because all her wiggling and adjusting had brought her a little closer than she had planned, and with her faux mini dress riding up and his silk PJ bottoms hardly a defense against a cold breeze, Charli found herself pressed up against him in the dark.

Pressed up against *all* of him. She couldn't be surprised that all of Rafe was rigid, strong and impossibly hard, straining at his elegant sleepwear, and making her mouth go dry and her breasts grow heavy and full behind the silk of her own sleepshirt.

If she knew what was good for her, she would pull back, give them both the space they needed to keep their relationship from spiraling out of control, but she'd been off-roading for days, and she wasn't ready to go back to the prim and proper Charlotte. Not ever, if she could avoid it, and certainly not yet.

So, she gave her hips an experimental wiggle.

Raffaello's hand came to her waist, pinning her in place. "Charlotte."

"Charli," she bit back, her own voice a little rough, the impression of his fingers on her hip like a bolt of lightning pulsing through her entire body. She needed more of his touch, more of his harsh, wicked words, and she needed to drive him to the absolute edge. "Call me Charli."

Raffaello leaned down, until he was a mere whisper from her throat, until she wasn't certain either of them would survive the encounter. "Stop that, Charli."

She wasn't sure if it was the victory over the powerful man, or the way he said her chosen name, like some kind of wicked spell, but she stopped, almost as if on instinct, even though every fiber of her being wanted to argue, wanted to buck and demand and push. But his command had been so direct, so intense, that even the warrior inside Charli wanted to admit, she liked it.

Rafe ran a single strong finger down the length of her neck, somehow getting even closer as he whispered in her ear once again. "Good girl."

Charli swallowed. Her breathing was heavy, coming from her tightening chest as her mind tried to catch up with her body. She had known there was an intensity to Raffaello she couldn't quite understand, but this was so much more than she could have ever expected.

So much more than she could have ever imagined.

"Raffaello..." It came out as a whimper, which thankfully only he could hear. "I need..."

"You need nothing, Princess," he murmured. "Nothing I can give you."

She could only imagine how difficult it was for him to push her away, when her own body was burning up from their contact, when all she wanted to do was writhe against him, when she ached for even the smallest touch, the very possibility of what it might mean for them to come together.

But he didn't waver, not when the movie ended and they began to chat, not when the bowls were collected and trash tossed, not even when several of his friends starting making thinly veiled allusions to heading off to their respective rooms in the club, which added even more tension to the space between them, a space that had grown much larger, as Rafe clearly tried to keep his distance from her.

And he wasn't the only one playing some kind of game with himself. Across the room, Rhylee walked past Van as if she didn't care about his reaction, but it was impossible to miss the swing in her hips or the flip of her braid, and Van simply stared at her as she walked by, as if he was deciding whether or not to hunt her down and push her against the wall and...

"I think I might like to go to bed now," Charli said, too loud. "Time zones and all. Thank you for a lovely night."

The others bid goodbye and Raffaello, ever the gentleman, guided Charli back to the suite they had shared the night before. With each step the sounds of chatting faded away, until they were standing outside the door to his apartments.

Completely and totally alone.

Chapter Ten

Raffaello opened the apartment door, but didn't go inside, instead, he lingered in the entryway, watching Charlotte. He had overstepped, he had no doubt of that. In the hidden spaces of the dark, with the fire crackling in the grate and the storm making the whole night seem more private and intimate, he had allowed the secret side of himself to slip through the cracks.

With absolutely the wrong person.

Rafe had no shame about his predispositions, the need to bring bratty subs to heel, for both their eventual pleasure. It was as much an extension of himself as his need to serve his country, even if he had indulged it less and less through the years. One day, when he was set to be married, he'd eventually have to give up that *thing*, whatever it was that drove him further into sin and depravity than other men, but that was an issue for well into the future.

The current issue he had to deal with at the moment was Charlotte.

Charli.

God, it had felt right, her name in his demand, the intimacy of using something other than her Christian name or title. It had felt too right, and Rafe had wondered if perhaps he'd been using her full name, against her wishes, to keep from crossing the invisible bridge.

Which had become a lot more visible after their shared moment on the couch. Charli—*Charlotte*—didn't make things easy, and that drew Rafe in most of all. He didn't want things to be easy. He wanted to rise to every challenge she set down before him, until they were evenly matched and battling for their very souls.

And for that reason, he had made a decision.

"I'll be sleeping elsewhere tonight," he said, not crossing the door threshold, as if he might find himself stuck in some fae land, unable to escape. "To give you some privacy."

Charlotte whirled. "You didn't care about that last night."

Raffaello shrugged, affecting nonchalance as best he could. "I thought you were going to try to run," he admitted. "The storm has worsened since we arrived, so that's not my concern anymore."

Charlotte crossed the room to come stand before him. Her rich, brown eyes were full of demanding and curiosity and a need Raffaello couldn't bring himself to answer.

Couldn't bring himself to stop answering.

"What exactly *is* your concern, Highness?" she asked.

Raffaello crossed his arms over his chest. "I believe you already know the answer to that question, Charlotte."

She met his stance, which made the hem of his night shirt ride up her legs, creating dangerous and enticing shadows. "I want to hear it from you," she replied.

"Don't push me, Charlotte," Raffaello replied, gritting his teeth and clenching his fists, anything to hold onto the small control left to him. This woman insisted on pushing his buttons, and despite all his training in matters of state and matters of desires, Raffaello couldn't help but rise to the bait each and every time she dangled it.

"You're not as big and scary as you seem," she said with a grin, one he knew was meant to make him mad. It worked, of course. "I've been sitting at tables with princes since I was old enough to walk."

She ran a dark gaze up and down his entire body, and it made Raffaello feel like he was waking up for the very first time, muscles burning to life, cock turning to steel in his silken pants.

"As for the rest of it," Charlotte continued, "well, I'm just not sure I see what all the fuss is about. Sex is just sex, right?"

Wrong.

He ached to show her just how wrong she was, how the kink and eroticism he found at the club was carnality renewed, connection and power and freedom in its truest form, how it allowed even the most controlled and demanding princes a chance to escape the binds they were given for the ones they chose, and how it had opened up a whole new world for him he could never have expected.

But since she was never ever going to patronize the club herself — over his dead body — Rafe could say none of those things. To tell her all that the lifestyle meant to him would be admitting too much, and it would open doors he was struggling with all his might not to walk through.

"I'm not playing with you, Charlotte," he said, knowing it would make her more angry than anything else. This wasn't a game to her, he was certain of that, because it wasn't a game to him either. "Hopefully the weather will let up tomorrow and I can take you home. But in the meantime..." He unfolded his arms and came to tower over her, finding it difficult to ignore the visions of her on her knees in his shirt, her hair mussed, her lips swollen, her pink tongue darting out to...

He cleared his throat. "In the meantime, you stay in this room, do you understand? I don't want you wandering, and I especially don't want to see you checking out the club. Any of it. Do I make myself clear?"

Something in his tone must have registered, because Charlotte held his gaze as she bit out her response. "Crystal, your Highness."

* * * *

Charli couldn't sleep. The snow was still falling, for days it felt like, though she'd only been in Montana for the better part of a weekend, and it lit the whole room with a soft, gray glow. She'd gotten up to close the blinds, put on a silk sleep mask she had found in Raffaello's closet, played ocean sounds, read through old law proposals, and still, she couldn't fall asleep.

For some reason.

Yeah, you have no idea what's keeping you up right now. None.

Of course she did. Her entire body was burning with need, and her mind was racing a million miles a minute. Each time she had gone head-to-head with the prince, Charli was certain it would be the breaking point, the moment when the volcano finally burst free after centuries of lying dormant. Hell, the fact that Raffaello had chosen to sleep somewhere else for the night meant he was clearly closing in on his edge, and Charli was rather certain she'd passed hers the moment he'd thrown her over his shoulder and carried her to the car.

She didn't know much about the lifestyle they supported at his club, but there was no denying the intense rush she felt every time they exchanged blows, when she lunged and he dodged, and when his deep blue eyes faded near to black and he made demands she couldn't help but agree to.

You stay in this room, do you understand?

In the moment, she'd been so overcome by the intensity of his tone, by the potent look in his eyes, that she'd felt bound to respond in kind. But now in the dark of the lonely bedroom, with her whole life being planned and pledged for her, Charli wanted to fuck the rules and fuck doing what she was told. This was *her* life, for as long as she was able to claim it, and prince or not, Raffaello had no right to tell her where she could or couldn't go, no right to make her feel like the fucking princess trapped in the tower — the way she had felt her whole damned life.

Charli climbed out of the enormous bed and pulled her socks back on before slipping out the door of Raffaello's apartments. If he wanted to stop her from exploring his club so badly, he was going to have to do it himself.

He had mentioned that the club was closed for the weather, so Charli didn't expect to see much when she wandered down the forbidden hallways. Likely, one or two of his friends had found their way to their respective rooms, implying as much after their movie night, but it was late and all too possible that she was the only one still awake in the expansive club.

Still, that just meant more time for exploring, and she peeked into the first door she could find, loving the thrill of doing what she shouldn't, loving the aching heat growing in her belly at the very possibility of being caught.

The first room nearly resembled a classic Montana lodge apartment, fireplace and hot tub and large bed, but there were thick leather straps on the headboard, and the cozy-looking hammock in the corner of the room seemed to be made of crisscrossing leather bands that could be tied or retied as needed. It was elegant and sophisticated, none of the tawdry kink she knew from popular culture, and it sparked a deeper need in her belly, to be the one tied to the bed, held in placed, forced to beg for the things she wanted.

Charli swallowed hard and continued down the hallway, realizing too late that she was passing the main lodge.

And that it wasn't empty.

Raffaello sat in the near dark, lit only by the light of the dying fire in the grate. All his friends were strong and muscled men, but she was too quickly learning how to recognize his powerful form, even at a distance, and as he sipped at the drink in his hand, she took the rare opportunity to study him.

He was so classically elegant, a prince from the fairytales, with broad shoulders and impressive height. His dark blond hair was well styled, but a few loose curls spilled free, giving him a boyish, playful appearance that was so rare for a man with such weight on his shoulders.

"Charlotte."

She startled at hearing her name and tried to take a step back into the shadows.

"Charlotte, come here."

It was as if her two feet moved of their own volition, her body and mind at war about whether to give in or fight back, the need growing all the more complex as she took in the sight of the disheveled prince.

"I couldn't sleep," she managed. "I thought it might help to walk around."

"You thought it would help to do the one thing I told you not to do," Raffaello said. He leaned forward on the barstool and placed two fingers under Charli's chin, which forced her to look up at him, into those deep-sea eyes that help so many secrets.

"I have to know, Charlotte, why exactly are you so determined to disobey me?"

"I just wanted to know," she admitted quietly, swallowed at the burning heat of his simple touch on her skin. "I... I need to know."

"You need to know about the club," he demanded. "You want to know what it's like to engage in dark, heathen desires, Princess?"

Charli didn't hesitate. "I do."

Raffaello moved his hand from her chin into her hair, stroking slowly, until he grabbed a fistful and pulled her head back. Charli knew the bite of pain shouldn't have made her lower belly ache and burn, but *hell*, it did, a deep, aching need awakening from somewhere inside her.

"Then I'll show you."

He released his grip on her hair and stood, indicating for Charli to go first.

He wasn't drunk, she was sure of that. His steps were steady and certain, and there was a look of absolute determination in her eyes that made Charli trust him, even as she knew he was trying to make her back down first. Even if he had swayed on his feet, Charli would have known that the ever-so-controlled prince was in charge of his faculties. For better or for worse, Raffaello was always in control, and she knew how much it must be frustrating him to no end that she didn't seem to bend to his every will.

Up until the moment he brought her back through the club, one hand firmly planted on the small of her back, and Charli had to reconsider if she, perhaps, did want to bend to *some* of his wills.

Because there was something altogether different about walking through the club with the man you were aching for, the anticipation rising with every room they passed, need and nerves and aching, carnal desire warring until they found purchase in Charli's belly, in the tight points of her swollen nipples, in the hot apex of her thighs, where need bloomed to life like it never had before.

Raffaello crowded her space, pressing her against one of the windowed walls that looked into a playroom. "Since you want to know what goes on here so badly," he practically growled in her ear, "I'll tell you. Everything."

He turned her body, responsive as she was to his touch, and leaned into her as he whispered in her ear.

"This is one of our exhibitionism rooms, Princess. Our patrons can watch through the window as the scene unfolds."

She could picture it now, a leather-clad submissive tied to the bench at the center of the room, arms and legs pinned, spread and welcoming, a powerful partner pacing around them like a predator.

"You see, we have Dominants and submissives here," Raffaello explained, his voice dark and coffee rich in her ear, like melted chocolate running between parted fingers. "Do you know what that means, Charli?"

She shook her head. She knew enough, but much more, she wanted him to be the one to explain it to her.

"It means power," Raffaello murmured. "It means total submission, the gift of control. Submissives want to be told what to do, and Dominants *need* to tell them."

"You're dominant," she whispered back. It wasn't a question. Anyone who knew Raffaello knew he was a man to grip control in an iron fist. "Always in charge, Highness."

"Yes," he replied. "I am. It's innate, in the blood, I couldn't any more submit than you could dominate, Charli."

She whipped her head around at that, finding him so much closer than expected, a mere breath away. "I could."

He chuckled, dark, a little wicked. "No, Princess. You couldn't. You'll fight to the very last, I have no doubt of that, but you'll give in eventually. And you'll be grateful for it."

She hated that he was right, that she could picture herself as the one tied to the bench, while Prince Raffaello paced around her. She hated, even more, that she needed to see more of the picture in her mind.

"How?" she whispered.

"There are ways," he replied. "Some are pleasurable, some balance burn and desire, some are like fighting, until the moment they're not."

"Tell me." Charli was certain she was begging, but there wasn't anything for it. "Please, I…I need to know."

It did feel like a need, like something innate, in her blood and bones. This wasn't a choice or a weekend game, not for her, and certainly not for the prince. This was woven into the very fiber of her DNA, until she found herself imagining crawling on hands and knees to do his bidding, and wanting it.

"Tell me what you're running from, Charlotte."

"No," she replied quickly, shaking her head. "Not here. Not now."

"Then no," Raffaello said. "I don't think you get what you want."

It felt like being split apart, to imagine him walking away, losing his warmth, his nearness, his demands. Too much and again not nearly enough, and she was completely and totally out of her depth, with only Prince Raffaello to hold onto for her life.

"It's my father," she finally confessed, hating the very thought of it, of him, of all that had driven her from her home in the middle of the night. This club, the lodge in the mountains, it had become a safe place in such a short amount of time, and Charli didn't want to taint it, not yet.

But her desire for answers seemed to outweigh all the rest, and maybe there would be a way to move forward if she cleared the poisonous plants on the trail.

"Go on," Raffaello's tone brooked no argument.

"He's forcing me to marry," she admitted. "Lord Wagner. To strengthen our households. For *unification*."

She had heard the word so many times in recent weeks it had begun to lose all meaning, but she had never truly believed her father would go through with such a thing, that he would honor an archaic and outdated contract, that he would sell off his only daughter.

Raffaello pulled back. "He's nearly sixty."

Charli pursed her lips together and nodded, afraid to let him see her expression, afraid to let him know just how close she was to breaking away at the edges. She had been running for weeks without a plan or a friendly ear, and in such a short amount of time, Raffaello had become a safe port for her. With the weight of the world finally off her shoulders, she was coming dangerously close to crumbling to dust.

"There was a marriage contract signed," she explained. "Before I was born. To marry the two houses together. Wagner never had children. Technically, it is legal."

"My father would never allow it," Raffaello said, his voice rising, the tone haughty and princely and strong, that of a man who fought for principle and justice.

It made it all the more frustrating that he knew so little of what went on just under his nose.

Knew, or acknowledged.

"Your father knows little of the goings of his nation," Charli replied. "You may be the only one who doesn't see it, Highness, but he is no longer the man he once was."

"Charlotte." The warning in his tone was different now. Charli had quickly come to realize she wasn't scared of this man, and especially not when it came to matters of politics. That, she could challenge him on any day.

"It's the truth, Raffaello. You've been running the nation for months now, but things are falling through the cracks. Things like me."

She hadn't realized how much she had blamed him for her circumstances until just that moment, until she had pushed the buttons on her own hidden doors and found spite and frustration and simple, lingering sadness. To avoid being wed to the contract and Lord Wagner she would have to leave her entire life, her entire world behind.

Otherwise, her future would be one of misery.

"You could never fall through the cracks," he bit out, as if it pained him to say.

"Then prove it," Charli replied, frustrating and need building within her. She wanted to fight, to rage and scream, and she wanted to be held and calmed at the very same time, two beasts warning within her, both yearning to break free.

"I shouldn't," Raffaello said, and Charli knew they were no longer speaking of the marriage contract or life in Contanari. They were speaking of that moment, in its shadows and haunts, in its promises and offerings at the altar of desire and sin.

"I'm telling you, Highness," Charli replied, "that you *should*."

Raffaello spun her around and pressed her against the wall, the cool glass on her cheek, his large, powerful body at her back. "You're not telling me *anything*, Princess," he murmured against her throat, as if her body was his canvas, to do with which as he pleased. "You think you're in control but you're not."

He ran a strong finger along the edge of her shirt hem. "I thought bringing you here, to look down at the depraved promises of these rooms would scare you off, but I can see it wasn't enough, so let me give you some details about what *exactly* goes on here."

She didn't move, for fear he would stop. Charli knew that using the club to warn her off was the lie Raffaello needed to tell himself to take the next step forward, but even if he had meant it, it still wouldn't have worked. Even with the little she knew and understood about the rooms, about the lifestyle, she knew it to be the missing piece, the part she had never understood, and now fell into place as if she had been waiting for it her whole life.

"What exactly goes on here, Prince?" she fought back, pressing into his hold. He gripped her hip, much as he had done during the movie, and the sensation sent sparks of desire racing up her spine. When he held her like that, she felt safe, protected, under his powerful control, and she wanted so much more than a single rough touch.

"In this room," Raffaello explained, "Dominants tie their submissives down to the bench, or lock them into the cross." He ran his hand through her hair, warm fingers occasionally brushing the skin of her throat and making her swallow hard. "With their submissive's arms legs tied, Dominants have easy access to all their pleasure points, their breasts" — he ran his hand up her side, barely ghosting the outer edge of her breast — "their asses" — the same hand, running over her curves, so light she could have imagined it, if her body wasn't burning up from the connection.

"Their pretty, needy holes," Raffaello continued, the word heavy in the thick air between them. "Some Dominants get pleasure from giving pleasure. Others from inflicting that perfect level of pain to feel like release exists inside the bursting of the sun or the volcano's explosion."

"You give pain," Charli managed, her voice so breathless it barely sounded like her own.

"Not entirely," Raffaello replied. "I give punishment when it's due. I tame, Princess. Mouthy, bratty little submissives who don't like to take an order, they come to me. And I bring them to heel."

"How?" Curiosity raged through her. Curiosity and so much more. Need, pulsing and heavier with each dangerous word he shared. She should have been turned away by his filthy desires, Charli knew that, should have been put off by the darkness in his voice and in his needs.

But she wasn't.

"Sometimes with my hands," Raffaello responded, using one of those hands to slip under the hem of her sleep shirt. "You wouldn't believe how *wet* some submissives get when they've been properly spanked."

Charli was rather certain she *would* believe it.

"Sometimes," Raffaello continued, "I'll bring them right to the edge, until they're whimpering with pleasure and losing all control, and I'll keep them there, right there, until they learn to behave themselves. You want to know how I do that?"

Charli nodded.

"I love the look of a submissive all filled up," he murmured. "Ball in their mouth, plug in their ass, my cock pulsing in and out of their tight little pussy. If they're especially ill-behaved, I'll put the clamps on their nipples and clit, so every time they arch their back in pleasure, it pulls."

She couldn't help herself, she arched her back at that, right into him. Against her ass, Charli felt

Raffaello's swollen cock, straining and throbbing, and she leaned into it, wishing she could have so much more than a touch.

Raffaello squeezed her hips, then ghosted his finger along the seam of her panties. That would be all it took for him to realize how much she wanted him. Her pussy was throbbing, and her panties were soaked with desire from all his dangerous words and impossible promises.

"Tell me you need to be filled, Princess. Ask me nicely."

"You want me to beg."

Raffaello's chuckle was harsh and dark, and make electricity burst in Charli's chest. "You have no *idea* how much I want you to beg," he replied. "On your knees, pussy wet and leaking, aching for my cock in your mouth, in your tight little holes. I am craving you to the point of madness, Charli, and each denial makes me want so much more. So yes. I want you to beg."

"And if I don't want to?"

God, she did want to, she really, really wanted to. His fingers were under the shirt now, skating her skin, never touching her where she needed to be touched most, and Raffaello knew it. But the urge to push back, to return every volley with a powerful play of her own, was too much to ignore. It was almost as if she needed him to beat her fair and square before she could surrender over her hard-won control.

"If you won't beg for me, Princess," he continued, pinning her in place with his enormous body and continuing his teasing touches, "then I'll send you back to the apartment with your legs shaky and your sweet little pussy dripping wet. I'll make sure you never get the relief you need to sleep tonight."

He nipped at her ear, the pain sending bright bursts of molten desire across her heated skin. "I'll tell you not to touch yourself, not to take the edge off, but we both know you will. And the whole time you're defying my orders, Charlotte, you're going to be wishing it was my fingers inside you, making you come."

"Raffaello…" His name was like something from a holy text on her lips, sacrificial and reverent. But it wasn't begging.

"Master Raffaello, Charlotte."

She parted her lips, already understanding how the words would shape in her mouth, tasting the submission, the acknowledgement, the sacrifice of her control. "No."

He squeezed her ass cheek hard, and to her great mortification, it made a flood of wetness spill from her pussy. The rough edge, the demand, the intensity of this man who when he was his true self, it didn't scare her the way she knew it should. It delighted, excited, inspired, and made her feel freer than she had in a very long time.

"Say it, Princess, two little words and I'll let you come all over my hands."

She turned to glare at him, their faces so close she could see the storm in his beautiful eyes, a wreckage at sea that only stoked the flames inside her. "Make me."

Raffaello chuckled the way Charli imagined Lucifer himself would chuckle, as if he were the most powerful being in the land, and she was his sacrifice on the altar. "With pleasure."

He ran his thumb down the seam of her soaked panties, pausing only to circle her swollen clit with the tiniest, lightest of motions, not enough, not nearly enough for all she needed and craved for him, but with each touch she climbed higher and higher, the pleasure like a dull roar growing in her ears.

And then Raffaello began to talk again. "The steam room, that's the room I designed, Charlotte, just like the beaches at home. But tucked into the tiles are metal hooks. Have you ever been pinned down under the spray of the water, arching and aching toward your release, coming over and over again under the shower?"

She shook her head. "No."

"Do you want to be?"

Charli didn't hesitate. "Yes...."

"I'll give it to you, Princess. You just need to say those two simple words."

"Raffaello..." she dragged his name out.

He stopped his movement all together, the pleasure edging out like watercolors off the page, then he began to pull his hand back.

Charli clenched her legs together. "Wait, please..."

"Why should I?" Raffaello asked. "I've given you your chances, Charlotte. You've made your choice."

"Wait..." She swallowed hard, aware that she was taking the final step over the bridge. "Please... I need it. I need you... Master Raffaello."

His chuckle was warm honey, decadent and thick, sunshine spilling over fingertips, and he slipped his finger under the band of her panties and stroked her wetness. Charli jumped, but he held her tight, caging her in, forcing the pleasure to burn hot and bright right at the center, and she leaned into him, knowing he could catch her, knowing he would hold her up even when her world fell apart.

"Good start, Princess," he growled into her ear. "But I believe I asked you to beg for me."

She was too far gone. Charli knew it and so did Raffaello, and she didn't bother to fight when all her energy and focus was on pleasure now, on the place where their bodies connected and he answered some unspoken, unknown question that made her feel alive like she never had before.

"Please...please can I come?"

"You're going to have to do better than that," Raffaello murmured. "Tell me how much you need it."

"*Fuck*," Charli couldn't help but swear. "I'm so close...so wet, I need to be filled up. I need your fingers inside me..."

"Inside where?" he asked, pushing, always pushing, until there was nowhere she could hide.

"My...pussy," Charli managed. "Fuck my pussy, *please*."

And finally, blessedly, he did just that, curling two large fingers inside her and hitting the spot that made stars burst behind Charli's eyes, sliding and pressing and teasing until she was rounding the very top of the mountain, until all her focus had narrowed and the only thing she could think about, the only thing that mattered at all in that moment was his touch and her impossible, burning pleasure.

"Thank me, Princess," Raffaello said, "and I'll let you come."

She didn't hesitate, not then, when he could take away what she wanted most, not when she was so damned close. "Thank you...Master Raffaello."

He kissed the sensitive skin behind her ear. "Good girl. Come for me, Charlotte."

And because he had said it, demanded it, she did, spilling hot release all over his stroking fingers, bursting and bursting and bursting free from the intense, overwhelming pleasure of it all.

At her back, Charli registered the feeling of Raffaello's cock throbbing, hard and insistent, and her pleasure-laden brain moved to reach for his pajama tie, but Raffaello grabbed her wrist and stayed her movements.

"Go back to bed, Charlotte," he murmured. "I'll take care of your father, I promise."

He pulled the hem of her shirt back down and, as if he couldn't help himself, leaned over and placed one more kiss on her neck, before disappearing down the hallway and out of sight.

Chapter Eleven

For the first time in three days, Raffaello was grateful for the snow. It meant they had an excuse to stay in Montana until he sorted out the complex web of Charlotte's potential marriage. Perhaps Anthony didn't know anything about the ancient marriage contract, but it had been all too clear to Raffaello the night before that she wasn't lying and she wasn't making things up. Chances were, her father was the one responsible for the decision, and Charlotte's father, Prince Johan, was not known for his kindness or diplomacy.

Which Raffaello should have considered when Charlotte had first made mention of the arranged marriage. He should have thought beyond the information in front of him, and for that, he owned her an apology.

As her prince, he owned her a solution, which was why he was dialing Madison for official unofficial state business when he was still meant to be resting and recuperating.

"Your Highness," Madison answered the phone with the same droll tone Raffaello had heard over the years, and it provided him with a sense of security and balance. In three short days, his entire life had been thrown into a wind turbine and tossed about, all thanks to a small blonde woman who couldn't seem to keep her mouth shut. He had a life back home, responsibilities, and here he was, giving into his desires like a schoolboy unable to hold his control.

"Madison," he said, instead of sharing any of *that* damning information. "I was wondering if you could look into something for me. The Prince of Fontaine, did he draft a marriage contract? It would be two to three decades old now."

"I'll look into it," Madison replied. "How is the princess?"

"She's..." *Sin incarnate, a fantasy come to life, sweet, hot, and needy for my touch. My touch.* "Well, I think. We're both enjoying our time away from the palace."

"Good to hear," Madison said, though his tone wavered ever so slightly with his reply. Madison had never been a man to waver, and he had always told the truth. It was the reason he made for such an excellent confidant and advisor.

"Speak your mind," Rafe said, his voice that of a prince. "What is the matter at home?"

"You're traveling abroad to rest, Prince," Madison said. "We can contain things here."

"Contain *what* things?" Rafe asked through gritted teeth.

Madison sighed on the other end of the phone. "Your father's condition...seems to be, well, he has his good days, Raffaello. And his not so good days."

"Am I to believe one is starting to outweigh the other?" Rafe managed, his heart suddenly feeling too big in his very tight chest. It had been a mistake to take an absence, a mistake to leave his father and travel so far from home, and now he was stuck in a snowstorm and unable to return, even in the event of an emergency.

Your father knows little of the goings of his nation. You may be the only one who doesn't see it, Highness, but he is no longer the man he once was.

Charli's words rang through his mind, bright and unyielding. She had spoken them in true anger, as a citizen of the country, and in his heart of hearts, Raffaello knew that there was a harsh truth to them. She had been wrong, in believing he didn't see the developments with his father, wrong in thinking he wasn't planning for the future, but the rest had been increasingly true in recent months.

The king was losing his capacity to rule the nation.

"Your assumption is correct, Highness," Madison said finally. "The doctors are taking every care with his needs, I can assure you, and Lords is managing our best in your absence."

Raffaello could only remember the meeting on the day of his little spell, when the room had been filled with bored, glassy-eyed representatives, who could barely be bothered to read the proposals sitting in front of them. He had little faith in their capacity to rule.

And yet, he had no choice. He was in Montana, at least through the blizzard, and there was nothing to be done for it.

"I trust you," Raffaello said. "I know I'm meant to be recuperating, but there simply isn't time. Run major decisions by me as you are able, and keep me abreast of my father's condition. But prioritize the Fontaine situation. I want to hear about that as soon as you know."

"It's done, Your Highness," Madison replied. He paused, as if grappling with his next words. "But please do try to rest. For the sake of the nation."

Raffaello nodded, though his advisor couldn't see it through the phone. "For the sake of the nation."

For the sake of the nation, he was going to need to be as focused, prepared and productive as possible.

Nothing could distract him now.

Nothing.

No one.

* * * *

Charli wrapped her hands around her hot chocolate and blew, trying to cool it down. While she regularly drank coffee and tea back home, she had always associated hot chocolate with winter, ski trips to the alpine and Dutch Christmas markets. Of course, it was still snowing outside, with temperatures continuing to drop, so when the other women had invited her to Skylar's cabin for cocoa and cookies, she had agreed in an instant.

They were so welcoming, so easy to be around, and she had spent so much of her life longing for female friendship, for camaraderie and secrecy and loyalty. In a few short days they had already given her so much, and Charli knew it was a gift she would take with her when she left.

"Okay." Morgan settled down on the chair in front of Charli and crossed her legs, as if preparing for business. "What's going on between you and Rafe? We're *dying* to know."

"Way to ease into it," Skylar said from the kitchen.

Morgan scrunched her nose. "Okay, yes, I'm sorry, that was very blunt. But he's so rigid and controlled, I have to know."

Rigid and controlled. Rigid and controlled enough to walk away from her the night before, when all she'd wanted to do was drag him into the nearest room and find out everything there was to learn about the lifestyle he had been hiding.

"Nothing," she choked out, swallowing some of the cocoa, which was still way too hot to drink. "He's friends with my brother, is all."

"That's not a *nothing* blush," Rhylee pointed out. "And I was sitting next to you two during the movie last night. I have ears like a bat."

Charli laughed. "I'll admit to it *if* you tell me what's going on with you and that Van guy."

The other girls hooted, and Morgan shot her a conspiratorial wink. "Now that's a mystery we've been trying to solve for years."

Rhylee shrugged, though her attempt at nonchalance fell a little short. "Like you said, he's friends with my brother. He's super protective because we've known each other so long. I'm sure he thinks of me like an annoying sister."

"He doesn't *look* at you like you're an annoying sister," Saint put in. "He looks at you like he's going to go all caveman and storm out with you over his shoulder."

"Rafe did that to me," Charli admitted. "When he found me at the club the other night."

Rhylee jumped on the subject change. "See, this is way more exciting than the nothing going on with me and Van. Tell us."

She wanted to say there was nothing to tell, that the tension between them was all in her head, and that she was eventually going to have to return to her country and fulfill her duties. But memories of Rafe's touch on her skin were still so strong, making her feel bright and hot and alive, and she had missed out on so many years of talking about boys with her friends.

And I want to seduce him.

Charli could pretend it was about the lifestyle, and the world of kink he had opened up to her. But it was more than that. It was *him* and the intense rush of power she felt in defying her prince, in making him work for her submission, in eventually giving in...

"Okay, I know that face," Emerson said, settling onto the couch. "What's on your mind right now?"

"I think want to seduce the prince..." she blurted out, covering her mouth with her hands the moment the words slipped out. So she'd been thinking them all but nonstop since waking up alone and oh-so-frustrated in a room that smelled that Raffaello, but that didn't mean she had to go around sharing it with all her new friends.

"I knew it," Morgan yelled. "You look at Rafe the way Van looks at Rhylee."

"Hush," Rhylee said, shooting a glare Morgan's direction. "And Rafe is way worse. He practically had his fingers up her shirt yesterday."

"About that..." Charli muttered.

The other women moved in close, clearly excited for any tidbit of gossip.

"He dropped me off at the room last night and said he was going to sleep elsewhere, and he told me not to go poking around the club."

"Let me guess," Emerson teased lightheartedly, "you went poking around the club."

Charli gave her a sheepish grin. "I couldn't sleep. But Rafe was there, in the lodge, like he'd been expecting me or something."

"How familiar are you with the lifestyle?" Skylar asked gently. She wasn't much older than the others, but she had the air of an older sister about her, and she immediately put Charli at ease.

"Not very," she admitted.

"No shame in that," Skylar said, pouring more cocoa into her mug, "but I think I know why Rafe was waiting for you."

"I think the astronauts know why Rafe was waiting for you," Rhylee added. "You can see it from space."

"See what?" Charli asked, feeling completely out of her depth. Maybe Raffaello had been right. Maybe she didn't have what it took to explore this world of kink and sin. Maybe she'd have to go back to the responsibilities of her life as a princess and hope the need for freedom eventually shriveled and died.

"You're a brat," Rhylee explained.

Charli shook her head, as if trying to clear the cobwebs. "Okay, explain. Slowly."

"It's nothing bad," Morgan said quickly. "It just means you like challenging him. Pushing his buttons, you know. And if anyone needs their buttons pushed, it's the prince."

"That man *loves* a challenge," Rhylee agreed. "And you are a damn cute challenge."

Charli couldn't help but grin at that. "Thank you. But I'm not trying to be a...brat. I'm just...me."

"That's the best kind," Emerson said. "It means you're not pretending. And when he tames you and you finally give into him, it'll be that much sweeter, you know?"

This is insane.

That was what she should have said. This world, this lifestyle, the casual way that all these beautiful women were so easily discussing kink and desire, it should have been completely and totally insane.

But Charli could only remember the feeling of absolute freedom that had accompanied her eventual submission the night before. She could only remember how it felt to give in after a hard-won fight, and how each challenge had pushed her further and further toward abject pleasure and needed. The sparring wasn't the *before*. It was the during, the hill to climb, the sparks to the flame that would cause them both to combust.

"I think she gets it," Morgan said, her tone gleeful. "Which means you two already scened together, didn't you!"

"No," Charli protested. "I wanted to... I would have, but..."

She quickly explained the events of the prior evening, knowing implicitly that the other women would keep her secrets, knowing she needed expert advice before she could take the next step on her wild journey.

"And he just...left you there?" Emerson asked. "In the hall?"

"He pulled down my hem," Charli explained, "kissed my neck and told me to get some sleep..."

Shame burned hot at the memory. She would have done anything he wanted in that moment, and had been halfway to figuring out all the things *she* wanted.

"These men and their self-sacrifice," Morgan murmured. "They're all such Doms, they'd rather walk away from something you both want than hurt you."

Saint laughed. "Dante almost had a coronary when he found out I was a virgin. I thought he was going to lock me in a nunnery himself."

"You should have seen Gabriel when Em took off," Morgan put in. "He ate like three trays of Rhylee's brownies in one sitting. It was so bad."

"I know they all seem really different," Skylar said quietly, "the baseball player, the adventurer"—she nodded to Morgan—"the banker, the soldier, the artist, but at their hearts and souls, they're cowboys. They have strong senses of right and wrong, and they'll do absolutely anything for their women. And, of course, they can be bullheaded and stubborn, each in their own way, but there's no one luckier than a girl loved by a cowboy, I'll tell you that much."

She caught and held Charli's eye. "Even your prince, he has the heart of a cowboy."

Charli smiled. "He's not my prince. Not... not like that."

"Yours for a day, then," Skylar replied. "And if you need help making that happen, I'd say you have just about the finest group of teachers ready, willing, and able."

Chapter Twelve

Rafe ran his hand over the horse's thick mane. It was still too cold and snowy for them to attempt a ride, though no doubt it would do him good to exercise his frustrations, but even standing in the stables, the familiar scent of horses all around, was enough to put him at ease. Too much had happened in too short a time. Charlotte, dropping like a firecracker into his life, bold, unapologetic, fighting for her place in the world, even if she couldn't see where she was going, the possibility that his own royal subjects were resorting to antiqued and inhumane practices, the truth about his father.

Raffaello sighed, and leaned his head against the horse, taking in deep, calming breaths. Madison hadn't told him anything Raffaello didn't already know, that the king's grip on reality and memory was slipping, that some days Raffaello looked at his own father, and wasn't sure the man recognized who he was. But it was a reminder, of all that lay waiting for him at home, of the country he'd soon have to inherit, to run as king.

It had been the job he'd been training for his entire life, and even well into his third decade, a known prince and strong fighter for his nation, it still felt impossible to see himself on the throne.

"Thought I might find you here."

Raffaello turned to see Van step into the stables, closing the door to the whirling storm behind him. "You always loved the horses."

"I needed to clear my head," Rafe said finally. "My father is… I won't be back here for a while."

Van nodded. In his time as prince, Rafe had turned to the solider more than once. Van was a warrior, to be certain, his tours of duty and the scars he returned home with, both the ones that could be seen and the ones that couldn't, marked him as such. But he was also an expert strategist, and had helped Raffaello work through more than one complex issue of military and state. While not as bold as Reece or amusing as Dante, he had been a stalwart friend and ally many long years.

"We all knew the day would come eventually," Van said, sitting on an overturned bucket and stretching out his legs. "Not that your father would — That you would be king, I mean."

He studied Rafe carefully, and Raffaello felt exposed, seen in a way he hadn't been in a long time. That was the problem with having brothers, as the other of the Seven were to him. They always knew you better than you knew yourself.

"You'll be a good king, Rafe, if that's what you're worried about," Van said eventually. "A just king. Your country is lucky to have you."

Rafe nodded. "Feels like I've been training my whole life for a job I'll never be ready for."

Van shook his head. "It's not a job to you, though," he said. "For some people, sure. Some people rise to the occasion, wear the crown, smile for the cameras. But you were born to be king because it's in your blood. It's not a job, Rafe, it's a calling."

The words reminded Raffaello of all he had said to Charlotte the night before, how he had asked her what she would have chosen to be, if she hadn't been born a princess.

A teacher.

A noble calling, to be sure. One he wouldn't have expected, but understood to be true. But then again, so much of Charlotte was unexpected and undeniably the truth.

"You know," Van said, and the nonchalant tone of voice immediately made the hairs on the back of Raffaello's neck stand on end. "You'll feel better about ruling if you have the right person at your side."

"Did you pick the shortest straw?" Rafe asked, leaning against the door of the stall. "You're the sacrifice to talk about my love life?"

Van shrugged. "The guys fell in love, made 'em soft. I'm not in love, so you know I'm being objective."

"Right," Rafe couldn't help but tease. "Not in love. Not at all."

Van glared at him. "Say your piece. Or better yet, don't."

"No piece," Rafe said, holding up his hands in surrender. "But I can't imagine I'd get the same reaction from you if *I* wore a Future DILF shirt."

Van rolled his eyes. "You are a future DILF, Rafe. Rhylee isn't."

"Rhylee is trying to get a rise out of you," Rafe replied. "I don't know if you're trying to fool yourselves or you're just too thick to see it, but the rest of us definitely, definitely do."

"Let's go back to your love life," Van said. "Charli's cool, man. The girls love her, and she'd be good for you. Someone to challenge you, make you your best self, you know?"

Rafe *did* know. It had been haunting him since he'd woken up on the couch in the lodge with a crick in his neck and visions of her falling apart dancing through his head. She had dipped her toe into a brand-new lifestyle and given him fantasies on a silver platter, the perfect mirror to his needs, never backing down or giving up, right until the moment she did.

Nothing in his entire life had been more difficult than walking away from her, but he had known that if he stayed in the hallway even a second longer, her shirt would have been bunched around her waist, and his cock would have been buried deep in her sweet, tight pussy. He had told her that he would show her the club to scare her off, but the truth was he had wanted to know just how far she was willing to go, how much her adventurous spirit could handle.

And he'd gotten so much more than he'd bargained for.

And so much more than he could have ever hoped for.

"It's a terrible idea," he told Van, instead of any of that. "She's Anthony's sister for one, and tangled in a messy situation. And—"

"And what?" Van prompted. "Morgan was running from corrupt politicians. Saint escaped the mob. You could untangle the mess, if you wanted to."

"Maybe I don't want to," Raffaello replied. Because he was trying to build his walls back up faster than they were coming down.

"Suit yourself," Van said, standing up. "But you should know that she dropped this off with Caleb this afternoon." He handed Raffaello a rolled-up pack of papers. "Oh, and she's up at the club with the girls right now."

* * * *

With the club closed down for the snow, the group had found themselves in a smaller gathering space than the dance club where they normally started the night, Charli's new friends had explained. It was the first room she had seen, with its large expansive view over the mountains and touch of alpine elegance that made it easy for Charli to forget where she was.

Well, *easier*. Everywhere in the room were hidden messages, discreet and sophisticated as she had first assumed, enticing nonetheless, as if drawing her in and making her answer questions about herself she had never asked before.

With the exception of that afternoon, when the other women had given her the official waiver and information packet for all the goings-on of The Ranch. It was strange, to learn the name of the club after all she had done and nearly done within its walls. But even though she'd gone about the process somewhat backwards, Charli had been impressed with the level of safety and security the club prioritized. The packet was extensive, providing information on lifestyle basics, such as safe words and limitations, and requiring an interest rating for pages of kinks and erotic interests.

She'd had to ask for translations on several.

But even though it was completely out of her world, it felt…right, signing the club waivers, with her latest royal physician's assessment attached, and trying on different outfits with the others, ranging from bedazzled to neon to practically nothing at all. And eventually, walking into the club and splitting a bottle of champagne among the six of them, while the storm continued to rage just outside the windows.

It was so much like the life she could have had, and Charli promised herself that whatever Rafe did or didn't do, she was going to enjoy every minute.

Though she had rather high hopes for what he *was* going to do.

Because he had expressly told her not to go to the club, and here she was, dressed to kill and drinking bubbly in a playroom.

"Okay, my turn." Morgan pulled a card from a deck. "Would you rather join the mile high club or have sex in a submarine?"

Rhylee sipped at her champagne. "Emerson's in the mile high club!"

"*Ew*," Saint muttered. "Airplane bathrooms…"

Emerson grinned. "Private jets. Of course, this was before I turned him all moral and he sold it, but I'd say we made good use while we could."

"Charli," Morgan called. "Mile high club or submarine?"

Charli shook her head. "Neither, ask another one."

"Okay." Morgan had a dangerous grin on her face. "Where's the most daring place you've had sex?"

Charli bit her lip in concentration. Life as a princess hadn't allowed for much privacy, and members of the press were always lurking around corners waiting for a scandal. But though she'd only just begun embracing her bold and exciting side, there had been a current of rebellion running through her blood for as long as she could remember.

"Reminding you all I *cannot* have nudie pictures showing up in the papers," she said, pointing at them with her champagne glass, "I did deface my English Literature classroom in university."

"No!" Rhylee clutched her chest. "Was it with the professor?"

"It was with a very nice literature major named David," Charli replied. "And it was entirely adequate."

"*Unacceptable*," Morgan said, throwing the card down on the counter. "You need dangerous, forbidden professor sex with the prince and you need it stat."

"She's first aid certified," Rhylee added. "She's practically a doctor, which means that is practically medical advice."

"Ooh, what about a medical fantasy?" Emerson put it, practically sloshing her champagne on the couch. "The doctor will see you now" — she made an exaggerated show of looking Charli up and down — "*all* of you."

The others devolved into laughter, but Charli's mind snagged and caught on the vision of Raffaello as a professor in her old literature classroom. He already looked the part, with his fitted suits and sense of subtle superiority that spoke to lineage and education and excellence. And when he wore his glasses…

"Mmm, I'll have what she's having," Morgan said with a grin, drawing Charli from the fantasy. Charli's ears warmed when she realized she had been off in a fantasy world of her own making. "Hot for professor?"

Charli shook her head, but before she could respond, the men all began to file into the room. Dante let out a low chuckle. "Professor is a classic for a reason. Though I'm more the bad boy type, I like to think."

Every bare inch of his skin was covered in tattoos and his ears glinted with spikey piercings. He most *definitely* fit into the bad boy category. And he most definitely had Charli wondering if Raffaello had tattoos he was hiding, and exactly what kind of man he was beneath his tailored suits.

Gabriel poured a glass of whiskey at the bar. "I prefer the sexy maid."

Emerson put one hand on her hip. "Do you, now?"

Rhylee grinned. "Someone's in trouble..." She leaned down to whisper conspiratorially to Charli. "She does it on purpose, riling him up like that. Of course...you wouldn't know a thing about that, would you?"

Charli couldn't argue the point. Maybe she didn't have all the terms and phrases yet, but it was like fire in her blood to deny Raffaello, to volley the taunts and teases, to make him work for the connection that was obviously growing much faster than it had any right to. She wanted to submit because she lost the fight, not simply because he told her to.

The other women had explained some of the power exchanges in their world, and while Charli knew she still had a long way to go, the power she felt from disobeying Raffaello's orders was all consuming and impossible to deny.

It shouldn't have been so exciting to ignore and disobey orders, but she had spent her entire life at the whim of her father and brother and the strictures of her royal position, and there was something incredibly freeing about just doing what she wanted to do.

The door to the room opened and all of them turned to see Van stick his head inside. "Fair warning, Princess. Rafe is on the warpath."

Each of the other women turned their gazes back to Charli, conspiratorial looks on their faces.

Charli feigned a nonchalance she didn't feel and sipped from the bottle of champagne. "He can do whatever he wants. He's not in charge of me."

Except excitement bubbled low in her belly at the thought of *exactly* what Raffaello would do to her when he walked through that door. The very first night he'd found her in the club, he'd picked her up and thrown her over his shoulder, and this, being in his secret place, playing games he had explicitly told her not to play, was sure to rile him up even more.

Charli grabbed Rhylee's hand. "Let's dance."

Rhylee was clearly up for any kind of trouble, and pressed a few buttons on her phone. The lights dimmed, giving the room an intimate and almost dangerous feeling, and a second later, pulsing dance music came on over the hidden speakers. Charli let the music move her body, just as it had done that first night, a base, instinctual kind of movement that made her forget all about the world outside, and made her feel like a person, made her feel like *Charli*, not Charlotte, not the Princess of Fontaine. Just *Charli*.

A moment later, the other women joined them on the makeshift dancefloor, moving in smooth, unrelenting rhythms to the anonymous music, and soon, their men followed, capturing and caging in their bodies, dance, but so much more, promises of nights of pleasure and power.

Charli draped her arms over Rhylee's shoulders and they moved to the music, the way girls had always danced together when out with friends, the way Charli had never had the chance to do, and she was so caught up in the freedom and novelty of it all, in the sense of true belonging, that she almost forgot Raffaello was on his way up to the club.

Right up until the moment the door slammed open.

He looked disheveled. Well, as disheveled as the prince ever looked, his top shirt button unbuttoned, his perfectly coiffed hair mussed, no doubt from him running his hands through it, and a look of raw, driving intensity on his beautiful face.

Rhylee gave Charli a look of devilish delight. "Exactly how much trouble do you want to get into tonight?"

Charli could read the look in her new friend's eyes, and the charged, demanding expression made her nipples pebble to tight points behind her dress. She didn't hesitate when she said, "All of it."

Rhylee grinned and leaned down, capturing Charli's mouth with her own. Charli had never kissed another woman before, but her body responded before she could stop it, a harsh river of heat spilling free from where their lips connected to the tips of her fingers, her lower belly warming and desire blooming hot and undeniable between her thighs.

She ran her hand through Rhylee's hair, tugging slightly, which made Rhylee groan, and pressing their bodies together for more contact, because *fuck* she needed more. So much more, kissing and touching and teasing and doing all manner of things she had always been told she shouldn't.

"Charlotte." Raffaello had crossed the room in the same time Charli had crossed all of the lines she had never known were drawn in the sand, and he stood at her back, imposing and dangerous, like a lion capable of great power.

She ignored him.

And in the next second, Charli felt herself being lifted — again — over Raffaello's shoulder.

It was too familiar a scene, and just like the first time he had done it, Charli was drawn to the strength and intensity of his body, his ability to carry her without breaking a sweat, his need to dominate, no matter much she fought back.

He walked toward the door, Charli still hanging over his shoulder, and paused only to speak to Van who stood by the door. "Sort out your woman."

Rhylee protested from across the room, but Charli barely heard, as Raffaello carried her out into the hallway.

"You can put me down now, you brute," she said, pounding on his thigh. His firm, muscled thigh.

"No," Rafe replied. "Every time you leave my sight you get into trouble."

"What's the plan, then?" Charli asked, the banter between them making her breath shallow, heightening her senses and her need... There was just something about pushing Rafe's limits, about teasing away at the edges of his self-control until he cracked that made her...

Wet. Hot. Needy beyond belief.

"Are you going to tie me up and keep me prisoner all night?"

Not that she hadn't imagined as much, hadn't imaged how Raffaello would pin her to the bed and tease pleasure and desire from her until she was begging for release. Her body ached for him in a deep, innate kind of way, like they were meant to connect the way stars were meant to explode, and Charli knew it wouldn't take long to push her over the edge.

"No," Rafe said again. "You think you know the rules here, Charlotte, but you don't. You think you're in charge here, but you're not. I decide what happens next. Not you."

Charli bucked against his strong hold, but he didn't even slow his pace. "And if I don't like what you decide?"

"Then that's too fucking bad."

He pushed a door at the end of the hallway open with one fluid motion. It shouldn't have turned her on to hear the prince swear, but *fuck* it did, the reserved, polished man, normally so diplomatic and controlled, giving over to his carnal needs, to the instincts that had carved men from stone and bone at the dawn of time.

She wanted to see all of this version of him, stripped bare and without the trappings of the world they had left back in Contanari. She wanted to see him release the lion within, and leave all sense of humanity and decorum on the other side of the door.

And then he placed her on the bed.

No longer swinging over his shoulder, Charli could see the room Rafe had brought them to. It was dark, shades and leather and mahogany, the bed he had dropped her on in the middle of the space, with rings at each corner, a wooden desk pressed up to the glass of the window, outside which the storm still continued to rage.

And along the walls, leather tools of different sizes and shapes, whips and paddles, cuffs, bars, the trades of the dangerous and depraved.

And Charli wanted to try them all.

She shouldn't. Her upbringing was still whispering in her ear, but her desire won out against the shame and the nerves. She wanted to push Raffaello until he had no choice but to make her submit, wanted to see what each and every one of those leather straps felt like against her skin as he made her beg for relief.

Rafe had been busying himself at the desk for a long moment, removing his suit and rolling up his sleeves, and when he turned back to her, Charli knew the prince was no longer in charge. *This* man was a predator, powerful and undeniable, driven by control, and coming for her.

"You signed the papers," Raffaello said, stepping toward her with slow, deliberate movements that only made Charli's heart beat faster, made her swallow hard against his approach. "You know what goes on here in the club."

Charli nodded. "I do."

"And you remember your safe words. Say them to me now."

She struggled with the command, but finally made her mouth move. "Green for good, yellow for slow, red for hard stop."

"Good," Raffaello said. "And tell me, Princess, what color at you at now?"

She shouldn't have been at any color, shouldn't have been in this space asking for these things, but it was too late for all that now, too late to pretend she didn't want everything that Raffaello was offering.

"Green."

There was almost a look of approval in his beautiful blue eyes. Almost.

"I'm pleased to hear it. Now, before we go forward, am I correct in assuming the others told you what goes on in my room?"

Over bottles of wine that afternoon, they had. Just as the others had read Charli's innate desires, they had shared Raffaello's, and the words they had used had made Charli's body buzz to life. "They said…they said you like to discipline."

Rafe nodded, his smile almost imperceptible, the tug at the corners of his lips more of a threat than an approval. "I do. You see, Charlotte… I like a good challenge. I'm a prince. People have been telling me what I want to hear all my life."

He looked at the wall of tools beside him, the whips and paddles and items she couldn't even begin to know how to use. "But not you, Princess. Oh no, you…you have been nothing but mouthy, disrespectful, and rude since the day I found you at the club."

Charli bristled. "I didn't ask for you to find me at the club."

Raffaello stepped forward, and Charli swallowed hard. Fear mingled with her desire, heightening it, making it brighter and more electric, and her body pulsed with a dangerous kind of need. "That's *exactly* what I'm talking about. You think you can act out without any kind of consequences."

He stepped to the edge of the bed then, mere feet separating them, and Charli got the distinct impression that she was about to be devoured. "But that's where you're wrong. See, Princess, I *am* the consequences."

Chapter Thirteen

Rafe moved and Charli dodged out his reach, scrambling across the bed as fast as she could. Her heart was pounding a million kilometers a minute, and her survival instincts were telling her to run, run, *run*, but she couldn't move fast enough, not to escape the strong hand wrapping around her ankle, dragging her back across the bed.

She bucked against his hold, almost breaking free, but Raffaello didn't let her go, trapping her between his grip and the soft covers below. "Like I said," he repeated, "consequences."

With a fluid movement, Rafe hauled Charli across his lap. The position was demeaning, exposing, and filthy, the way it made her dress slide up her thighs, the way it gave him access to the heated space between her legs, how it pushed her head into the mattress and exposed far too much skin for a man who no doubt knew exactly what to do with all of it.

Raffaello ran his hands along her curves, *tsk, tsking* as he stroked her, each touch sending her body closer to complete and total destruction. "You have been badly behaved this week, haven't you?"

He inched the dress up, the tiniest amount at a time, until Charli was holding her breath and desperately searching for any rational thought. "I'm a grown woman," she bit back. "I can do whatever I want. You're not in charge of me."

Rafe brought his hand down on her ass so fast she barely had time to register the whistle in the air before pain exploded around her skin. It was a firework, bursting and combustible, and then, to Charli's great surprise, twinkling at the very edges with light flashes of pleasure that made her breath catch.

"But you want me to be in charge of you, don't you, Princess? You want someone to take you by the throat and tell you exactly how to believe yourself."

He slid one hand under her chin, until his powerful fingers were stroking the line of her throat, the touch incendiary in the darkest way.

Charli barely managed to get in a breath. "You're not my father."

"Oh, no," Raffaello whispered, leaning down so his warm breath brushed her ear, "I'm not your father, Princess. But I am your Daddy."

Charli's bucked against him, aware that she was asking for so much more than she should, aware that her body was aching and burning up, searching for touch, release, pleasure of any kind. She needed with a kind of intensity she had never needed before.

But she also needed to show him she wasn't going to give in that easily. "No."

Raffaello massaged one of her sore ass cheeks, the touch at once comforting and demanding. "No? That's a shame."

He danced his fingers below the curve of her ass, making Charli arch back into him, practically against her own will. "Because if you don't give me what I want, then I can't give you what you want."

Charli summoned all the power she had left. "You don't know what I want."

Raffaello chucked, dark and deep, a promise without words. "I most *certainly* know what you want, Princess. You want me to push your panties to the side and pulse my fingers in and out of your tight little pussy until you slick me with your cum. You want me to fill you up with my cock and my fingers and my toys, making you come over and over and over again, until you're begging me to stop.

"And… You want me to spank you again. Maybe with my hand on your bare skin, maybe with one of my toys, maybe both, whatever it takes to show you that I'm in charge."

"Raffaello…" His named spilled from her lips like a broken prayer.

"Try again, Princess. I know you can."

She shook her head. "No."

She could hear the grin in his voice. "Yes. Just once."

Charli knew a losing gambit when she was the one moving the pieces, and nearly burning for his touch, for edges of the relief that was clouding her judgement and making her buck and arch against him, meant she was past the edge of her own control. "Please… Daddy?"

Raffaello ran small circles over her ass, which made the fabric rise up, exposing more and more of her. In a second, he would know all of her secrets. "Please what, Princess? You need to be specific."

She tried to move out of his grip, but he pinned her down with one strong hand.

Charli sighed. "Please…finger my pussy."

He didn't move. "You're going to have to do better than that."

"Fuck…" Charli tried to move against him. "Please finger my pussy until I come all over your hand… I need… I need to come… Daddy."

He leaned down and whispered in her ear, "Do you have any idea what I want to do you, Princess? The depraved, sinful things I've been fantasizing about? I'm going to make you dream of me for the rest of your life."

And then he slipped his finger under the hem of her dress.

And paused. "*Mmm*, and tell me, was it your idea to skip the underwear?"

Charli shook her head.

Raffaello stopped moving his fingers, and she practically cried at the loss of contact. "Fine, yes. It was my idea…"

"Tell me"—he started teasing her sensitive skin again—"what *exactly* did you think would happen when I found out you were bare under your dress…?"

Charli took a deep breath, and it smelled of Raffaello, of his fancy French cologne, of his ink pen and the wooden desk he always sat at while he worked. "I had hoped you'd push my dress up to my waist and fill me with your cock."

Raffaello slipped a finger inside her pussy and Charli gasped.

"I like it when you're honest with me, Princess," he said. "Be honest again. Do you like misbehaving because you know you'll get punished?"

She didn't want to answer, but as long as it kept his fingers pulsing insider her pussy, Charli didn't have a choice. "Yes…sometimes…sometimes I want to see if I can make all your control break."

Raffaello pushed another finger inside and Charli clawed at the bed. The pleasure was hovering at the edges of her vision, but it wasn't enough, wasn't nearly enough to satisfy her cravings.

"You want to break my control," Rafe asked, as if he wasn't finger-fucking her slow enough to make Charli lose her mind. "You want to push me to my edge."

"Yes," she managed. "Even the rigid prince has his breaking point."

He leaned down and whispered to her, "I'm much more interested in finding your breaking point, Princess." And then his rhythm changed, hard and fast and unyielding, and he brought his other hand between her thighs to tease and stroke at her clit, and it didn't take much, not much as all, for Charli to reach the edge of her pleasure like it was where she had always been destined to go, close, so fucking close and…

"Ask me for it," Rafe said. "Nicely."

And she couldn't fight him then, not when everything was on the line, so she bucked back into his touch and murmured the words she knew he wanted to hear, "Please, Daddy, make me come."

With a single stroke of his finger over her swollen clit, he did, sending Charli shattering over the edge, her body tightening around him, squeezing and pulsing and chasing that sweet fucking relief, until it was just them in the center of the whole universe, just them and her submission and the incredible pleasure of finally, finally, finally giving in.

Chapter Fourteen

Rafe was close to breaking.

It had been far, far too long since he'd played in the club, his responsibilities at home taking him away and keeping him up most nights, and he had resigned himself to that reality.

But if he had known just what it would be like to scene with the woman in his arms, he would have abandoned the throne and country for a taste.

Because she was *perfection*.

Charlotte was new to the lifestyle, no doubt about it, but there was something natural and innate about the way she played, about how far she pushed, and he had taken the bait and risen to the challenge each and every time. Because he hadn't been lying, he liked a challenge, and Raffaello was fairly certain that no one in his life had ever challenged him quite the way that she did.

Which was how he found himself sliding two wet fingers from her tight pussy, not hesitating a second before slipping them into his mouth. The taste of her was ambrosia, intense and full of desire, and he suddenly needed to have his mouth on her pussy like he needed to breathe.

But there were more pressing matters to deal with first.

"How are you feeling, Charlotte?"

Her voice was rough and thick when she responded. "Green... Master Raffaello."

Fuck, his title on her lips made his cock harder than steel. Not that it hadn't been straining since the moment he'd walked into the club to find her lip locked with Rhylee, since the moment Van had handed him her papers...

"Good," he murmured, stroking her soft hair because he couldn't quite help himself, "because now you need to take your punishments."

"For what?" she asked, like she hadn't been defying and disobeying him since the moment he had found her in the club.

"You tell me," he said, teasing the sweet valley where the curve of her ass met her thigh. "And I might be lenient."

"And if I don't?"

Fuck, he loved that mouth, the way she never hesitated and never backed down. When she submitted to him, it was because she wanted to, because she had finally deemed him worthy, and that was far more decadent, feeding his soul and his body.

Well, right now, he was ignoring his body, his throbbing cock and aching balls, but she was right, he had always been a man of total control.

"Then you don't get what you want, Princess."

"I don't want to get punished."

He squeezed her ass. "You can't lie to me, Charlotte. You're dripping all over my thighs and practically begging for more. You want your ass turned red and your hands and legs cuffed so you can't escape." He leaned down, nipped at her ear, and whispered, "You want to be totally at my mercy."

She turned her head, and he was struck the harshness of desire in her eyes, the glaze and intensity, the part of her lips and the flush on her cheeks. Her words were barely above a whisper when she said, "Fuck you...*sir.*"

Rafe couldn't help himself, he claimed her mouth in a kiss, gripping the back of her neck to drag her closer, taking the connection in an almost brutal claiming, but *fuck* he had been waiting too long, needing so much more than he had wanted to admit, desperate for a woman who saw him as something other than the prince. There was no future for them, not in the world they walked, but he could steal his pleasure and give her so much more in return, just for the night, just for the few moments they got to share, and he wasn't going to deny himself any of it.

Finally, he pulled back, dragging his hand to her chin and holding her in a firm grip. "Tell me what you have to atone for, Charlotte, and I'll give you what you want."

She pursed her lips and tried to square her jaw in defiance, but he still held her chin. The rebellion sparkled in her eyes anyway. "You want me to say I went to the club because you told me not to, that I looked into every room to see what was inside because you explicitly forbid made from doing it... Not everything is about you, *Prince.*"

For a traditional submissive, that would have earned a punished. For Charlotte, it was all part of the game.

"I don't believe you," Raffaello said quietly, his tone lethal. "I think you went to the club because you wanted to act out, to get my attention, to push me...to my limits." He slid her dress all the way up then, exploring her beautiful round ass. "And I think you kissed Rhylee today to make me angry. To make me lose control."

"No," Charlotte whispered on a breath. "She's very beautiful... And I've never kissed another woman before... I was curious."

"Curious, right," Rafe murmured, "curious about how it would feel to have your ass spanked red and your orgasm denied."

"No," she said again. "And you have to admit, it was hot..."

He did have to admit that, but certainly not out loud. Charlotte didn't need to know exactly how her unabashed desires, her willingness to explore and adventure, or the sight of her hands digging into Rhylee's hair made him feral. She didn't need to know that he had practically taken her right then and there in the room with all his friends because he'd been turned in a slavering beast at the sight of her.

Instead of responding, he brought his hand down on her bare ass. It wasn't too hard, just a way to test her limits, and to Raffaello's delight, Charlotte bucked into his touch and swallowed her sound of pain.

"So hot," he said, massaging the spot that was now turning red. "But I'm not a man who likes to share, Charlotte. I like to claim what belongs to me."

She twisted around to look at him. "I don't belong to you."

Raffaello leveled another spank across her ass. "You're wearing my marks," he said, fascinated with how her skin turned pink under his touch. "Now, do you want to tell me what else you're sorry for, or do you want to take your punishment?"

"I don't have anything to be sorry for," Charlotte bit out, much to Raffaello's delight.

"Mm, I thought you'd say that," he responded. "So be a good girl for once and do as you're told... Count the punishments, Charlotte, and thank me for each one."

And before she could protest, he spanked her ass again.

Charlotte bucked up, brushing his swollen cock, which nearly made Raffaello swear. "Fuck you... One."

"And?" he prompted.

"Thank you," Charlotte said through gritted teeth.

"Good," Raffaello replied, before giving her another.

On and on they went, and with each strike against her ass, Charlotte settled into his touch a little bit more, the ice around her responses melting away, until she was practically writhing in his lap and begging for his touch.

"One more, Princess," he said. "Take your punishment like you know you deserve it."

She strained and arched against him, but finally relaxed, the perfect submission, earned and given after a fair battle. "Please..."

And he didn't make her beg, not then, when Raffaello felt he'd crossed over a threshold of his own, not when he was straining at the very edges of himself to push her to the limit, just as far as she thought she could go, and then that little bit further. No, she deserved the release in that moment, the sweet release of pain and pleasure dancing together, and he deserved to watch her find it.

"Good girl," he whispered, as he brought his hand down one more time. She did cry out then, no doubt from the pain of his punishment hitting the same red and raw spot on her flesh over and over, and he gently, carefully pulled her into his arms and leaned against the headboard, so he could stroke her hair and tell her that she had done so well, taken what was owned to her and atoned. The words spilled free like an unstoppable tide, too true and raw to be spoken in anything but the intimacy of the club, in the breath when the scene stood still.

"Rafe..." Charlotte murmured against his chest, her tone a little rough and low, a kind of intense eroticism in the need there.

"Yes, Princess," he replied, unable to keep from kissing the top of her head. It was a temporary truce, one born from the ashes of destruction and need, but it was a truce, nonetheless.

"I don't want you to send me back to my room without..."

"Without?" he prompted, know what she was asking for and wanted to hear her say it all the same.

"Without touching me," she replied. "I need... I need more than your fingers and hands..."

"What do you need?" Raffaello asked, as if either of them could ignore the way his cock pressed against her thighs.

"You," she said finally, just a hint of uncertainty in her tone, like she wasn't sure if she could be asking for such a thing. "I...please... I need your cock inside me..."

She paused and pulled back to look at him, determination in her eyes, clouded by need and aching, hot rebellion. "Please, Master Raffaello, I need you."

Chapter Fifteen

Charli didn't quite know where the begging had come from. She had been so capable of denying his charms, of pushing back when Raffaello pushed forward, but she had passed the point of no return with each spank against her ass, and instead of turning her off, the punishment had become a kind of reward all on its own. It made her body ache for something she couldn't quite name, but all Charli knew for certain was that her nipples were hard, painful points, and her pussy was clenching on emptiness, as if she were desperate to be filled and taken again and again.

"Say it again, Charlotte," he whispered, stroking along her cheek. He was such a universe in one, strong and controlled most days, but with a softness there, a tenderness that made him a good leader and a good Dominant. "I need to hear you say it."

Because, she realized, he was at the edge of his control, the slight cracking to his voice, the way he held her tight, as if afraid she might bolt. He was far better at hiding it, but Raffaello was losing himself to the moment between them.

And Charli wanted him to fall over the edge with her.

"You heard what I said," she muttered, and *fuck* if that didn't make her pussy pulse and ache, the pushing, the knowing he was going to fight back, the knowing he would always meet her on the field.

"Then hear what I say right now, Little Brat," Rafe murmured in her ear. "If you don't stop giving me fucking attitude, I'm going to put a gag in your mouth and not let you come for the rest of the night."

Charli arched against him, her sore ass and thighs pressing into his hard, throbbing cock. He was huge, thick and strong as steel behind his tailored trousers, and she needed him inside her like she needed to breathe.

"I don't believe you," she whispered, the twin tendrils of fear and desire weaving up her back and turning her body to a hot, aching mess. "I think you're making it all up."

Raffaello reached down and undid his button and fly with a single deft motion. The movement brought his fingers closer to her aching pussy, but not nearly close enough, just a teasing taste of all the possibilities he might have to offer, if only she were willing to behave herself.

"If you're good for me, Princess," Raffaello said, carefully, slowly pulling his cock free from his trousers, "I'll give you permission to ride my cock."

She was so close to him, nearly bare skin to bare skin, and it was all Charli wanted in the world right at that moment to take him inside her, to feel him stretch her and fill her. She knew the club required screenings to play, and she also knew in her gut that Raffaello would never let anything happen to her, which meant she would be able to feel him, all of him, and the thought was nearly overwhelming.

"Simple words, Charlotte," he whispered into her ear. "I know you can give them to me. I know you *want* to give them to me. You must be so needy right now, so wet and desperate to feel a hard cock filling you up."

"Yes..." It was barely a whisper. "So wet."

"So don't fight it." His words were thick as honey, the sweet promise of the devil at the crossroads, and Charli was ready to make a deal. "Give me what I want, and you'll get what you want, to be filled and fucked and pleasured like you deserve."

"Raffaello..." she managed, the desire making her fuzzy and the need pulsing through her body like a molten river. She was nearly ready to combust with the intensity of it all, and no doubt Raffaello knew that. "I need... I need..."

"I know what you need," he replied. "But you know what you have to do first, Charlotte."

"It's Charli," she pushed the words out, harsh and deliberate, and Rafe smiled with his canines.

"If I call you Charli," he teased, stroking his cock with long, deliberate motions, "will you call me by what I want to be called?"

She swallowed hard. "Fine."

"See, that wasn't so hard, was it, *Charli?*" he asked, rolling her name over in that dark, demanding voice of his, making her squirm and arch until she was nearly, nearly pressing against his cock, and at that same time, not nearly close enough to what she wanted.

"Seems plenty hard to me," Charli tried to tease, but it came out as a whimper, need roiling in her every word."

"Yes," Rafe replied. "I'm hard as a fucking stone for you, Charli. I've wanted to fuck you since the moment I found you in that club in the city dancing with some stranger." He bit her earlobe. "There is no shortage of the filthy, wicked things I want to do to you. But it's up to you, now. Say the words and I'll give you what you want."

Charli swallowed. She'd passed the edge of where she thought she could hold on to a dozen times over and could no longer keep her control, the tether getting tighter and tighter in her hands until it finally snapped. "Please fuck me... Daddy."

Rafe didn't wait, not a second, not a breath. Before the words were out, he positioned his cock at her entrance. "Take it, Princess. Take it."

And she did, sliding down his hard length, until he was buried deep, so fucking deep inside her, stretching her, filling her the way Charli had known he would. It was everything, the connection, the intensity, the absolute surrender, and she wrapped her arms around Raffaello's neck to leverage herself up and down, adjusting to the intense size of him with each harsh entry. She loved it, each pinch of pain, followed by almost blinding, bursting pleasure, loved the sounds he made in her ear as she took him, the dark intense whispers that propelled her forward, the building, impossible ache that was sure to burst like the sun as she chased it.

"Do you feel that, Princess?" Raffaello asked, pulsing his cock inside her full pussy. "Do you feel what you do to me?"

"Yes..." she barely managed to get the word out. "It's so good, I need... I need to be fucked harder..."

Because she couldn't get the speed or leverage she needed, not straddling his lap, and she knew Raffaello was holding back.

"First, you're going to come all over my cock," he said. "Maybe twice, and then I'll fuck you like you want."

"Raffaello…"

Raffaello moved his hand between their connected thighs, brushing over her swollen clit. "It's Master Raffaello, Charlotte. Don't forget that…"

Charli pressed against his fingers, aching for more friction on her sensitive bundle of nerves. "Yes, Master Raffaello."

He didn't respond with words. Instead, he pinched her clit hard, which sent Charli careening over the edge, an absolute storm of pleasure bursting free all around her, hard, intense pounding in her ears as she came hard and fast, as she rode, rode, rode Raffaello's cock, spilling hot, wet release between them.

"You just love to get your punishments, don't you, Charli?" Raffaello asked. "Just love to ignore the rules and do whatever you want, like not calling me by my title, like coming without permission. Just for that, you're going to have to come again before I fuck you like you really want to be fucked."

"Please…" Charlotte wasn't past begging, her body was still on fire from her release, but she knew that Raffaello could give her so much more, so much more of a pounding, intense pleasure that might just wreck her.

She didn't care. She needed the roughness and intensity, and he was holding back.

"I don't think so," Raffaello replied, stroking her clit again. "You're misbehaving on purpose just to get a rise out of me, and I don't reward that kind of behavior. But if you do as you're told, I'll put you on your hands and knees and drive into you from behind until all you can think about is the feel of my cock in your pretty little cunt, until you're begging me to fill you up and mark you as mine."

Charli thought she might lose the plot right then and there. It was filthy and depraved to want such a rough fucking, but his words only served to make her pussy wetter and hotter and she knew she would never win the battle, let alone the war.

"I'll be good," she managed. "I'll be good, Daddy, please, just fuck me."

"You want to come on Daddy's cock?" Raffaello asked. "You want to make me slick and wet with your sweet release?"

She nodded. "Please..."

"Fuck, I love that word on your lips, Princess. Like you can't even help yourself from begging for my cock." He slipped a finger into her mouth. "I can't wait to see you all filled up, a ball gag in your mouth, my cock in your sweet, tight cunt, a thick plug stretching your sweet little asshole so you can take me there, too. I'm going to wreck you with pleasure, Princess."

"I can take it," Charli managed through the fire of her need. "I can take it..."

"I know you can," Raffaello said, sliding his finger over her bottom lip. "So beg to come all over Daddy's cock..."

"Please," she bit the word out. "Please can I come on your cock, Daddy? I need... I need to be fucked harder and faster, I want you to mark me in your cum... Fuck, *please*." It was an erotic, string of hot, filthy words, but they seemed to hit Raffaello with the same intensity they hit her, and soon he was pistoning his hips up and down, moving her body to take his cock, stroking her clit, and just when she thought she couldn't hang on a second longer, he leaned over and whispered into her ear. "Be a good girl and come for me."

Charli did as she was told, giving into the pure, intense sensations of Raffaello driving into her, taking her again and again, into the sweet, bursting release that coated his still-hard cock in her cum, in the knowledge that she was about to get everything she had been hoping for.

She came hard and fast, and was still riding the waves of her release when Raffaello spun her around without breaking their connection and pushed her onto her hands and knees on the bed. The position, the vulnerability and intensity of it, built her pleasure and desire right back and up, and then Rafe was giving her everything she wanted, the harsh intense thrusting of his cock, driving relentlessly into her, his strength at her back, his demanding, commanding presence keeping her locked into place.

He put his hand on her lower back and pressed her harshly into the bed. "You wanted to be the bad girl, Charli, this is what bad girls get. They get fucked hard and fast from behind, they get taken and owned and claimed."

"Are you going to claim me?" she asked, adding, "Sir" just long enough after to be disrespectful. "Are you going to mark me?"

"Do you want that?" he asked, reaching down to stroke the apex of her thighs, right where their bodies met. It was slick and hot and demanding, his fingers moving nearly as fast as his cock. "Do you want to me be covered in my cum, Princess? Hot and sticky?"

She didn't really have a retort for that because, all at once, Charli did want to be covered and claimed, taken by this man and forced to pleasure over and over again. "Yes," she managed. "Come all over me. Fill me up."

"Mmm, but I'm so enjoying the view," Raffaello said. "You look so good on your hands and knees... Tell me, *Charli*, have you ever worn a man's collar before?"

She shook her head. "Never."

"Good," he replied. "I want to be the first one, the one to leash you up and make you crawl to me on your hands and knees. My sweet little princess, dripping wet because she loves having her pussy exposed for my pleasure."

"I'm not your toy," Charli managed, even as she gave him all her pleasure, all her need, even as she took his demanding, driving cock so deep in her needy body. "You don't get to fuck me whenever you want."

"No," Raffaello said. "But I'll fuck you whenever *you* want. And that's going to be all the time when I'm done with you."

"Will not," Charli fought.

"Little Brat, by the time I've had my fill, you're going to be begging for me to come in every one of your holes. You're going to be ravenous for me, demanding, promising, whatever it takes. No one else will ever compare."

She feared he might be right about that, as the thrust of his hard cock pushed her higher, further, closer to the sweet fucking finish line, stronger and more real than anything she had ever felt in her entire life. "Never going to happen," she whispered. "I won't crawl for you."

"You'll *beg* to crawl for me," he replied. "And you'll beg for my plug in your ass and my cock on your tongue and the sweet release only Daddy can give you. Try it now. Beg, Charli."

"No," she said. "No... I'm so close, please..."

"So close," he repeated, "so close to spilling in your sweet tight cunt, which is what you really want, isn't it, to be filled up and claimed?"

Charli pushed back into him. "Yes... I need to be claimed. I need you to claim me... Fuck. Please...please make me come."

"First," Rafe said, slicking his finger through her wetness, "say you'll crawl for Daddy. Say you'll be so good for Daddy."

She was going to do it, Charli knew. She was going to give everything over to this man, her body, no doubt, but likely so very much more. Because he pushed her, he demanded of her things no one had ever demanded, and he saw in her things no one else had ever seen.

Because she wanted to do everything he said, and so much more. She wanted to crawl, to beg, to fight and fuck and submit, she wanted to be owned and claimed in ways she didn't quite understand, but knew to be the total and honest truth in her heart and soul.

"Fuck...yes," she muttered, the words so fucking sweet, freedom on her tongue. "Fuck you and fuck yes. I want to craw for you, Daddy."

Rafe swore under his breath and thrust once, twice, once more, each thrust sending her closer to that invisible peak and taking him with her, and then it was too much, far, far too much all at once, intense and blinding and overwhelming, the impossibility of pleasure taking her under, taking them both under.

Charli came hard and fast, and a second later, Raffaello was pumping hot sticky cum deep inside her, bursting pleasure and connection and sweet relief from the world, from the demands, from the denial. Just desire and need and release in each other's arms.

Chapter Sixteen

Raffaello watched as Charli slid her fingers between her legs, the motion making her back arch until she pressed up against him. He knew what she was doing, testing the waters, playing the games she knew would get her into the trouble she clearly liked so much, and he planned to let her dig herself in just a little deeper.

At least, he planned to let her until he lost his own sense of control and caved to the desires he had finally submitted to when he'd walked into the club and found her in a tiny dress doing exactly what she knew she wasn't supposed to do.

Because *fuck* she played that role perfectly, didn't she. The dominate side of Raffaello, the side of himself he'd been ignoring and denying for so long, it wasn't a costume. It wasn't a *sometimes* feeling that came out to play on the nights he needed a little bit of distraction. It was who he was deep in his bone, innate, like he couldn't exist without the dominant, without the need to control and temper and deliver.

And he knew without a doubt that Charlotte was the same way. She had been raised prim and proper and royal to a fault, but free from the confines of court, there was no denying who she was beneath, and that true version of her called to the true version of him in a dangerous, explosive way.

If the night they had spent together had been any indication.

She was new to the scene, and yet, she seemed to act on instinct, pushing the limits, taking what she wanted, giving him the challenge he had been craving for so long, the true respite from how heavy his world had become.

And she was challenging him all over again.

Raffaello slid his hand between her thighs and gripped her wrist, staying her motions. Then he leaned over and whispered very low in her ear, "What exactly do you think you're doing, Little Brat?"

Charlotte gasped, the sound laden with heat and molten desire that made Rafe's cock jump and press against Charlotte's lovely, round ass. "What I want to," she replied. "You never said I couldn't make myself come."

And there, the twinkle in her voice, like she knew she was pushing the limits, it made Raffaello *ravenous*, like he wanted to steal the sarcasm from her lips with a bruising kiss, wanted to bring her to the very edge and leave her hanging on until she repented and atoned and begged for her punishment. Charlotte made him creative in entirely new ways, and he nipped at the smooth skin of her shoulder, only barely resisting the urge to bite down.

To mark her.

This was dangerous enough, this dalliance that couldn't never be anything more. But the aching need to claim her as his own, that was a reality Raffaello had no interest in unpacking.

"I know for certain, *Charlotte*, that I told you your orgasms belong to me, your pleasure belongs to me..."

You belong to me. For the moment, and no longer.

"I don't remember agreeing to that," she said, that devilish spark in her tone. "And you were asleep when I woke up."

"So, you did exactly what you knew would piss me off the most?" he murmured, his voice low and dark, even to his own ears. "So you touched yourself when you knew you shouldn't, slipped your fingers into your tight, wet pussy, even though it was against the rules..." He placed his hand over hers and moved them both, so he was the one in charge of exactly how Charlotte touched herself. "You made yourself come, even though I claimed your releases..."

"I didn't come," Charlotte said on a gasp. "I promise."

"But you're so wet..." Raffaello slicked a finger along the desire staining her thighs. "You're dripping, Princess. And already so ready..."

"I know..." Her voice was teetering on submission, but he knew she wouldn't give up quite so easily. "Can you help me?"

"No, Charlotte," he said. "I only help my little subs when they've been good. And you haven't been good. I don't even think you know the meaning of the word."

"I do too," she replied. "It's just so much more fun to see you get angry..."

Raffaello took the opportunity to press Charlotte's own fingers between her thighs, guiding one inside her tight hole. "I get angry when you go against my orders.

When you touch yourself when you know that's not allowed."

Charlotte stroked her fingers, the sound making her gasp. "But it feels so good... Raffaello."

A deep heat bloomed in his chest. Every time he thought she was about to give in, there was more, one more push, one more dangerous response, one more teasing comment to make him rock hard and dangerously close to tying her up and taking her like the animal inside told him to.

"Try again, Little Brat."

"Or what?" she asked. "Raffaello is your name, isn't it, *Highness*?"

"Or I put you in a chastity belt for the rest of the day," he threatened. "One that puts just a little pressure on your swollen clit, but never enough for you to come. One that makes you drip and ache all day long, with no relief. And when just when you think you're going to lose your mind, I'll remove it" — he pushed one of his own fingers inside her — "and fill you up with my cock...and tell you, Charlotte, not to come."

"What makes you think that'll stop me?" she asked. "I don't like being told what to do."

He chuckled, low and harsh. "I know, Princess. But I like punishing you."

He pushed a second finger in and brushed his thumb over her clit at the same time, so she was arching and bucking back into him, pressing against his swollen cock and making Raffaello burn with need. The need to control her, to rise to her challenge, to win her submission.

"Tell me you're sorry for playing with this sweet, pretty pussy," he murmured, "and I'll give you what you want."

"Raffaello…"

He stopped pulsing his fingers in and out of her hole. "Tell me, Princess."

"Please…" It came out on a whimper. "Fine… Yes, I'm sorry for playing with my pussy and trying to make myself come…"

"Sorry…?"

"Sorry… *Sir*." She bit out the last.

And God, if that word wasn't like lightning to his senses, bursting and bright and beautiful in its destruction. Because he had *earned* it. Because she had gifted it to him, because neither of them was handed what they craved for most simply because of who they were or the positions they had been born into.

"So good," he murmured into her ear, his words carved from stone. "So sweet in your submission, Princess. You deserve to be rewarded." He bit the sensitive skin right at the base of her throat, loving how she arched and caved into his touch, loving how responsive and needy she was for him. "Come all over my fingers, Charlotte. Give me your release."

"It's *Charli*…" she managed on a gasp. "*Please*."

And because Raffaello found he just couldn't help himself when it came to her bite, her innate power and sense of self-worth, the way she fought with everything she had, he kissed where he had bit, and whispered, "Come for me, *Charli*."

She did, hard and fast, clenching around his fingers and rocking back into his cock. Her free hand grasped for the blanket, dragging the covers back in a wild frenzy as she rode her waves of pleasure hard and fast.

It was all Rafe could to do hold onto his control and need as she shook in his arms. There was no propriety in her release, no politeness or subtly. She was bold and unapologetic and without fear or reservation, and there was something so incredibly honest about seeing Charlotte in such a moment of freedom, that it stirred a truly carnal need to life within him.

"How are you feeling after last night?" he asked, as she slowly began to come down from her release. Her skin was warm against his, and her breathing finally began to even. "Are you sore?"

Charlotte nodded. "A little. But..." She blushed, and he was surprised to see the color pinken her already stained cheeks. "I kind of like it..."

"Little Brat," he replied, unable to keep the admiration from tone. "You just like being marked and claimed."

She let out a low laugh. "I thought we had already established that." Then Charlotte looked up at him with those big brown eyes, the pure falsehood of innocence as she climbed to her knees, a position that pushed her breasts up and her ass out. "Now, what are we going to do about your needs..."

Raffaello leaned back against the headboard. "Who said we're doing anything, Princess? I make the rules, not you."

Charlotte grinned. "You think you make the rules. But I have to wonder. If I were to lean down and take your cock in my mouth..." She held his gaze. "If I were to take you so far down my throat I choked, would you stop me?"

Raffaello knew he still had his control. Somewhere. Surely. But he couldn't quite seem to figure out where that control had gone... Because now that she had planted the beautiful picture in his head, it was all he could think about, the pulsing of her throat, spilling across her tongue...

"Ask me nicely and we'll see."

Charlotte shrugged. "I'm pretty sure you'd prefer if I wasn't nice at all…"

It was Rafe's turn to grin. "See, I think you want to suck my cock. I think it makes you wet to even imagine it, dripping and needy, your pussy *aching* to be filled. I think you're craving that feeling of taking me, and hoping I'll just let you have what you want." He took her chin in his hand and held her face steady in a strong grip. "So ask me nicely."

Charlotte took a deep breath. "I think we established I don't need your help to get off."

Raffaello slid his thumb across her lower lip, loving how she parted her mouth on instinct, as if she didn't even realize she was doing it. "You'll look so pretty with your mouth full," he murmured. "Why don't you just do as you're told this one time, and we'll both get what we want."

Charlotte slid her tongue along his thumb, the sensation sparking hot need, making Raffaello's cock surge and pulse. Then she wrapped her lips around his thumb and sucked, taking him into her mouth in a teasing display of the obscene way she would no doubt suck his cock.

"Do you want more, Little Brat?" he asked. "Do you want to come down here, take the thing you really want? You know how to get it."

She swallowed hard and finally pulled away from his hand. Her eyes were glassy with desire and need, and he knew she was already wet and aching from their play.

"Where are you, Charlotte?" he asked quietly. "Tell me now."

It was the one thing she didn't fight him on. "Green."

"Good." He held her gaze. "Now, what do you want?"

Charlotte took a deep, shuddering breath. "I want…to suck your cock…"

Raffaello raised a brow.

Charlotte ground her teeth together. "Please…can I choke on your cock until you come down my throat…" She lifted her chin in defiance. "Master Raffaello?"

He ran his hand down her neck, loving the way her body seemed to melt into his touch. "You want my cock," he murmured, "come take it."

She didn't wait to be told twice. She kneeled between his legs, her ass in the air and her beautiful breasts on full display, pressed together and so incredibly soft to the touch. And then she took his cock in her and, and Raffaello gasped at the sensation, reaching for the headboard behind him to squeeze tight at Charlotte leaned down and swallowed the head of his cock.

He swore low and harsh, but she barely seemed to realize, as she set about her task, sliding up and down his cock with a slick, wet mouth that felt like fucking heaven. She sucked her cheeks in and took him to the back of her throat, until she was choking, but it didn't stop her. Each kiss, suck, and lick brought him closer to the edge, and Raffaello reached for her hair, guiding her up and down with a strong hand.

"Look at you taking my cock like it was meant for you," he growled. "So fucking pretty with your mouth full. All the way down there, Princess, all the way down."

He was close to his edge, and beginning to feel his control ebbing away as she took him like she had been begging for, and he knew he wanted to be inside her when he came, spilling hot and thick in her tight little hole, filling her up and making her come around his cock one last time.

With a strength he didn't know he possessed, he pulled his cock free from her mouth, and dragged Charlotte up to sit on his lap. Her pussy brushed his swollen cock, and *fuck* but she was absolutely soaked, so wet and so ready all from choking on his cock.

"Did that make you wet, Princess?" he asked, while slipping two fingers inside her. "Did that make you so needy?"

"Yes…" she managed through bared teeth.

"And do you need to come again?" he asked. "To relieve a little of that…pressure?"

"Yes…" that was a whimper.

"Tell me what you need…"

She was quite only for a second. "I need to ride your cock. *Sir.*"

Raffaello reached out and pinched her nipple. "Are you going to get me all wet, Princess? Are you going to cover me in your slick need?"

She had a defiant expression on her face when she finally nodded.

"Say it."

"I want to get your cock wet… *Please…* I need to feel you inside me." And she held his gaze, strong and intense and needing so much. "Daddy."

Raffaello pulled her onto his lip, giving her barely a second before seating her on his cock. "Take what you what, Princess."

She slid down his cock, not hesitating to take his length, and when she bottomed out against his hips, both of them sighed in relief. Raffaello couldn't keep his hands to himself, not a moment longer, and her buried them in her hair as he pulled her in tight, kissing the top of her head and murmuring how sweet she felt, how well she took him, how proud he was of her.

And then they were moving, slowly, too slowly for both of them at first, but their bodies were both still so sensitized, and the moment was too sweet, too decadent to give up so easily, and so they moved much slower than either of them wanted, feeling every single inch of each other, taking in the shape and feel of each other's bodies, until Raffaello knew that he was quickly crossing over that invisible bridge, that barrier that kept him from unleashing the monster, giving over to the side of himself he'd been denying far, far too long.

He captured Charlotte around the waist and spun them over, never breaking their contact.

"Grab the bar," he said, indicating to the metal bar over the headboard. She didn't fight him, just reached overhead and grabbed the bar with both hands, which brought their bodies somehow closer together, sealed their connection in an intense, almost blinding way.

"Hold on tight, Princess," Rafe practically growled in her ear. "And come as much as you can."

He didn't give her the chance to respond, just slid his cock down hard and fast into her, and then out, and then they were fucking like the storm they had become, intense and unyielding, dragging them both closer to the precipice, until it wasn't a matter of *when*, but how many, not of *how* but how hard.

He felt like a madman unleashed, but every time worry snuck in that he was pushing her beyond her limits, Rafe found Charlotte right at his side, giving as well as she took, riding his body like she was laying claim.

"Eyes on me," he demanded. "When you come, I want to see you lose control…"

For the first time in long, pleasured-filled moments, his words broke through her haze "I can't…"

"You will, Princess," he said. "For me."

And then he slammed hard into her, and Charlotte clenched her fingers around the bar and surrendered to the pleasure, and he saw every ounce of her fight as she kept her eyes open and her gaze locked on him with the riotous, pulsing orgasm that took her, until she was spilling hot and wet along his pounding cock.

"So good," he murmured, trying to keep from losing his head. "I know you need to be bad, Charlotte, but look at how it can be when you're my good girl."

"I guess you just need to make it worth my time," she whispered, her voice thick with pleasure and need.

"That can be arranged, Princess," he replied, bringing his fingers up to the heated space of their connection and stroking her swollen clit, and then sliding his other hand to cup the back of her neck, his thumb at the base of her throat, just where she swallowed and…

"Say thank you," he murmured. "Be good for me…so good for me…"

She parted her lips, thrust up to meet his pistoning hips, and held his gaze. "Thank you…Daddy."

And then Charlotte crashed hard, squeezing, tightening, arching into and all around him. She held onto the bar only long enough for Raffaello to spill his hot, thick cum, and he reveled in the feeling of filling her up, of marking her sweet body, claiming in an undeniable and impossible way.

For both of them.

Chapter Seventeen

Raffaello gently guided her hands away from the bar and pulled her into his arms. He carried her through an adjoining door, and Charli realized in the bleary haze of her pleasure that they were back in the steamy shower room she had first discovered. The warm air relaxed the muscles in her back, tightened from holding onto the bar, and soon Raffaello was guiding her into a private soaking tub. He turned a few knobs and streams of water began to spill into the tub from each side, adding to the steamy, almost fantastical feel of the place.

There were no windows in the steam room, and she had the impression that the room was Raffaello's to use at his discretion, and it felt as though they could have been the only two people in the world, right at the edge of the Mediterranean sea, or in a kink club in the mountains, living their freedom and truth for as long as they could.

The steam room had been modeled for the ones back home, which dotted the many mountainsides of the islands, and for a moment, Charli was thrust back into her real life, into all that she was running from, all that she had to worry about.

All that could never be between herself and the prince.

Because, despite how incredible the last night had been, Charli knew it would be temporary. Neither of them had been able to say as much out loud, but that was the truth of it, and their lives, their responsibilities, were far too complicated for any kind of connection to survive in the outside world.

But then Raffaello poured a thick stream of bath oil into the tub, and the room filled with the scents of lavender and jasmine and sage, and Charli let those worries fade away, just for the moment. If she had limited time to enjoy this fantasy, and there was no doubt that the time was limited, she wasn't going to waste a second worrying about the things she couldn't change.

"Are you coming in?" she asked Raffaello. Not that she minded watching him from the tub. In all their play, there had been precious few moments to actually look at him. But she looked at him now.

Even in the dead of winter, his skin was deep olive, rich and warm. His dark blond curls had come slightly loose in the steam, and one spilled over his forehead, giving him a rakish charm. He walked around the room collecting towels and such, and she could only admire the strength of his flank, the strong curve of his hip, the line of rippling muscles that led to a deep vee...

And down further, where his thick cock hung between strong, powerful legs. She felt no smaller measure of pride at having taken him, and her body offered tinges as reminders of that taking. Tinges that felt like trophies.

"Only if you stop looking at me like that, Charlotte," he said. "You need rest."

"Maybe you're the one that needs rest, old man," she said, leaning her head back against the cool tile wall. "I could go all day."

Raffaello chuckled. "No doubt." He settled at the edge of the tub and handed her a glass of pineapple juice. "But it's my job as a Dominant to make sure you're taken care of."

Charli didn't want to admit how those words made her feel. Instead, she sipped at her juice, the flavors feeling particularly bright and sunshiny on her tongue. "How did you find all this anyway, this...lifestyle?"

Rafe grimaced. "You're not going to want to hear the answer to that."

Panic laced through Charli's belly as she considered the only possibility. "Not... Anthony."

Raffaello bit his lip to keep from laughing. It truly wasn't fair for a man to have such beautiful lips. "He doesn't practice, don't worry. But he did take me to my first club in Amsterdam when we were in university. He left. I stayed."

"So when your friends all talked about opening a club together..."

Raffaello nodded. "The lodge came first. It was the last gift Beau Sinclair gave us, tying all the lost young men he'd saved together for life. And the more we were together, the more we all realized we had in common. It made sense, in a way. That summer, we were wild stallions. Eventually, we all sought order and control in our own ways."

"It's hard to imagine you on your Servizio trip," Charli admitted. "The young prince."

Raffaello finally joined her in the water, his large body adding a heat and intensity that the steam could never. "The greatest decision of my life. My father thought it best for me to live like a normal person. I would never have done that back in Contanari, even on my community service trip. So, he sent me here. And it changed my life."

"Which is why you came back," she prompted, "after you fainted in Lords. It's your safe place."

Raffaello considered this. "First, Little Brat, I did not *faint*. Men don't faint. I...passed out. But yes, I suppose. It's a place out of time. A place to be free."

Charli felt those words in her heart and soul. She had been snowed in on the mountaintop for days, locked into a strange and wild world with people she had only just met. But already she felt more alive, more herself than she had in such a very long time. Maybe it was the lifestyle, but she suspected it was more. Or perhaps, the lifestyle simply allowed her to be honest with herself, about who she was and what she wanted.

"I can see why it's important to you," she murmured, the steam giving the room a sense of intimacy that allowed her to speak more freely than she was used to. "I don't know if I understand all of it, or if I ever will, but it feels...special."

Raffaello watched her with clear, knowing eyes, and it was the expression in them that told Charli just how dangerous this thing between them was. Of course, the relationship between a Dominant and a submissive — as she had learned from her new friends — was always more complicated than just sex. But it seemed to go beyond that somehow. It seemed like Raffaello...

Saw her.

No one had ever seen her. She had a few friends in the royal courts, though it was always difficult to know who her friends were from one day to the next, and the time she had spent in her volunteer work had netted her some of the truest friendships she'd ever enjoyed. But Raffaello seemed to see her in a way Charli had never been seen before, and she couldn't help but think about how much trouble that would signal for them both.

Thankfully, he spoke again before she could spiral any further. "It is important," he agreed. "People have tried to shut us down before. They only see the depravity of it, the raw sex, filthy words. But it's not like that. There's nothing...untoward or harmful here. It's consensual power play, relief, freedom. It's nothing more or less than humans have been doing since the dawn of time."

Charli considered this and knew in her heart she agreed with everything Raffaello said. Even the kink of calling him *daddy*, the very thought of which made her pussy clench and squeeze, was about the power play, the taming, the submission. Anyone who saw it as something more tawdry was missing the point.

"Thank you," she said quietly, holding his gaze, even as he drifted his fingers along her legs, the touch instantly awakening her body. "For showing me your world. For...for the freedom."

Raffaello was entirely serious when he responded. "Thank you for appreciating it."

Chapter Eighteen

Raffaello had been reading the same paragraph for the third time when his phone rang. He reached for it quickly, hoping to silence the call before it woke Charlotte. After the recovery in the steam room, he had brought her back to his quarters, applied salve to the red marks on her beautiful skin, and held her until she had fallen asleep. It hadn't taken long. No doubt the play had been intense and overwhelming, and he knew she needed to rest.

He, on the other hand, couldn't keep his eyes closed. Because his thoughts were busy and overwhelming, wracked with all the ways a dalliance between them could go wrong, not the least of which being the feeling that every time he looked at Charlotte, he felt a deep, innate need to claim her and mark her as his own.

So he'd tried to work. But instead of actually completing any proposals, Raffaello had been stuck remembering the way Charlotte's body had bucked and arched against him, how she'd fought his commands only to finally submit when the pleasure become too strong, how she'd made him come so hard and fast he had seen stars.

He answered the call practically out of desperation.

"Raffaello." Madison's voice was matter of fact. "I have the information you asked about."

Right, the information on Charlotte's claim that her father was trying to sell her to the highest bidder. The information Raffaello had pushed far out of his mind, because if it were true, that had serious implications for how his nation was being run, and how members of his aristocracy were being managed. It also significantly complicated matters between himself and Charlotte, but he absolutely couldn't figure out how to navigate *matters between himself and Charlotte.*

Raffaello stepped into the adjoining living room of the suite and closed the door behind him. He could have been working in the office the entire time, but he had liked the view of a tired-out Charlotte curled up in his bed a little too much.

"What have you learned?" he asked Madison, his stomach suddenly turning. It hadn't truly occurred to him that Anthony and Charlotte's father, Prince Johan, would be capable of such a practice. Perhaps he had simply hoped the man wasn't, and hoped Anthony wasn't caught in the crossfires and guilty by association.

"Likely not the news you were hoping for," Madison replied. "But Lady Charlotte does seem to be telling the truth. I searched records, and there was a marriage contract drafted on the day of her birth. It was amended and approved to include any member of the Wagner house recently, not only an heir."

Thus, paving the way for Charlotte to marry the elderly lord.

"Approved by whom?" Raffaello asked, though he already had a sneaking suspicion. One that made his chest feel tight and the same familiar sensations he'd experienced in the House of Lords return, an overwhelming dizziness that clenched his temples and burned a hot pain behind his eyes.

Madison hesitated only a fraction of a second. "The king, Raffaello."

Rafe's father. His own father had approved a *marriage contract*. Like they were still living in Regency days, where a lord could sell his daughter off as easily as a parcel of land or a flock of sheep.

Raffaello sat down, not entirely certain he wouldn't fall over. He pinched the bridge of his nose, chasing some relief from the sudden, unyielding pain behind his eyes. "Can you send me the information you have? And is there anything else to verify this?"

"Unfortunately, there is," Madison said. "I have anecdotal testimonies from several reliable witnesses to back the fact. But the most...revealing. Lord Wagner filed a breach of contract suit against the Marchand House. He's suing unless she agrees to the marriage."

The marriage. That was an eloquent way to put it. Charlotte would be no type of equal in an arranged, legally coerced marriage to man three times her age. She was spirited and bold, and the last few days had shown Raffaello a wild streak in the girl he had once known, that showed the world just a taste of what she was capable of when the strictures of society weren't choking her.

To imagine her in a forced marriage, to a man who would do whatever it took to break her...

It made Raffaello see red.

He clenched his free hand into a fist, felt the beating at his temples like a war drum, and took up from the seat, suddenly needing to pace. "Send that, too," he said. "And keep looking. I want any information I can on this matter. And, Christoph, I trust in your absolute discretion on this topic."

Madison agreed. "As in all things, Raffaello. You have my total allegiance."

That settled a small amount of the rage bubbling in Rafe's body and threatening to spill over. He ran his hand over his face. "I don't know what I would do without you."

Madison made a small noise of agreement. "Likely never get another night's sleep in your life." He quickly changed the subject. "I've been in constant communication with the FAA and your pilots. The storm winds are still strong where you are, and visibility is low. Even if you could get down the mountain, you'd be grounded."

Rafe nodded, even though Madison couldn't see it. "Gives me time to figure out the situation with Princess Charlotte, so not to worry. Just…stay connected."

"Of course, Your Highness. But first, matters with the King are…accelerating. It might be best to discuss a temporary course of action."

"I'm sure it will stabilize itself," Raffaello said, his mind distracted and overwhelmed, and the long-standing worry he'd felt for his father just one thing too many to handle at the moment. "Father will be fine.

Madison quickly signed off, and Raffaello took a deep breath, trying to calm his pounding heart.

Right up until the moment he heard a voice behind him.

"What situation with Princess Charlotte, exactly?"

He turned to see Charlotte, wearing another one of his shirts that fell to her strong thighs, her hair mussed and a sleepy expression on her face, but her eyes were focused and clear, and she was staring directly at him.

Because, of course, she had most definitely heard the last part of that conversation.

And Raffaello couldn't come up with any alternative explanation beyond the truth.

More than that, he was overwhelmed with a sense of guilt that he had been so unwilling to believe her. Of course, he had *hoped* it wasn't the truth, that no one in his family's court would ever stoop so low, that the system of checks and balances would help to protect her and others like her.

But Rafe knew in his gut that he simply should have trusted Charlotte, believed her, because she had asked him to.

"That was my advisor," he said finally, tossing the phone onto the couch, like it was at fault for the entire situation.

"Christoph Madison," she replied. "I'm familiar."

He filed away her knowledge to consider later, not allowing any detail to keep him from sharing the truth she deserved.

"I had him...look into your situation."

Charlotte crossed her arms. The action made the shirt she wore ride up, exposing more of her long, beautiful legs, and it took all the power in Rafe to maintain eye contact.

"You mean," she said, "you had him *verify* the information I told you. Because you didn't believe me."

Raffaello nodded slowly. "You're right. I needed to know the situation for myself. It's a good practice for a leader."

"Perhaps for a leader," Charlotte said. "But I told you as a friend."

"I couldn't help as your friend," Raffaello replied, taking a step toward her because he couldn't quite seem to help himself. "But I could as your Prince."

"So" — Charli threw her hands in the air — "do you believe what I'm saying when someone else tells you? Specifically, when a *man* tells you."

Raffaello shook his head. "That has nothing to do with this."

"It does, though," Charlotte replied. "Because I ran across the world to escape this horrible fate that my family is putting me through, and you needed to verify the facts."

"I tried," Raffaello said. "I called your brother right after you told me. He said he knew nothing about it."

Charlotte got very, very still. Her face was a mask that, for the first time since finding her in the city, Raffaello couldn't read. And he hated that he couldn't.

"Has it occurred to you" — her voice was like ice — "that he was *lying*?"

Until that moment, it actually hadn't. Charlotte and Anthony's father was an old-school leader, with harsh principles and a strong sense of his own importance. Raffaello had spent enough time at their house to believe that Prince Johan was capable of the kind of antiquated bullshit required to force his daughter into an unwelcome marriage.

But Anthony.

Raffaello had always prided himself on his ability to read people, and if he had been that wrong about the man he had considered his closest friend and confident these many years...

"Is he?" he asked Charlotte very calmly.

Charlotte swallowed. "I don't know," she answered. "He's been traveling a lot lately, leaving me home alone with Father, and when I tried to tell him, when I tried to figure out what he knew and how to ask for help, Father always seemed to interrupt us."

Her mask cracked a little, reveling abject pain and sadness. "I believe my father is monitoring my calls and messages. So, I went to Anthony's apartments to tell him. I left in the middle of the night with just a small bag packed, in case I needed to stay there and... When I arrived..."

"Your father was waiting," Raffaello filled in the blanks.

Charlotte nodded. "So, I didn't go inside. Instead, I called a cab to the airport and left town. Went to Barcelona, then Amsterdam, and when I realized my father was tracking me, I took the first flight out of Schiphol Airport."

"To Montana," Raffaello said. "But Anthony was tracking your phone. If Anthony doesn't know, and perhaps it's possible he doesn't, what reason could your father possibly have given for you running off like this?"

Charlotte shrugged. "Father lies. He always has. He treats Anthony much better than me, so perhaps my brother...simply believed those lies."

"Or perhaps," Raffaello said, "your brother is also a liar."

"Perhaps," Charlotte replied. "I don't know. And frankly, I don't much care. If Anthony is stupid enough to believe whatever lies my father told him, without trying to figure out how I feel or what I need…he's not exactly a reliable, loving big brother, is he?"

"No," Raffaello managed, his chest too tight again, the pain beating a resounding tempo behind his eyes. "He's not."

The room fell into a weighty silence, and finally Raffaello took the last step toward Charlotte. "I'm…sorry. For not believing you earlier. And for going behind your back to gather more information. I should have told you."

Charlotte leaned her head on his chest, and the sensation of her soft touch, of the scent of her, it made his tight strings loosen, made it that much easier to breathe. "You believe me now," she murmured. "That's enough."

"It may have to be," he said after a moment. "Charlotte, this complicated. Maybe…"

She pulled back, a look of anger in her pretty eyes. "Don't you dare, Rafe."

"Dare what?" This time, the frustration he felt was sweet and delicious, heady with the familiar eroticism of their battles. "Do what's best for you? *Protect* you?"

"Protect me?" she scoffed. "You've been trying to protect me this entire time, and look where that's gotten us. I don't want your protection, Raffaello. And I certainly don't need protecting *from* you."

"You don't know what you need," he replied, rising to the bait despite himself. "What you need is stop fighting me on every little thing."

"This is not a *little* thing." They were circling each other now, two caged lions, waiting to see who would pounce first. "This is you about to shut down the best experience I've had in maybe my entire life because you think you know what's best for me."

"Maybe I *do* know what's best for you," he said. "Maybe the answer isn't a fucked-up affair in the mountains while you're running away from home."

She let out a deep, frustrated sigh. "Don't dirty it," she bit out. "You're the one who said the lifestyle isn't tawdry. Don't *do* that. I am so *sick* of people telling me what to do." Charlotte squared up to him, and even with her small frame and bare legs and sleep-mussed hair, she was a still a formidable opponent. "If you want to give this up because you don't like it...don't want it, that's your prerogative. But don't you dare try to make my decisions for me. I know what I want."

Raffaello backed her against the wall, his body flaring to life with the very proximity to her, his cock throbbing hard and thick in his briefs. "So, what, Charlotte," he asked, crowding her in, taking up her space. "So, what do you want?"

She glared daggers at him, defiance to the very last, but he could read her now, and he could see the burning lust in those beautiful eyes, the need bursting through, promising, demanding, all for him.

"I want all of it."

The last word was barely past her lips when Raffaello slammed his mouth on hers in a brutal, demanding kiss.

Chapter Nineteen

Charlotte met his kiss beat for beat, kissing him back with the same ferocity he offered her, demanded of her, pushed her to, pushed her past. It was a kiss of apologies and explanations and promises, but it was also a challenge, hers to meet, to rise to, to push back against.

She had been so incredibly fucking furious with him when she had overheard his phone conversation, furious all over again that he would simply believe her brother on face value, but not her. But that fury had turned to something else entirely when he'd tried to shut down their future, temporary as it was.

The experimentation, the power play, the domination and submission, it was all so new, but it didn't *feel* so new. It felt like the only way to shed the skin she had been wearing her whole life, skin that had never fit just right. It felt like the truest, most natural way to be who she was meant to be, and she refused, *refused* to let him take it from her in some kind of misdirected noble act.

Because Charli knew, from the way his cock pressed against her thigh, from the dark look in his eye, from everything big they had shared in such a small amount of time, that Rafe felt it too, the innateness of their connection, the very rightness of how they came together—and *how* they came together, a freedom in finding that missing puzzle piece to give when she took and take when she gave.

And he was taking, harsh and demanding, full of the challenge she had been craving since the day she was born, the challenge she had never been able to rise to or act on or fight against because she'd always had to be the perfect princess.

Not for Raffaello Chiaramonte.

When she was *his* Princess, his Little Brat, she was tart and bold and demanding and she spoke her mind.

And he liked it.

"You are committed to driving me crazy," he said, sliding one hand to cup the back of her neck in a strong hold, a hold that made her feel strong. "I say jump, and you say why. I say stop and you run faster and farther. I say, this is a bad idea, and you give me that fucking attitude, Little Brat."

He kissed again, harder and more bruising, and demand and a consumption all in one. "That attitude that makes my cock hard as steel, that makes me want to take you fast and rough whether you like it or not."

And hell, that shouldn't have turned her on the way it did, but familiar heat bloomed between Charli's thighs, and she arched her back to get more of the contact she so desperately needed.

"You'd like that, wouldn't you," Raffaello practically growled into her ear. "You'd like it if I took what I wanted, if I pinned you and cuffed you and chained you and took everything I wanted."

"What do you want?" Charli asked, her voice only a little glazed with lust. Only a little.

"I want you to be good for me." He nipped at her ear, which sent a burst of hot need racing down Charli's back.

"No, you don't," she bit out. "You like it when I'm bad so you can punish me."

"Too bad you like getting punished," he replied. "Too bad it makes you wet and hot and needy. That's no kind of punishment."

"We could always try again," Charli pushed. "Just to make sure."

Rafe spun her around so quickly Charli barely had a second to protest, and then he pushed her against the wall and shoved the shirt up around her waist.

"You want to be punished so badly," he murmured, the threat and promise mingling in his voice. "Then you're going to take what I give you, Princess. All of it. And if you come even once, you don't get fucked for the rest of the night."

Charli snapped her teeth. "Better get to work then, instead of talking all day."

Before she even knew what he was doing, Raffaello, the Royal Prince of her kingdom, was down on his knees and burying his face between her thighs.

He lapped at her pussy like a man possessed, and Charli knew without a doubt that he was trying to do whatever it took to push her past her breaking point.

Well, she wasn't going to let that happen.

Even as Raffaello continued to lick and suck, spreading her cheeks and exposing her to the room, to his dangerous touches, each one pushing her higher and closer to an edge that would surely wreck her. She slammed her fist against the wall, reaching with all her might for the control that would help her rise to his challenge.

But he was just so...*good*, finding her hotspots again and again, sliding one thick finger inside her until she was riding him and bucking against his touch, whimpering with need, with a demand for something she had needed for so very long.

"Don't come, Princess," he murmured, pulling back to place a rough kiss on her ass. "Don't come all over my fingers and tongue. Take your punishment for being a mouthy little brat."

"I am *not* a mouthy brat," she muttered, proving exactly how much she was what he said. But it felt so good to be *his* mouthy brat when he wrapped his strong hands around her hips and held her in place, when he devoured her pussy, pulsing and licking and sucking, when he pushed a third finger inside her, spreading her wide, making her ache for even more than his fingers.

And then he slid those wet, slicked fingers free, and in the next moment, Charli felt the warm tip of his finger at the tight, sensitive entrance to her ass, not pushing in, not pressing, just teasing, whispering, the nearness enough to make her feel overwhelmed and hot and needy for something she had never tried before.

"Where are you, Charlotte?" Raffaello asked.

She didn't hesitate to answer, not when she wanted to know so much more, not when he was offering to teach her *everything*. "Green," she whispered. "Sir."

"Oh, very green then," he replied. "You must desperately want me to play with your ass if you don't even need to be told twice to address me properly."

"No...not desperate." She tried to come up with some kind of sarcastic response, but he just began edging one large finger against her tight hole, and the sensation was overwhelming, intense, drawn-out pleasure that came as much from the forbidden as the touch itself raced down her back, filled her belly, made her breasts tingle and ache.

"You should see how pretty you look right now," Raffaello murmured, pausing to nip at her skin. "Your pussy is glistening, and your asshole is taking my finger so good, Charlotte. I just know you want more."

She did want more. And she wanted him to push her to it.

"You don't know what I want."

Raffaello's chuckle was low and dangerous. "I know *exactly* what you want. You want to know how it feels when I push it all the way inside, how it feels to get your ass fingered when my cock is filling your pussy..."

His voice got even darker then, richer and more potent, like honey wine. "You want to know if this tight little hole can fit my whole cock..."

"Fuck..." It wasn't going to be his fingers or tongue that sent her over the edge. It was going to be his words, his filthy, damning words, his promising, freeing words.

"Fuck, indeed," he replied, like he wasn't teetering right at the edge of his sanity. "So, I'll make you a little deal. If you confess that I'm right, I'll let you come. I'll tongue your pussy and finger fuck your tight little hole and let you come like I know you so desperately need to do. But you have to do something for me first."

She was going to die for the pleasure, each of his words ratcheting up her need, pushing her control further than she had ever thought possible, making Charli wonder if it was even possible to hold on a moment longer.

"Fine…" She huffed out a breath, as if that would stave off her impending release. "Fine…I have fantasized about how it might feel…"

"To what?" he pushed, pausing his motions, which nearly made Charli cry in frustration.

"To have your cock in my ass," she confessed. "To feel full and stretched and taken like I know I shouldn't want to, and God, it's so fucking hot…" She was babbling now, nearly incoherent in her admissions, each one pushing her past that invisible breaking point. "And I've even fantasized about begging you for it, Daddy. Begging for you to fuck my ass."

"Charlotte." His voice held the kind of admiration and pride that bloomed something completely overwhelming within, and she knew that was going to be it, the end of all of it for her. "So good for me. Take your reward, Princess. Come for Daddy."

Charli didn't have to be told twice. She rocked forward on his finger, taking him deeper in her ass, and when Rafe leaned down licked at her wetness, fingering her swollen clit with his free hand, Charli managed a single curse before the ground fell out from under her, the pleasure cresting in an impossible, undeniable wave, too much, far, far too much, and yet, she took it all, each beautiful, decadent burst of pleasure and need, her body arching, lights flashing behind her eyes, and Raffaello catching her when her legs finally went out.

Chapter Twenty

Raffaello carried Charli back into the bedroom. She nuzzled up against his chest, her body limp with pleasure, and the look in her eyes enough to make him lose all sense of himself. No submissive, no brat he'd ever tamed before, had the same innate attitude, the same perfect balance of fighting back and giving in, and he wondered if he would ever find it again after her.

If he would ever want to.

But if his time was ticking away, there was no question he was going to enjoy every fucking second he got.

"Don't go," Charli murmured, as Raffaello placed her down on the bed.

"Just turning the light down," he said. "And getting a few things."

She roused a little. "Things for me?"

He raised a brow, amazed at how quickly she seemed to slip back into her demand for pleasure, how responsive she was to his promises.

"Maybe," he replied. "Depending on if you deserve them."

"Well, I think I do," Charli said. "And isn't that what matters?"

Rafe hid a grin as he walked over to the closet and collected a few items, then he lowered the lights in the room. With the press of another button, cuffs and bars slid free from the corners of the bed. Perhaps it wasn't becoming for a prince to have a custom-made kink bed with all the tools he needed for pinning down unruly submissives and teaching them a lesson, but Raffaello couldn't bring himself to care, not when Charlotte was pulling off his shirt and sitting on the bed on her knees, the perfect submissive pose, even if she didn't know it.

Except, of course, her head wasn't bent down in supplication. Not his Charlotte. No, she sat with her shoulders squared and her head high and a look in her eyes that teased and challenged and made him hard as fucking steel.

As had ever filthy word that had come out of her mouth.

"You almost look like a proper submissive like that, Little Brat," Raffaello murmured. "Almost."

She raised a brow and grinned that sinful grin that made him feel like maybe he was the one pinned down.

Or the one flying high.

"I'd be a proper submissive if you could figure out how to be a proper Dominant. *Sir*."

Of course, the word was anything but respectful on her lips, and God, Raffaello loved it, the bite, the teasing, all the ways he could make her pay for both.

Too many things in his life had come too easily, at the whim of the title and crown. Not Charlotte's submission. That, that was worth fighting for with all he had.

"You want a proper Dominant." He prowled over to her, teasing at the edges of his leather toy, the soft material so perfectly painful in the right hands. "Lie down on the bed or I'll whip your pretty pussy until you're coming all over the leather."

Charlotte sucked in a breath but held her position, right up until Raffaello walked to the edge of the bed. Then she scampered to lie down, arms behind her head, legs folded and knees pointing to the sky.

"You want a proper Dominant," he repeated, "then you shouldn't behave so badly he has to tie you down and chain you up, just to keep you from acting out."

He reached over her, aware of the heaving of her beautiful breasts and the soft glaze of pleasure in her eyes. With a single motion, he wrapped a pair of cuffs around both hands, teasing the throbbing vein on her inner wrist as he slowly made his way down her body. "But the good news for you is that it's my all-time favorite thing to tie my submissive up and make them...*atone* for their behavior."

"You're assuming they've done something wrong," she bit back, pleasure coloring her words. "I haven't."

"Haven't you, Little Brat?" he asked. "You're the one who is always saying you like to be bad."

He reached for her ankles and took his time there, spreading her legs apart and revealing her sweet, glistening cunt. Then he pulled each leg down toward the bottom of the bed, where he latched the cuffs around her ankles.

And stood back to admire his handiwork.

Because Charlotte was spread wide, wet and achy and absolutely at his mercy.

"Give me a number," he said, looking down at all the toys he'd arranged on the settee.

"Why?" she demanded.

"Give me a number," he repeated calmly, playing with the cat-of-nine tails, "or I'll double it. And I promise you don't want that."

"Six," she huffed out. "It's my lucky number."

"Yes," he replied, turning on one of the small vibrators. "It will be."

He placed it on the inside of her thigh, low enough to avoid putting pressure where she wanted it, but still able to send intense sensations across her skin. Charlotte arched and keened, trying to get closer to the toy, but the restraints held her in place.

"You're going to count every orgasm I give you," he explained, climbing on the bed for better access to her spread body. "All six of them."

"It's too much," Charlotte protested. "No way."

"Yes, *way*," Raffaello responded. "And if you're good for me, I promise I'll fuck you right through the last two and fill your pretty pink pussy with my cum until you're leaking."

"Raffaello..." It came out as both a denial and a request. A demand.

"No, Little Brat." He gently ran the leather along her body, and ever so carefully tapped it right against her clit. Charlotte practically screamed. "You're going to thank me properly for each one or we start all...over...again. Do I make myself clear?"

She squared her jaw as well as she possibly could in her trapped position. "Yes."

He tapped her clit with the toy again and she bit out, "Yes, *Sir*."

"Good girl," Rafe murmured. He moved the vibrator up her inner thigh and then, because he couldn't wait any longer, her pressed it right against her quivering pussy.

Charlotte did scream then, a hoarse cry of need that reverberated through her entire body, and in the next second, she was coming hard and fast all over the toy, riding it like it was his cock, thrashing against the restraints and unable to escape the pulsing pleasure.

"Thank you…" The words were clearly forced from her lips, which made them all the more delicious to Raffaello. "Sir."

"See, you can be nice when you want to be," he said. "Now I'll let you pick this one. Do you want the paddle or the tails?"

"For what?" she managed, her eyes widening when he held up the small paddle.

"Take a guess," he replied, loving the fire in her eyes, the dark, burning heat in her gaze. "Where do you think I'm going to punish you with this?"

"My breasts, *Sir*."

"Very good," he replied, toying with it. "And?"

"And my pussy."

He nodded. "Where are you, Charlotte?"

She scrunched her face, obviously annoyed with the question. "Green. *Master Raffaello.*"

"Good, Princess. Then hold on."

And before she got the chance to brace, he brought the paddle down on her pink, slick pussy.

Charlotte arched into the touch, as if she had known exactly where the blow would land, and she seemed to ride the razor thin line of pain and pleasure, like she welcomed the burst of heat the paddle leveled on her body, like she took it because she wanted it, craved it.

And that was why Raffaello didn't hold back from wielding it again, another rough touch to her skin, fast and undeniable, until she was begging arching, and aching into his touch.

And then she was coming hard and fast, like the orgasm was being stolen from her, a wave of intense, overwhelming pleasure that she couldn't control, couldn't do anything but bear down and take, a burst of desire and heat so intense that she seemed to lose herself to it completely.

Well, not completely, since the pleasure was clearly still wracking her body when she whispered low, "Two, thank you, Sir."

Raffaello *ached* for her, for the sweet need she embodied and embraced so easily, for the strength she held as he bore down with his demands, how for all she fought and kicked and bit, she so clearly wanted to make him proud.

"I did promise you the tails too," he said, sliding the ribbons of leather between her parted thighs, "but you're already so shiny and pink. Maybe we'll just see how it feels when they tease your pretty little cunt."

And he did just that, sliding the toy between her swollen pussy lips so slowly it was clearly driving her to the edge, a tiny little push at a time.

"Please," Charlotte begged. "Please, go faster…"

He kept his pace. "Please go faster…*what?*"

She huffed at him, apparently not pleasured to the point of forgetting how to bicker. "Please go faster, *Daddy.*"

Fuck if that word on her filthy lips didn't make him want to forsake everything and take her right then and there. But he knew exactly how sweet it would be when he finally did, and Raffaello had always valued his sense of patience.

"Do you want me to fuck you with the handle of this toy, sliding in and out until you're staining it with your cum, Princess?"

She nodded. "*Yes…*"

"Right answer…" He turned the toy around, the handle a silicone toy with a round ball head, and he pressed it right against her hole. "Tell me where you are, Charlotte."

"Fuck… Green. In me, now. I need…I need…"

"I know, Princess, you need to be fucked again and again." He pressed the ball gently in and she lifted her hips to meet it the best she could. "You need to be taken and filled and pumped full of cum, don't you?"

"Yes, Daddy…" she murmured. "I need all of it…"

"Good girl, taking the toy," he replied honestly. "You're stretched so pretty and wide, but not nearly as wide as you'll be with my cock in your tight little cunt."

"Fuck, say that again…" she demanded. "It's… Fuck, it's so hot."

"You love the dirty talk, don't you…" He twisted the toy. "Then it's a good thing I like telling you each and every one of the filthy, depraved things I'm going to do to your tight little body. I'm going to fuck you and fill you, tease you and take you, claim each of your holes until you know exactly who you belong to."

And that was when she came, a soft whimper escaping her like it was too much for her to take, the release carrying her along in twisting, writhing pleasure, and he coaxed her through the fall with words of praise that had come from deep, deep within his soul.

Finally, Raffaello pulled the toy free, slowly, telling her all the while how good she had taken it, how proud of her he was.

"Let's slow down a little," he murmured, dropping to his knees between her spread legs. "You tell me how fast to go, Princess."

And then he buried his face in her sweet scent, inhaling her release and her desire, tasting pleasure like it was fucking ambrosia, and Charlotte did as she was told, begging and demanding for him to go faster, then slower, then so slowly it was like he was barely moving his tongue at all, each tiny motion making her buck and arch against the cuffs.

He pulled back and reached for two more of the items he'd brought from the closet, first opening the lube and then unboxing the small, bejeweled plug. "Tell Daddy," he said quietly, his cock hard as steel and his heart about to beat out of his chest. "Tell Daddy exactly where you want this plug, Princess."

"You already know," she whispered, a valiant effort to argue when she was so clearly gone to the pleasure and need. "You know what I want."

"I know I want you to tell me," he repeated. "Say, Daddy, I want the plug in my tight little asshole…"

She shook her head.

He generously coated the plug in lube and pressed it right against her tight hole, teasing her sensitive skin. "Be good for me one more time, Princess. And I'll give you what you want."

"Daddy…I want the plug in my tight little asshole…"

He didn't think his cock could get harder, but Raffaello was straining at the thinnest of leashes now, almost bursting out of his own seams, control a long-lost memory. "And why do you want the plug in your tight little hole?"

She twisted, but there was nowhere for her to go to escape his touch. "Because I have filthy fantasies, Daddy. Because...I want you to stretch me and train me so I can take your cock in my ass..."

He could picture her doing just that, practicing with his plug and fighting him on every turn, only to claim exactly what she wanted in the end. It was a mutual claiming with them, and he knew he wasn't going to walk away from her dangerous mouth unscathed.

"So good." He pressed the toy gently against her hole. "Relax for me baby, let me get the plug in."

She did, slowly, as he leaned back down and licked at her sweet, wet pussy, more wetness spilling as the plug edged inside her, until finally, finally, it was seated all the way in her tight little hole.

"Okay, Princess?" he asked.

"Yes," she whispered. "Fuck, it feels big, but good... Green, so, so green."

"Good." He leaned down and licked at her pussy once more, and then because he couldn't help himself, began devouring her wet cunt, sucking and licking and sliding his fingers deep inside her waiting hole, and then Charlotte was crying out for him and coming hard and fast, spilling her sweet release all over his tongue and fingers and toys, begging, pleading, promising and thanking as the orgasm broke free and took her tumbling with it.

The sensation of coming with the plug in her ass was so overwhelming Charli thought she might just come again, but she managed to remember Raffaello's orders in the very last second. "Four, Sir. Thank you."

"You are so welcome, Princess," he said, his voice rough, teetering at the very edge of his control, and she wanted to be the one who took him over it.

"Will you fuck my pussy with the plug in?" she asked. "I want to... know what it feels like."

He brushed her swollen clit with his thumb. "Only because you asked so nicely, Princess. Fuck, look at how pretty you are, all spread out and filled up. Are you ready for me?"

She nodded. As incredible as he had already made her feel, there was no substitute for his cock.

He slid in slowly, she knew to make sure she could take the size of him with the plug filling her ass, but Charli wished she could wrap her legs around his waist and pull him in deeper.

Rafe clearly realized this. "My speed this time, Princess," he said. "And I promise I'm going to make it worth your while."

And he did, slowly bringing her right up to the top, not like before, with harsh intense movements and wicked words, but like carrying her up a mountain, power and potent and achingly slow, and when it was too much, all way, way too much, she felt like she was floating free, released and flying high and riding a way of slow, molten pleasure that soaked into her bones and pulled her back into the earth.

"Five," she managed. "Thank you, Sir..."

Because the words were barely her own and she was barely tethered to her own body anymore, just that blazing point of connection where Raffaello filled her, and she knew the very last time would wreck her in a whole new way, as he picked up his pace, just the smallest amount, just enough to drag her pleasure from the very depths, to bring her to heights she had never before known she was capable of reaching.

"So good for me," he murmured, his voice achingly raw, like he was as close to the end of all he could control as she was. "You'll come with me one more time, Princess, I know you will."

And because he wanted her to, because he believed she could, Charli let herself fall that one, last, beautiful time, spilling and arching and taking him, pulling him right over the edge with her, as he spilled hot, thick cum inside her swollen pussy, and they both gave over, to the power, to the pleasure, to control, together.

Chapter Twenty-One

"I don't understand," Emerson said, her tone very serious. Early on, she had explained to Charli that she had been a campaign manager for American politics, and now co-ran a philanthropic foundation with Gabriel, and Charli could see that now. Emerson was all business, powerful, forward, intent on problem solving without any delay. "What do you mean a *marriage contract?*"

Because after she and Rafe had fallen in a sweaty pile of limbs, and he'd finally released her from the cuffs, massaging her wrists and ankles, they had showered and gone in search of food.

And his friends.

Raffaello had asked if it would be okay to share their current predicament, and Charli hadn't hesitated. She had only known his friends' girlfriends and wives for a few days, but she already felt comfortable and connected to them.

And he had said *our predicament.*

Not hers. Theirs.

In the shower, soapy and tired and without games or artifice, he had promised her that he would find a way to make things right.

And she had believed him. Because Charli knew that when Rafe put his mind to something, he achieved his goals. Whatever they were.

So, they had gathered back in the lounge, bowls of snacks and fruit in hand, and settled in to share with his friends.

"It's an antiquated practice," Raffaello explained. "That's why I didn't..." He glanced at Charli. "That's why I made sure to verify that it's all technically true and legal." The gaze in his eyes was apologetic, his atonement for not believing her the first time.

With space to think about it, Charli could almost understand. Who wanted to believe such a thing was happening in their country, right under their nose?

"And it is?" Gabriel confirmed, tapping away at his tablet.

"It is," Charli replied. "My father had it amended last year."

"What was the reason for the amendment?" Emerson asked.

Charli glanced back at Raffaello then squared her shoulders. It wasn't her fault. *None* of this was her fault. But there was something so humiliating about admitting to the terms of the contract about her life, one which she had no control over or say in.

"The original contract was signed the day of Charlotte's birth, twenty-five years ago," Raffaello explained. "It promised that a female child of the Marchand family would be legally bound to the heir of the Wagner family."

"So, what changed?" Morgan put in, handing Charli a cup of hot tea from the tray they'd brought over.

"Lord Wagner never had an heir," Charli said bluntly. "None of his wives…lived long enough for that."

Her new friends' faces seemed to morph in mixtures of horror and panic, and she knew she had to get through the rest of the information quickly or she would lose her nerve.

"So last year, they changed the contract. Now the female child of the Marchand family, my family, must marry any member of the Wanger bloodline."

"Meaning Lord Wagner, himself," Raffaello confirmed. "That's what her father told her."

"Forgive me," Skylar put in, "but how do these amendments to these contracts work? Wouldn't you, as the subject of the contract and now of age, have to be present and consenting?"

Raffaello grimaced. "There is…one way around that."

She could tell that the subject had been more bothersome to him than he had wanted to let on, but in truth Charli simply found it odd. She didn't know King Claudio very well, had only spent time in his presence at formal events of state and official celebrations, always when there was a great deal more for him to be doing than passing time with her.

Why he would go ahead and make such a choice about her future was…strange.

"Typically, yes, the parties listed in the contact, if of age, would have to consent to the amendments themselves. As the original contract was written at her birth, Charlotte's father acted in her stead, if not in her best interest. But…if you are able to obtain the King's written approval, it would overwrite everything else. It's rare, but it's been known to happen."

"And did your father...approve?" This came from Dante, who looked every part the tattooed, pierced bad boy, but who seemed to have an air of understanding about him that Charli could appreciate in that moment. Whatever she felt of the king, he was Raffaello's father, and she knew a thing or two about complicated relationships with fathers.

"He did," Rafe said, not expanding further.

No one pressed. Instead, Emerson directed the conversation back to Charli. "Can you counter-sue?"

Charli shook her head. "My father acted on my behalf. If Lord Wagner decided to sue for breach of contract, he is within his rights, horrid as that may be."

"What if you sue your father?" Emerson asked.

Charli glanced as Rafe. "We considered it. Unfortunately, there is a great deal of protection around the royals, and a lawsuit may not be successful. Likely, it wouldn't be. My father may have made terrible choices for me and without my consent, but they were...legal choices."

"And there's the matter of the press," Rafe added.

Emerson gave Charli a sympathetic smile. "Always kinder to powerful men than young women." She shared a secret look with Gabriel.

"Okay, we're obviously not going to let you marry some murderous leech of a lord," Rhylee said from beside Charli on the couch. "What if you just stay in the States for a few years? We could always use more brilliant minds teaching America's youth."

For the briefest moment, the possibilities flashed before Charli's eyes, a life spent in the wilds of Montana, horseback riding and playing in the snow. Teaching, really teaching, with her own classroom and her own books, giving back as a member of the community like she had never been able to truly do as a princess.

Living with these new friends of hers, and playing in the club every night.

With a man who was *not* Raffaello. Since Raffaello was heir to the throne, and because she would have to break the law to stay, even if the law were unjust and unfair.

"There are extradition laws," she explained. "And technically, I would be breaking the law. If Wagner or my father wanted to come get me, they could."

"Or if her brother's friend wanted kidnap her and bring her back to Contanari," Rafe muttered, a hint of self-loathing coloring his words.

She gave him a small smile. "I think we can both forgive you for that by now."

"Okay, I have...a strange one," Dante said, his eyes alight with creativity and possibility. "It's out of left field, but bear with me a for a second."

Charli shrugged. "No such thing as bad ideas."

Rhylee elbowed her. "See, you already sound like a teacher."

Dante stood and muttered something under his breath, bits and pieces of Italian slipping through. Finally, he paused. "All right, I'm no expert on Contanari law, but if you can override these contracts, any contract, with the king's approval, that recognizes the royal palace as the highest office in the land, correct?"

Charli nodded. "Correct."

"And that means, *arguably*, that a contract with a higher-ranking royal, say one of the royal palace, would, *presumably*, overwrite the existing one."

Rafe cocked his head to the side. "Maybe. It would have to depend on the specifics of the contract."

Dante shrugged, the movement far too innocent. "Say, a marriage contract."

Rafe rolled his eyes. "*Andiamo, Dante, rapido, per favore.*"

"Fine." Dante threw his hands up. "What if instead of marrying Lord Wagner, you married a higher-ranking royal? What if you married Prince Raffaello?"

Chapter Twenty-Two

"Why exactly can't you marry the prince?" Rhylee asked. After the bombshell Dante had dropped, Rhylee had suggested that maybe they all take a break and come back to the brainstorming later. And then she and the other women had grabbed Charli and raced off for what they referred to as mandatory girl time. "He is...very handsome."

Charli tried to ignore the strange warmth she felt at hearing another woman call Raffaello handsome, even one she liked as much as Rhylee.

"It's not that I can't," she said, looked around at the others. It's just... All my life, I've done what's expected of me, been the dutiful princess and daughter. I've made decisions for my country and my people and my family. I guess... I guess I just didn't want to have to make this one decision because I was being forced into it."

"That's completely understandable," Saint said. "Sometimes...sometimes we lose ourselves to taking care of others and forget to live our own lives."

Charli let out a humorless laugh. "I wouldn't even know where to begin."

Rhylee gestured at her with a glass of wine. "You said you wanted to be a teacher. Why not start there?"

Because she was a princess of the realm, who likely wouldn't be able to return home without being kidnapped by her own father. Because she didn't even know where to begin, what degree she would need, what age to teach...

It all started to feel very overwhelming. Not just the question of what she was going to do with her life, but all of it, the new and intense affair she was having with Rafe, the introduction to a lifestyle she had known nothing about but taken to with an unsettling ease, the contract ruining her life... the question of marriage to the prince.

Because the very worst part of all of it was that she didn't *hate* the idea. It was far easier than it should have been to picture herself married to a man like Raffaello, with his reserved brilliance, his dedication, his work ethic and care for his people...and everything they had shared in the last few days.

But that had never been on the table, any kind of future for them beyond the time at The Ranch, and knowing as she did about Raffaello's more...noble nature, Charli knew she would always worry that he had agreed out of a sense of obligation and responsibility, rather than true feelings for her.

And she hadn't been lying to Rhylee either. Charli's entire life had been decided for her, had been decided without anyone once asking what she might want. Taking off on a midnight flight had been one of the very few choices she had ever made for herself, and marrying a prince to avoid marrying a lord felt like just another decision that was out of her grasp.

Saint shook her head in Charli's direction. "This is overwhelming you, so let's start smaller. My Gram...I pretty much put my life on hold to take care of her. And Dante was the first person in my life to actually ask me what I wanted, not just to survive. So, we made a silly list."

"Okay," Charli said, feeling slightly more at ease now that she didn't have to have all the answers to all the questions all at once. "What was on the list?"

Saint pulled her phone out. "Okay, I wanted to ride his motorcycle..."

Morgan coughed, "*Not all she wanted to ride.*"

Saint rolled her eyes, but a light blush tinged her fair cheeks. "And to see the stars in the mountains, both of which might be a little tough right now. We bought art supplies, scratch-off cards, and ice cream and...oh, you can do this one right now — we did tequila shots."

Charli shrugged. "I've never had tequila before."

"Perfect!" Rhylee scampered out of the room with Morgan hot on her heels, and a moment later returned with a large bottle of tequila in hand.

Charli felt her eyes go wide. "Maybe just...one, to start."

Rhylee laughed. "I hope you didn't think we'd make you do tequila shots *alone*."

She handed out shot glasses and poured each one to the brim. Then she passed the Charli a small saltshaker. "Okay, lick, shot, suck," she said, indicating to the lime slices in a bowl on the table. "Don't sip, it's...not a good idea."

Morgan leaned in conspiratorially, and whispered, "We all know Rhylee prefers to take it to the back of the throat."

Rhylee smacked her with a pillow. "At least I can get myself out of a climbing harness without help."

Morgan stuck her tongue out. "Those were not regulation knots, which Reece *fully* knew."

Charli couldn't help but smile. There was such honesty and freedom in the experience of sitting in a sex club lodge with open, care-free women who were so knowledgeable and excited about the lifestyle. It took away all the taboo, and made the kink into a conversation about connection and boldness and refusing to apologize for the things she wanted.

She leaned over to Saint. "Are they always like this?"

Saint smiled. "It kind of comes with the territory. I think there's a sort of comfort with exhibitionism and voyeurism with a club like this."

"Especially with Rhylee," Morgan said, elbowing Rhylee in the gut, like they were friends who had been roughhousing their whole lives. "*Especially* if she's trying to piss Van off…"

Charli cocked her head to the side. "I heard Rafe say something to him when he…" She blushed, her cheeks growing hot. "Dragged me out of the room like a caveman. What's that all about it?"

Rhylee scrunched her nose. "I'm much more interested in what happened after Rafe dragged you out of the room like a caveman, actually. He seems so…reserved. Except around you, apparently."

"Kiss and tell," Emerson said with a grin. "Please, it's my favorite thing."

"I think I might need to do this shot first," Charli said. "And maybe another."

"To princesses behaving badly," Rhylee said, raising her shot glass.

"I'll drink to that," Charli replied, licking the salt before downing the tequila shot. It burned all the way down.

But it also made her feel very much alive.

Chapter Twenty-Three

"I've been thinking," Raffaello said as Charli walked back into the room they had been sharing. "About what Dante said."

"Not going there," Charli replied. She was a little buzzed after a few more shots with the girls, and riding a little hot on the conversations that had flowed as freely as the drink. The rules of Domination and submission were still so new and different to her, but the more time she spent with the intelligent, well-possessed women of The Ranch, the more quickly she had learned about the true root of the power and the intimacy of control and submission.

It was fascinating, academically and theoretically speaking. Practically speaking it was also...very hot.

Because the other women all played with power in their own ways, handing it over willingly or pretending otherwise, and it turned out there were about a million nuances and flavors a person could play the game. Which made it all the more telling that they had clocked her as a brat with barely a day's evidence to prove it. But Charli had very much enjoyed hearing about all the different secrets and scenes and games.

And all the while, she couldn't help but feel like her secret games were the very best.

Which was a dangerous, *dangerous* way to think about her temporary affair with the prince, but the tequila had loosened her inhibitions and her thoughts, and she could admit privately to herself that whoever did end up marrying Prince Raffaello Chiaramonte, Royal Prince of Le Isole del Contanari would be a very lucky woman, indeed.

It just wouldn't be her.

It couldn't be her.

Right.

"We *should* go there," Raffaello said, sitting down at the desk. He wore those damned glasses again, the ones that made her feel like asking for extra credit, and the sight was making it very difficult for Charli to focus on the conversation.

"Nope," she replied. "There are about a million reasons we should not get married."

Raffaello looked at her carefully. "But we could. If we needed to. I had Madison look into the legality of it, and technically it would fall under a traditional statute, which to be honest we should have removed ages ago, but it would work. If we needed it to. And neither your father or Lord Wagner would have any legal foundation for a countersuit or other action."

"Great," Charli said, waving her hand around in front of her face. "I'm sure that's exactly how you expected to find your future bride. By blowing up a marriage contract."

Raffaello studied her, realization dawning in his beautiful eyes. "Are you drunk?"

Charli laughed. "No. What? You're drunk."

He shook his head. "I can assure you, I am not. But you should know, we are at a rather high elevation here. Alcohol is much more…effective."

"Nope," Charli stated with more confidence than she probably should have, as she almost missed the edge of the bed. "It's not the elevation. It's tequila." She slid down to the floor. "You know… I've never had tequila before."

Raffaello furrowed his brows. "I could have assumed. *Why* did you have tequila?"

Charli threw her hands in the air. "It's my *list*," she explained.

Raffaello nodded. "Naturally. What's your list?"

Charli sighed. "Saint had a list. It was…all these things she never did. Like, she missed out on them because she had to take care of her Gram. Well, I missed out because I'm a princess and I can't go wild because the paparazzi will take pictures and my father would kill me."

"So, you're going wild now," Raffaello confirmed. "The hair and the dancing and the…rest of it."

She grinned. "I do like the rest of it."

He shook his head. "We're not going there right now."

"I *know*," Charli said. "Two drink max at the club."

"Correct," he replied. "And how many did you have."

"Two," Charli said with total confidence. "No. Two times two. Times three, what's that?"

"That's a whole pot of coffee," Raffaello replied. "And food."

"I've never had a prince make me coffee before," Charli said. "Are you good at it?"

Raffaello gave her an indulgent smile. "No. I'll make Dante bring us some."

Charli nodded. "*Si, si, tre tazze di caffè per favore. E…
E biscotti e caramelle e pasta.*"

"Who's the third cup for?" Raffaello asked, shooting
Dante a quick text. "And how many languages do you
speak?"

"Two for me, three for you," she said. "And four.
Well, five."

"Two for you, one for me," he corrected. "Italian,
English, French, Spanish."

"And Arabic," she said. "And Turkish."

"That's six."

She shrugged. "No one needs me to count. I'm just a
princess."

Raffaello sounded frustrated when he responded.
"You have to know that's not true. Whoever told you
that is very ignorant about the nation and about you."

She smiled. "That's my father."

"Charlotte." Raffaello grew very serious. "I know
you're probably going to forget this, but I'll say it again
anyway. "I'm going to find a way to get you out of this
marriage. I promise."

She laid her head on his leg, enjoying his warmth,
the simple, innate power he offered, her and the world.
And then she wondered how often Raffaello let
someone else hold him up.

"You need a list too," she said.

"I do?" he asked.

"Yes. You need to learn how to have fun."

"I have fun," he replied. "Sometimes."

"Never," Charli said. "You're here to *relax*. And
you're always working. Always. It's bad for you."

"It's the job."

She shook her head. "What's on your list. Tell me."

Raffaello finally smiled. "I like horseback riding. I
come back here as often as I can to ride the horses."

Charli's heart softened a little bit. "I bet you're good with horses. Strong, powerful type. You don't have to be strong all the time you know."

"I do, Princess," he said, helping her back onto the bed. "I actually do."

"Nope," Charli said. "You can let someone else carry some of your burden. I could help. I'm good at policies, not that anyone every lets me help. But I could help you—I want to help you."

But before she could consider the implications of her words, or why they came so easily, Charli's head hit the pillow, and she quickly fell asleep.

* * * *

When Charli woke a little while later, there was a tray of coffee and food on the table, and a very cozy looking Prince Raffaello in bed beside her.

"How's your head?" he asked, placing his tablet down on the bedside table.

"Fine," she said. "Mostly. Coffee, please."

He grinned, that same, unexpected grin that seemed to take her breath away every time she saw it. Because Raffaello wasn't a man prone to intensity expressions of emotions, and it was always a special kind of treat to see, like she had earned something worth holding onto.

"You might have been right about the elevation," she admitted. "Do I have anything to apologize for?"

Raffaello shook his head, handing her a cup of coffee mixed exactly how she liked it. "Not at all. You did ask me what was on my *list* though. You have to be careful. At a club like The Ranch, that could mean something very different."

Charli choked on her sip of coffee. She hadn't been expecting the staid and controlled Prince Raffaello to allude to some kind of kink bucket list. But, of course, now that he had…

"Okay, forget what I meant before. What's on that list?"

He shook his head. "Not a chance. I didn't have six shots of tequila."

Charli scrunched her nose and gave him her sweetest smile. "I could get you some. Please, Raffaello, I know you're dying to tell me."

He let out a low chuckle, and the sound went straight to her belly, warm and hot. What was it about this man that could turn her molten with the merest look or laugh?

"I have a compromise."

Charli's belly warmed for an entirely different reason then, a feeling of foreboding and nerves, like her body knew what Raffaello was going to say before he said it.

Because, of course, she did remember some things from stumbling back into the room hours before.

"You want to know why I won't marry you," she said. "Even though it's the logical next step and the easiest way to fix this…situation I'm in."

He nodded. "I do. It seems like the lesser of two evils, if I do say so myself. Though perhaps I'm wrong on that count."

Charli couldn't help but give him a soft smile. "Of course not. Raffaello, you're…honorable and admirable and true. And no doubt my life would be far richer and more fulfilling if I married you rather than that lunatic Lord Wagner. But…" She hesitated. Why was it so much easier to tell the women about her fears and hopes than this man who was quickly becoming one of the most important people in her life?

Because he's quickly become one of the most important people in your life.

It lingered at the corners of her mind, the possibility that maybe she would want to say yes, but not because of some ridiculous marriage contract and not because Prince Raffaello was an honorable man.

"But," he prompted.

Charli took a fortifying breath. "All my life, every single decision has been made for me. I've never been allowed to pick what I wear, what I study, where I go. My father selling me off in an antiquated marriage contract, that's…not that extreme for him. I just… I just don't want to have to decide who I marry because I don't have another choice."

Raffaello studied her carefully, those bright blue eyes seeing past so many of her defenses, like he knew her, on some innate, true level, like he understood her in a way few people ever had before—or ever would again.

"Okay," he said. "Okay, I can understand that. I know what the life of a royal can be like, a gilded cage, at times. But this is still our best course of action and we're running out of time to figure out another solution."

She searched for some explanation, for artifice or agenda in his gaze, but found none. "I don't get it," Charli admitted. "You have the freedom to marry whoever you want. Why would you waste that on getting me out of the contract?"

He shook his head, like the answer was the most obvious thing in the world. "You need help. I can help you."

"And if I don't deserve it?" she asked, her voice cracking just as little as Charli realized the fear had been haunting the back of her mind for longer than she wanted to admit.

"Everyone is worthy of saving," Raffaello said. "Everyone is worthy of redemption."

"Including you." It wasn't a question. She had seen the dark circles under his eyes, had heard the story of his passing out in the House of Lords. When it had circulated, he was still just the prince, a friend of her brother's and member of the Royal Family, a politician. But now, he was *Rafe*, and Charli found she cared much more than she wanted to admit about how he cared for himself.

"Yes," he responded after a moment. "Something you want to say, Princess?"

She nodded. "I don't think you're getting enough rest. I think you're working too hard, and running away from something."

"Maybe I am," Raffaello replied. "But I promise, it's none of your concern, Charli. I have matters well in hand."

"If you need help, will you ask for it?" she pushed. "Not just with proposals and articles. But true help. Support from a friend. Will you ask for it?"

"Okay," Rafe replied. "But only if you consider the marriage."

She could live with that. "I'll give you an answer when the storm lets up," she said. "When the time comes for us to leave, I'll tell you what I've decided for my future."

"Before that, though," Rafe said, "you mentioned that you're good at proposals—and that no one ever lets you help, as I remember it. I'm asking for your help, Charlotte."

She studied him. "You're not supposed to be working right now."

Rafe shook his head. "It's routine. Well, it's supposed to be. But the numbers for Fontaine's annual trade routes aren't making any sense."

Charli smiled. "Happy to help — if you look over the education funding strategy I've been working on."

Raffaello laughed. "So many compromises and diplomatic statements between us. It truly is a miracle any legislation ever gets passed."

"Speaking of compromise," Charli said, aware that her voice had gotten a little husky, a little wicked. "I believe you were going to tell me what's on your list."

"I could tell you," he said, and the shift would have been imperceptible, if she hadn't been actively looking for it, hoping for it, aching to see him take up the mantle of his power and domination, "or I could show you."

Chapter Twenty-Four

Rafe dimmed the lights and settled down at the large desk. He knew that matters with Charlotte were far from resolved, and that they were going to have to have much longer discussions about her future, potentially *their* future, but he also knew she wasn't ready for that.

And, frankly, neither was he.

Because there was no denying that he'd been too quick to jump on Dante's suggestion, too quick and without good reason, and Rafe knew that if looked behind the curtain to figure out exactly what that reason was, well, it was only going to add kindling to an already blazing fire.

So, he reverted to the one thing he knew they were good at without question, the one element of their increasingly complex dynamic that felt right in his bones and soul.

So right, in fact, that he'd actually planned ahead for it.

"There's a gift hanging for you in the closet," he said. "Go put it on."

Charlotte raised an eyebrow at him and squared her jaw, but nodded, as if the decision was her own, and walked over to the closet.

Rafe's cock pounded a hard, pulsing rhythm behind his slacks, anticipation building with every moment Charlotte spent in the closet. It didn't matter how many times he had her, he craved her more each and every time.

Dangerous.

Unstoppable.

"When you walk out of that door, Princess," he said, his voice already sounding so low and so rough, "the scene starts. So, before you do, tell me. How do you feel?"

"Green."

She didn't hesitate. Fuck, he was beginning to love that, her surety and certainty. Her fearlessness, even in the face of new, heart-pounding experiences.

Heart-pounding, indeed.

"Good," he managed, a sense of relief filling his chest he hadn't expected to feel. He had been slightly worried about pushing too far, but Charlotte didn't seem to pause at any of it.

Except marrying me.

Which was a thought for another time.

Especially since every thought he'd ever had in his life fled the second she stepped out of the closet.

Because she wore the uniform of his old university.

He'd had it adjusted, of course, the skirt shortened, the sweater tight and cropped, the white button-down shirt straining to pop. It had been a long-standing fantasy, and the uniform had hung in the closet for some time, but he'd never found the perfect partner to play it out.

Until Charlotte.

And *fuck* she was perfect. The skirt skimmed her upper thighs, just a few bare inches between the hem and the tops of her high socks, and she had left the white shirt tails hanging out and the tie loose around her neck in an act of flagrant defiance so blatant and bold that it was like waving a red flag in front of a raging bull.

"You wanted to see me, Professor?" She played with her tie and snapped her teeth together, as if she were lazily chewing on a piece of bubblegum. And the attitude was enough to drag Raffaello so far and fast to the edge of his fantasy that he gripped the edge of the large wooden desk to keep from losing himself completely. Or falling over when the blood rushed away from his essential organs.

"Yes, Miss Marchand, I did," he said, reining it in the best he could. "Come take a seat at my desk. There's something we need to discuss."

She raised a brow. "Is there? And here I thought this was just a…" She scrunched her nose. "Social visit."

He indicated to the seat on the other side of the desk. "Your test scores are surprising, Miss Marchand," he said. "Given your obvious feelings toward this class. But it's your latest essay that has me concerned."

Charlotte shook her head. "You didn't like my thesis, *Sir?*"

Raffaello had placed a pile of folders and papers on the table, and he reached for one now. "I didn't like how it was a direct copy of the same paper handed in by a former student of mine last year."

"You're saying I plagiarized," she said, her eyes wide and her bottom lip jutting out so plump and pink it was all Raffaello could do not to lean over and bite it.

"Yes," he said. "Which is, as you know, an expellable offense."

Charlotte leaned back in her chair, as if she were already bored with the conversation. "That's assuming I did. Which I did not."

"I thought you might say that," he said. "Which is why I retrieved the former student's paper for a comparison and..." He paused, letting the moment build hot and heavy around them. "They are identical papers."

"Fine," Charlotte said, leaning forward so she looked up at him with those wide, dangerous eyes, eyes that could command surrender as well as they could give it. "Maybe I did...take inspiration...from a line or two. So what?"

"So, what, that is a *good* question," Raffaello said. "And I suppose my answer would be, so what are you going to do about it?"

"You want me to ask for extra credit," she teased, climbing up on the desk, the movement making her skirt ride up, exposing more of that long, slender leg. "You want to tell you that I'll do anything as long as you don't report me?"

She was teasing him now, the perfect bad girl, all spit and vinegar, and it was everything Raffaello needed — the challenge, the glint of mischief in her eyes, the confrontational pose that told him she wasn't going down without a fight.

"That depends," he said, leaning back in his chair to take in the full picture, and Charlotte made for a full picture, long legs, short skirt, sweater swelling over full breasts, her thigh-high socks teasing at the shadowed space beyond her hem. "Do you want to pass my class? Because I hear you're doing just fine in all the rest of your courses. In fact, you're one of the very best students in your university year." He watched her closely. "So, what it is about *my* class, Miss Marchand, that makes you behave so...badly?"

"Maybe it's not your class," she whispered, swallowing hard. He watched the bob of her slender throat, and thought about how it would feel to wrap his hand around her there, to pin her and hold her down until she begged for mercy. And he knew it would be a long time before she begged for anything.

"No?" Raffaello asked. "If it's not my class...then your issue must be with me."

She squared her jaw. "And if it is?"

"Then I have to ask," he said, drawing one finger down her thigh, loving how she shuddered with the touch. She was so responsive, challenging and full of fire, but her body always seemed to betray her, and Raffaello loved watching the internal struggle, loved seeing her fight against her own best instincts so she could continue to defy him, knowing it would be better for both of them. "What seems to be the problem?"

Charlotte parted her thighs slowly, her knees falling open and creating a canopy with the hem of the short skirt, creating promise in the dips and valley between and below, exposing more of her long, toned legs and beautiful thighs. "I can't stop thinking about you," she whispered, leaning back slightly, the position pulling her sweater tight across her swollen breasts. "I want things, wicked things...dangerous things."

God, so did he, his cock straining against his slacks, his heart nearly beating out of his chest, the need like a fire, all-consuming and impossible to ignore.

"Like what, Miss Marchand? What could be so distracting that it keeps you from performing well in my class?" Raffaello heard the rough growl in his own voice, heard the dark threat of need at the corners of his words, and judging by the heated expression in Charlotte's gaze, so did she.

"Like your fingers on my skin," she whispered like a confession. "Pushing up my skirt, until..."

"Until?" he prompted.

"Until you find out... I don't have anything on underneath..."

"And do you, Charlotte?" He teased right at the hem, at the bare skin between her skirt and the top of those fucking socks. "Do you have anything underneath?"

She darted her tongue out between swollen lips, more defiance, more challenge, and Raffaello didn't think twice about rising to it when she said, "Why don't you find out?"

Raffaello leaned forward in his chair and stared up at her. There was something so heady about being in the position of submission for her, like they both knew that she would eventually give over to his touch, and be all the more grateful for it.

He slid his hand up her leg, lingering at the top of the high sock, and then farther, to where her skirt hid just enough to make it all the more tantalizing, his fingers caressing warm, smooth skin, his cock jumping every time Charlotte released a low, shuddering breath at his touch.

"You know that it's a violation of the dress code," he murmured, never taking his eye from her. "If I find there's nothing under here, I will have to issue punishment."

She grinned, dangerous, teasing, the kind of grin that made men follow sirens to the sea floor. "What kind of punishment?"

Her back arched on the last word as Raffaello found her slick, hot entrance with his thumb. It was the most potent, intense aphrodisiac, to see that she craved the submission and domination as much as he craved giving it, to feel her arousal from the games they played that didn't feel like games at all, but like the solution to all the problems in their universes.

He tsked. "I know you like defying the rules, Miss Marchand, but this is just blatantly disrespectful to the school and to your professors."

"And to you?" She spread her legs wider, the skirt riding up, exposing more deliciously smooth thigh, which only made Raffaello's cock pulse with anticipation. He slipped a finger inside her tight, hot channel.

"Oh, most definitely to me," he replied. "Which is why I need to know you are capable of following the rules. So don't make a sound."

Before she could respond, Raffaello dove under her skirt, the tiny fabric no match for his need, pulsing and overwhelming as it was, and he took what he wanted, devouring her sweet, wet pussy like it was made for him and him alone, a burning, aching need to make her come, to make her lose all sense of herself. He licked and sucked, sliding his fingers inside her and brushing her swollen clit, and Charlotte arched to take more of him, his responsive, needy little princess.

She gripped at the desk's edges, but Raffaello could tell she was starting to lose control, soft pants and whispers escaping her lips, a deep shuddering moan that rocked him to his core, and then finally... "*Yes, Professor...*"

And with that, Raffaello slammed one more finger into her tight little hole, and Charlotte came hard and fast, her body tensing around him, her pretty cunt taking his every touch as she rode the waves of pleasure.

"I knew you couldn't follow simple directions," Raffaello said, his voice harsh and intense, rich with the desire pulsing a hot rhythm through his blood. "Stand up, put your hands on the desk."

"Or what?" Her challenge lost some of its bite with pleasure still hazing the words, but it turned him on just to see her try.

"Or I double your punishment," he said, not that he would have any issues with turning her ass pink all night long.

Charlotte raised a brow, but came to stand against the desk, her back ramrod straight and defiance in her eyes.

Raffaello took her neck in his hand and none-too-gently guided her to bend over the desk. "I've let his go on too long. Now you need to know what happens to students who defy their teachers." He reached into his desk drawer and pulled out a thick wooden ruler. "Now I need to know you're not going to do it again. So with every punishment, I want to hear you confess to your transgression."

"Yes, Professor," she bit back, her eyes still fighting.

He pushed her skirt up, massaging the soft globes of her ass, and then before Charlotte could brace, brought the ruler down hard.

"Fuck..." She bucked forward. "I apologize for plagiarizing my essay, *Professor*."

Heat burned a path down his back, making his cock swell and his balls tighten. It was his fantasy come to life, thicker and more intense than he could have ever expected, and it was already so difficult to keep from taking what he wanted, what they both wanted. But Raffaello knew the wait would be worth it.

He brought the ruler down again, on a different patch of her soft skin.

Charlotte took the blow with dignity. "I apologize for not wearing panties to class," she whispered, danger in her words.

Another blow, another cutting confession. "I apologize for fantasizing about you, Professor," she bit out.

He leaned down, pinning her against the desk, her lush body pressing against his own and making it difficult for Raffaello to think. "Be specific."

He brought the ruler down.

Charlotte swore. "I apologize for imagining how it would feel to have your cock inside me and your fingers on my clit, Professor."

"Is that all?" he asked, biting at the sensitive skin of her throat and loving how she responded to him.

She shook her head.

He smacked the ruler against her pretty little ass again. "Tell me everything. So I know you won't do it again."

"And if I want to do it again," Charlotte asked. "If want to touch myself imagining how it would feel to take your cock in all my holes…then what?"

"All your holes." He slipped a finger into her pussy, and fuck she was so wet, so aroused by the punishment, the perfect dark need to match his own. "You want to be fucked and filled up, do you,

Charlotte? Dripping my cum down your thighs as you sit in class. Maybe you want a toy in your tight little hole that makes it impossible to pay attention."

"Yes," she practically whimpered.

"You'll be squirming in your seat while I ask you questions, and when you get them all wrong because you *just can't focus*...I'll ask you to see me after class."

"*Yes...*"

"And then," Raffaello continued, "I'll take your plug out, even though you just love having it in...and I'll fill your tight little hole with my cock, instead...is that your fantasy, Charlotte?"

She nodded and then swallowed hard. "Except..."

"Except...?" he pushed, pressing a second finger into her tight hole.

"Except..." She hesitated. "I shouldn't tell you..."

Raffaello twisted his fingers around. "You really should."

Charlotte bucked against him, but he held her firm against the desk. "Fine," she bit out, "Fine, I fantasize about you coming in my asshole... Professor. And then putting the plug in, so I have to walk around all day with your cum in my hole, claiming —"

A harsh sound of need escaped Raffaello's lips. "Such a filthy Little Brat," he murmured. "But you've been honest with me, so I'll give you what you want."

With one hand, he opened his trousers and pulled his cock free. It was thick and hard, pulsing with an overwhelming need, and when he pressed it against Charlotte's sweet little entrance, they both groaned.

"You're going to take my cock, Charlotte. Be a good girl just this once."

"Please..." she murmured. "Please, I need..."

"I know what you need," he said. "You need to let me in, let me make you feel so good..."

And she did, relaxing just enough that his thick cock could press in, stretching her, filling her. He'd never get enough of her body's response to his, the way they fit together so perfectly, it was like the connection was predestined.

"When you sit in class," he murmured, sliding in an out in an agonizingly slow rhythm, "all I can think about is how it would feel to have you on your knees under my desk, sucking my cock...I bet you'd look so pretty with your mouth full."

She pushed back into his thrust. "You want me to kneel for you?" she asked, the words coming out in a rush of desire and need that only served to heighten his own.

"I want you to *crawl* for me," he growled against her ear, holding her throat with one strong hand. "I want you to think of nothing but taking my cock over and over again until you're satisfied. And then taking it again, just because I told you to." Her cunt clenched around him, and Raffaello gripped her thigh hard, bringing them closer together, tightening the connection that was sure to devastate them both.

"You should see how pretty you look with my cock buried in your pussy," he murmured. "But I know you can take more. Tell me you can take more, Charlotte."

She shook her head. "Your cock feels so big inside me."

Raffaello groaned. "I know, Princess. But you promised to be good, so you're going to have to try."

He slipped his fingers into her wetness, massaging the space right where their bodies met, which made them both groan and arch. Then he slipped between her cheeks, pressing one wet finger to the ring there. Charlotte nearly jumped at the sensation, and he tightened his hold on her hip.

"Ask me for it," he said. "*Beg* me for it."

She shook her head. "No..."

"Yes," Raffaello murmured. "I know you want to be filled like a filthy little slut. All you have to do is ask."

Charlotte swallowed hard, clearly overwhelmed by the intensity of the pleasure and need pulsing through them both. "Finger my asshole," she whispered. "Please... I need... I need to feel full."

Raffaello kissed the back of her neck, and then pressed one finger against the sensitive muscle, until it yielded and let him in. He pulsed it in and out a few times, and each touch seemed to drive Charlotte closer and close to the edge of her control, until she seemed so tightly pulled that she was about to snap.

"More?" he asked.

"Please," she begged. "Put another finger in my ass... I need...I need to be stretched."

He did as she asked, pulsing in and loving how her body responded. "Yes, you do," he muttered. "Stretched and filled and taken. Do you want to be taken, Charlotte?"

She nodded. "Now, please. Take me, Professor?"

"Try again," he said. "Tell me what you really want."

"I want to fucked," Charlotte whimpered. "I want to be fucked until I can't stand and then I want you to fill my pussy with your cum until you're dripping down my thighs."

Raffaello couldn't wait another second, not with her filthy demands, not with the way her body was clenching and claiming him with every pulse, not with how *fucking* perfect she looked in that university uniform, and so he slammed into her hard and fast, and then again and again. Each thrust pushed them both to their very breaking points, until Charlotte was muttering and demanding and confessing all the filthy depraved things she wanted, until Raffaello was responding in kind with dark intense promises, until she was begging, begging, begging for permission to come around his cock.

When Charlotte came, she squeezed him so hard Raffaello saw the vision at the corner of his eyes dim. "Again," he muttered. "Come again. Take me with you, Princess."

It only took a moment, the coupling harsh, too intense, too bright, flint hard and perfect, and Charlotte took his next thrust and then his next, and finally Raffaello pressed a third finger against the entrance to her tight little asshole, and Charlotte broke, coming with a busting intensity that had her squeezing hard, swearing and arching and begging and...

It took Raffaello with her, until he was holding tight to her hip and thrusting, pulsing long, hot jets of cum into her waiting pussy, spilling inside her until it leaked all over her thighs, the pleasure nothing short of a total claiming.

For both of them.

Chapter Twenty-Five

The next few days passed in a similar haze of pleasure and comfort. The storm continued outside their windows, keeping the lot of them locked up in The Ranch, and Raffaello took every opportunity to introduce Charlotte to new pleasures, which she took to with a natural instinct that only made him more aware of their innate, growing, and all-too-dangerous connection.

Raffello had shown her the trade route issues he'd be struggling with, and Charlotte had been completely shocked to share that they were not the right numbers at all. Rafe, for his part, hadn't been shocked in the slightest when she'd sent over her education initiative and it had been flawless. Despite his doctor's orders, Rafe and Charlotte worked together in their spare moments, strengthening arguments and building out plans for the future—and the time they shared seemed to make him feel relieved, refreshed even, work no longer draining Rafe dry.

Of course, that might have been because Charlotte was doing a fine job of it.

Between scenes, they spent time with his friends, more time than Raffaello had been able to spend in years, and with each other, warm and cozy in different beds around the club, watching the snow or the fire in the grate, talking about their lives with people who actually understood. Raffaello had grown up as a prince, and knew exactly what it was like to have his life planned out for him from the day he was born, but Charlotte, it seemed, had been all but locked away, restricted and decided for, with few exceptions.

He could almost understand her reluctance to agree to a marriage.

Almost.

Time was running out for them both, and no matter how he broached the subject of her future, of their one viable solution to the predicament they were in, she shut down, refusing to entertain the idea.

It was *infuriating*.

And the worst part was that Raffaello couldn't quite figure out why. It should have been simple. He asked. She said no. They moved on.

But the more sand that spilled from the hourglass, the more Raffaello found that it mattered why she hadn't said yes. It *mattered*. And that was... complicated.

What made matters all the more complicated was a call he received from Madison early in the morning, after a particularly late and intense night. Charlotte was still asleep, spread out and warm under the covers, and Raffaello took the phone into the other room, shutting the door behind him so as not to wake her.

"I'm assuming this is important," Raffaello said. He realized he sounded frustrated with the early morning wakeup call, which had never happened before. He was always grateful when Madison called, especially now that Rafe was stuck halfway around the world and his right-hand man was all but running the country.

Because it's all changing. Because she *changed it.*

Because for once, he didn't want to jump out of bed and race to start working again.

To his credit, Madison didn't say a word about Rafe's tone. But his response was so much worse.

"It is," he said, pausing uncharacteristically, the long seconds of silence making Raffaello's stomach drop, and his muscles tighten. "Prince Johan has left the country."

And there was the shoe dropping hard and fast.

Because he hadn't been quick enough or smart enough or whatever else he needed to be to find a solution for Charlotte's future. He only had the one, the one idea that forced into light the things he had been pushing down into the dark, and she had refused to even listen to the possibility, despite his best efforts.

Raffaello looked out of the French doors that led to his veranda, and realized with a start that the sky was no longer sleet gray and thick with snow. Even in the early hour, there was a tint of light blue right at the edges of the sky, and the storm clouds that had raged for days were turning to soft shades of white.

The snow had stopped.

No doubt, that aligned far, *far* too coincidentally with the departure of Charlotte's father, and Raffaello knew without a shadow of a doubt that Prince Johan wasn't running away from potential retribution or consequence. He was chasing Charlotte down.

And time had run out for all of them.

"How do you know?" he asked Madison finally, trying desperately to hold onto the sense of logic and calm that had served him well enough as a politician. "And when exactly did he leave?"

"I put surveillance on him," Madison said, as if it were the most obvious thing in the world, and not for the first time in their relationship, Raffaello had to wonder if his advisor had former intelligence skills and connections. Or current intelligence skills and connections. "The first time you called. He's been in the palace since."

"Except for today," Raffaello said.

Madison confirmed it. "I got a call from one of my men an hour ago. Last we have of Prince Johan is his drive to the regional airport. I'm still working on getting the flight manifest."

"I don't think you need to bother," Raffaello said. "He'll try to come here."

"Most likely," Madison agreed. "What would you like me to do?"

Wasn't that the question? It was the same damned one Raffaello had been going over and over since the goddamned day he'd learned about Charlotte's marriage contact. For better or for worse, Prince Johan was a member of his Royal Court, and held strong political and social influence, and Raffaello couldn't exactly go storming around the countryside arresting his royals, especially not in a country that wasn't his own.

It didn't stop him from wanting to, however. And wanting to do so much worse. Because no doubt Prince Johan deserved it. Raffaello couldn't shake the urgent, instinctual need to shake the very life out of the man who had made Charlotte's such a living hell for so long.

"Nothing for now," he said to Madison, instead of any of that. "I need...to figure some things out on this end. But I'll call you soon."

"Before you go," Madison said, "there's the issue of your father we need to discuss."

"Not now," Raffaello said. "Later."

And then before Madison could get a word in edgewise, Raffaello hung up the call, plunging the room into a kind of damning silence. Outside the lodge, snow blanketed every surface, as if cushioning the world, but the sun was cracking through the clouds above, like the celestial call of angels in a Renaissance painting, and it would only be a matter of hours before the snow and ice began to melt away, likely not even a day before the roads were clear enough to ford.

Time was up for all of them.

* * * *

Raffaello contemplated how to tell Charlotte her father was on his way for most of the morning. But the more he agonized over the perfect words, the more difficult it became to share them, like the truth of their situation was stuck in his throat, the reality that her father was coming to...what? Collect her, kidnap her, steal her back to force into a horrid arrange marriage, it was too difficult to wrap his head around.

He knew he should have talked to his friends. They were all still locked up in the big lodge, and they would understand better than anyone the confliction and worry he was experiencing. But voicing his concerns aloud, actually telling them what was going on, it felt too much like acknowledging the mess of the situation, like it wasn't real or true unless he told someone.

And he knew, deep in his gut, that he couldn't tell anyone else until he told Charlotte.

Who had been clearly picking up on his mood all day. He couldn't have hidden it for all the gold in the Royal Palace. Or maybe Charlotte was just too good at reading him, which was a much more damning possibility.

When it was clear she was finally getting too frustrated to deal with him, Charlotte all but dragged Rafe out of the main lodge and back to his quarters. If he were a different man or the situation were different in any way, he would have taken that for the challenge it was and used the moment to make the most of the small time they had left.

But Rafe knew they had passed the point of no return, and the expression Charlotte's face told him he was about to go to battle.

"What the fuck, Rafe?" she said, as soon as the door was closed behind them. He didn't want to admit that he really liked this side of her, the wild side of the sheltered princess who had finally come out, and it was clear Charlotte had no plans of hiding her again. "What's the problem? Is it because the storm is over?"

"Yes," he said, stepping toward her, because fuck, he couldn't seem to keep his distance from this woman. "Yes, the storm is over, and you told me that we would have an answer about your future, Charlotte. So, let's have it. Give me all the reasons you would prefer to marry Lord Wagner over me."

She glared at him. "It has nothing to do with that, Your Highness, and you damn well know it."

"Do I?" he felt like he was losing his cool. No. He was *definitely* losing his cool. "I thought every girl in the world dreamed of marrying a prince someday."

Charlotte threw her hands in the air. "I am not *every girl*, Raffaello. I'm already a princess, and it has been the absolute worst part of my life for as long as I can remember. So, forgive me for not immediately jumping up and down with gratitude at your very *honorable* offer."

"What is the alternative?" he asked very seriously. He knew, he *knew* he needed to tell her the truth, that her father was coming to America, that the rug was being pulled out from under them and they needed to find a way to land on their feet. But it absolutely smarted his pride that she couldn't see the benefit of marrying him over her current option.

Pride, sure.

It was his pride, of course. All Raffaello wanted to do was help a friend, because Charlotte had become his friend in the strange few days they had shared, and she wasn't going to let him. So, despite himself, despite knowing it was the absolute worst, stupidest idea he could have, he didn't tell her, not yet.

Because you want Charlotte to pick you for you, not because she has to.

He pushed that idea down about as far as it would go. There were far more complex and significant issues to be dealt with in the current moment.

"I don't know," she said. "I don't know, Raffaello, because I've never been in a situation like this before. But please, *forgive me* for not wanting to be pushed into one marriage just to avoid another."

"It has *got* to be preferable than being married to a man three times your age with a notable history of *killing his wives*."

She got up in his face then, and it was a terrible and telling thing that he noticed her delicious scent and the sweet crinkle at the corners of her eyes, and the blazing fury in her gaze that made him want things Raffaello knew he had no business wanting.

"Yes," she said. "You are a better prospect than an aged lord with a propensity for murder. I hope that's enough to soothe your wounded ego."

"Good *God*, Charlotte. This is not about my ego." Raffaello realized he was shouting now, and realized, also, that there wasn't a damned thing he could do to stop.

Because it was about his ego. It was about so much more than that, too.

"This is about me trying to keep you safe, trying to save your life, which you don't seem to have any interest in saving."

"What life?" she asked, shaking her head. "We go back to Contanari as what, *man and wife,* and I am still just a princess in a castle with no life at all to call my own."

"It doesn't have to be like that," he bit back. "Plenty of marriages are built out of friendship and respect."

"And I want *more*," she said, matching his tone. "I know you can't even begin to understand this, Raffaello, but for the first time in maybe *ever* I finally feel like a real person, like I can be *myself* and make choices because I want to, not because I have to. And I don't want to go back."

"I understand that far better than you realize," he said, his voice growing low and quiet. Because he'd been hiding in the mountains of Montana, far away from his country and his people, and it was time he got back to his real life of responsibility and demand.

"Fine," she choked out. "Maybe you do understand, Your Highness."

"I do," he said. "And as your Prince, I am commanding you to stay in this room. Don't go anywhere or do anything until I get back."

"You're commanding me," she said, incredulity coloring her voice. "Just like my father has my whole life. Just like you would if we were to marry, isn't that right? One gilded cage for another."

"It wouldn't have to be like that."

"Right," Charlotte scoffed. "Well, I hate to break it to you, *Prince*, but you're just like them. Even after this time, you still won't even call me by the name I've chosen for myself because isn't proper. You'd rather be polite, upstanding and honorable than do what needs to be done. If I married you, I'd survive. But nothing else."

Chapter Twenty-Six

The room went very silent, and in the long seconds that stretched between them, Charlotte realized she had opened a Pandora's Box she had no idea how to close. Because the look in Prince Raffaello's eyes told her that he had no intention of letting her statement pass without challenge, and when she and Rafe went head-to-head, neither of them came out unscathed.

"What do you mean?" he said, his voice lethally quiet, straining at the edges with the raw masculinity that had pushed her over edges of her own again and again. "What do you mean doing what needs to be done?" He indicated to her. "Here I thought marrying you to save your life might be one of those things."

"It's fixing the symptom," she said quietly. Her words spilled free, the melting ice caps flooding the valley below, with no way to stem the tide or prevent the inevitable hurt. "But it's not the cause."

"Then what *is* the cause, Charlotte?" he asked. "Please, *enlighten* me."

She shook her head. Because as angry as she was with him, and she was goddamned furious, she didn't want to break his heart, didn't want to pour salt into what was no doubt a long-ignored and festering wound. "I think you know," she whispered. "I think you've known for a long time."

"No," he replied, but his eyes said something different, and there was such an intense vulnerability there, such an incredible fear, that the powerful, dominant prince look every part the young boy in that moment, a scared little kid who didn't want to hear what he already knew deep in his heart. "No, Charlotte."

She gave him a small, supportive nod. "Yes, Rafe. You're a good honorable man. And you will be a true leader; I have no doubt. But being a leader means doing the hard things."

"I am trying to do the hard things," he bit out, fury mixing with sadness in his beautiful eyes. God, the man was beautiful. He would make another woman very happy one day.

And if that thought dug a dagger into her gut, well, Charli had other things to worry about just at that moment.

"I'm trying to protect you."

"You could have protected me years ago," she said quietly. "Your father signed that amendment, Raffaello. He signed it, even though he shouldn't have. Even though, in his prime, he never *would* have. And I think you know why."

"He is still your king."

Charli nodded. "And he's still yours," she said. "So think of him as a king now, Raffaello, not as a father. And tell me, do you believe he is still fit to rule?"

"I can't," he said. "I can't usurp him. He is a great leader."

"He was," she agreed. "But I can't help but think that the reason you passed out in the House, the reason you're out here working every minute you're supposed to be resting, is because you need to clean up mistakes that wouldn't be mistakes and soothe over hurt feelings and restore diplomatic peace, because your father…can no longer serve his people."

"It's simple lapses," Raffaello muttered. "Nothing more."

"Simple lapses that will cost me my life," she said. "My future."

Raffaello took a deep breath, shaky, uncertain, the one thing that seem to unsettle the staid and reliable prince, and Charli had to wonder if she had gone too far. But was there a too far when it was a matter of life and death, when it was a matter of ruling a whole country, filled with people who deserved the very best? King Claudio was Rafe's father. But he was also the king.

"You have *no* idea what you're talking about," he muttered, like tearing flesh with his teeth. "That man is your *king* and you will speak no treason against him."

"You can lie to yourself," Charli said, her heart, which had been filled with kindness and sympathy, now coloring in anger, "but the country will know soon enough and then you'll have to be the one who denied the truth."

"There is no truth to deny," he practically shouted. "There is nothing going on for me to acknowledge or deal with, and certainly no reason to even consider a coup."

"I'm not talking about a coup," Charli responded loudly. "I'm talking about *mercy*. For him and for yourself. You deserve a chance, Rafe, I know that much."

"It's Prince Raffaello," he said, the pain on his face cutting through to her very bones, because she knew he was fighting for a cause he could only wish he believed in, an argument built on a house of cards, sitting at the edge of an oncoming storm. "And you know *nothing*."

Before Charli could respond, however, his phone rang.

Raffaello looked at Madison's name on his phone, a familiar name, but he saw it in a whole new light, Charlotte's words coloring his world, lifting a blind he had imposed for his own survival.

A blind that could no longer hold back the truth.

Because Madison had been trying to tell him for days. And Raffaello hadn't let him, hadn't wanted to hear the truth about his father's condition, about the circumstances of his mind, about the deep fear that permeated Rafe's dreams on the nights when he couldn't fight hard enough.

Because, of course, it wasn't exclusively the words his advisor hadn't been able to give to life. It had been months of minor slips, strange exchanges, indecipherable messages, like codes, each one a part of a much large puzzle.

Decisions, like signing an amendment on a marriage contract that should never have been signed.

Raffaello looked at the phone and then back at Charlotte, fear for his father competing with fear for her, with the threat looming over their heads. "Stay here…" The phone rang insistently again. "I swear to God, Charlotte… just stay here."

He, however, couldn't stay in the room a moment longer, and he stepped out into the hallway, pacing quickly when he finally picked up the phone, a nervous energy filling his fingers and making his chest tighten.

"You have news on Prince Johan?" Raffaello asked hopefully, as if he could will the information into reality with sheer force. Maybe Madison was calling about Charlotte's father. Surely, that was a possibility.

"No," Madison said quietly. "We're still trying to get ahold of the flight plan. That's not why I'm calling."

Raffaello stopped pacing and squared his shoulders. "Okay," he said, forcing the resolve into his voice he didn't feel. He had left the argument with Charlotte in the worst way, but despite all that, he wished she were there by his side, right then, holding him up while he faced his words fears head on. "Okay, what news is there?"

"Your father is in the hospital wing," Madison said. "He injured himself in the garden in the night."

Rafe's heart dropped into his stomach. "What? How?"

Madison's voice was calm and strong when he responded. "He's going to be okay. He has a mild concussion, and he bruised his wrist when he fell. But he's going to make a full recovery."

"That's good," Raffaello said, "right, that's good?" The need to ask for reassurance was unusual, and it felt almost childish, but he couldn't seem to stop himself. He needed to know his father was all right. Would be all right.

"That is the good news, yes," Madison said. "But please allow me to be blunt here, Raffaello. I know you don't want to hear it. You haven't wanted to hear it. But that doesn't make it any less true."

Rafe shook his head, even though Madison couldn't see. "He's fine. There's nothing to know."

"There is." Madison's voice was kind and uncharacteristically emotional. "I've been trying to tell you, and we can't deny it any longer. You can't deny it any longer."

"No," Rafe said. "No."

"Yes," Madison cut through. "He was wandering the garden last night in his robe. Raffaello, he was looking for your mother."

His mother, who had been gone these past twenty years.

"Why?" His voice nearly broke.

"He said—" Madison took a deep breath. "He said he wanted her to come back to bed, according to the guards who heard him. He tripped on the edge of the fountain in the dark. That's how he hurt himself."

Because Charlotte hadn't been acting out of vitriol or anger. She hadn't been pushing back out of spite. She had been voicing her concern, both as a constituent of his nation, and as his friend. And if she could see it in just a few days, then no doubt Raffaello had been ignoring the truth of it for longer than he wanted to admit.

"You said he'll be okay," he asked his advisor, because *fuck* if he didn't need a little bit of advice right about now. "Does he...does he know what happened?"

"He seems lucid for the time being," Madison replied. "And he's being monitored for any signs of physical injury, but..."

"I know," Raffaello said. "I know, it's time to decide next steps." About everything in his life, apparently. "And I apologize for ignoring you about this before. I... It's difficult."

"He's your father," Madison said, as if that was enough to answer all the questions racing through Rafe's mind. "I'll be here when you're ready."

"Thank you," Rafe replied, grateful as ever for the support of his advisor and confidant. "It should be sooner than later, the storm is starting to clear."

"I'll inform the pilots," Madison said. "Once you've decided what to do about the princess, we'll be on standby."

Rafe quickly said his goodbye and ended the call. Then he looked down the hall back toward the room he had been sharing with Charlotte these past days. Because he couldn't quite decide *what to do about the princess*. She had been the one to see him in the moments he didn't want to be seen, the one to challenge him, make him better, understand who *he* truly was, not Raffaello Chiaramonte, the Royal Prince of Le Isole del Contanari, but Rafe. Just Rafe.

And instinct told him again and again that the best way to protect her was to marry her.

In that moment, though, the raw wound of his father's needs and all that Rafe had been ignoring for so long making him feel vulnerable and lost, Rafe had to wonder if it was more than instinct.

If it was...*desire*.

What if the need to protect her went further than simply want to take care of a friend's sister and citizen of his country. What if it was because he...

Wanted more.

Rafe closed his eyes and took a deep, shuddering breath. Because it didn't actually matter if he wanted more. It didn't matter the reason behind why he wanted to marry her at all. The point was, she would always wish she'd had more choices in her life, and even if they came to a comfortable, neutral kind of marriage, the way so many royals had before, no doubt Charlotte would always ask herself what would have been different if she'd had a choice.

I could tell her how I feel… Give her the choice to pick me.

But he couldn't bring himself to put one foot in front of the other right at that moment. Because if he laid his cards on the table and she still said no…he actually had no idea what he would do.

The spears and daggers they had thrown at each other just moments ago were still blooming red wounds in his chest, and Rafe knew he needed a minute to collect his thoughts, just to figure out what exactly he was going to do next.

And he knew just the person to help.

Chapter Twenty-Seven

Charli paced around the suite like a caged tiger. Certainly, she felt half-feral, vulnerable and raw from the fight with Raffaello, and wishing for something she knew she couldn't have, shouldn't even be wishing for.

Because in all his talk of honor and duty and doing the right, hard thing, he had never said the simplest words that would have changed her mind without question.

I want to marry you.

She didn't want his obligation or his honor, and she certainly didn't want to trade her current tower for the next, not when she had only just gotten a taste of the great wide world. Of course, the kink and intimacy between them had been nothing short of spectacular and lifechanging, but it wouldn't be enough, not in the long-term, not when she had spent so much of her life feeling so alone.

It's more than you want to admit.

Perhaps, but it was so much easier to pretend that it was just sex, and not the innate trust and honesty and freedom of truly connecting with another person. If she acknowledged how much their shared moments meant, Charli worried she was going to race down the hall and beg him for a life and future together, and she just…couldn't. Not if she knew he didn't feel the same, not if she knew he would say yes, just to keep her from suffering a worse fate.

And she *was* going to suffer a worse fate. She could hold firm on the decision not to marry Raffaello all she wanted, but that wasn't going to protect her from what waited back at home. The storm was clearing. No doubt he needed to return soon, back to his position as leader, and he wasn't going to leave her there, Charli knew that for certain.

But the second she stepped back on home territory, her story was written for her, and there would be no escape.

She sat down and buried her face in a pillow, and then screamed as loud as she could. Charli was trapped and she knew it, no escapes, no alternatives, just one way out, and it was absolutely going to break her heart.

It was time to find Rafe, to tell him that after all that, she was accepting the offer of his hand, and she was grateful for it. Charli reached for one of the many notepads Rafe kept lying around, and tried to clarify her thoughts.

Thank you for your offer of marriage. I have decided to accept.

Thank you, Prince Raffaello.

To the honorable Prince Raffaello. Thank you for your offer of marriage in this difficult time. I have decided to accept.

It wasn't her. And it wasn't him either, not the stilted politeness, not the practiced words. She threw the pad across the room, and the pen went flying after it.

Charli sighed and went to go retrieve them when she caught sight of a dark spot against the white landscape.

It had been days of snow and wind, days where she could barely see the trees out of the window, let alone the mountains or the distant horizon. But in the soft sunshine cracking through the clouds, Charli most definitely saw *something*.

And whatever that something was, it seemed to be getting closer.

Her feet were rooted to the floor, panic overtaking her senses and making it difficult to form a clear, coherent thought. Who could possibly be coming up to the mountain just after the snow, and what could they possibly want? Surely, it wasn't a mail carrier or delivery person. Nothing would be so important as to arrive on...snowmobile.

And they weren't even in the main lodge, where a regular person might have reason to visit. No, their small contingent had been spending the storm in the club, which was very much known for its secrecy and discretion.

So, whoever happened to be headed in Charli's direction, approaching rapidly, was most certainly on a mission, and almost definitely going to cause trouble. Like they didn't have enough of that already.

Th thought occurred to her that perhaps it was her father on the back of the snowmobile, come to collect her and drag her home by whatever means necessary. But the thought fled almost as quickly, squashed by the reality that her father was unhealthy and unathletic, and most definitely uninterested in navigating snow-covered mountains.

The rider approached, and Charli tried to force out a scream. She tried to move her feet or reach for her phone, or do any of the normal things people did when faced with a dangerous situation, but she couldn't get her limbs to work, and the scream got caught in her throat, and she didn't even think her phone was charged anyway, because she had been living in a dream world, an escape from the reality of her life where people actually saw her and believed in her and wanted her to be happy.

And this stranger, who was approaching on foot now, scaling the edge of the veranda out of the window, he was the harsh, damning reminder that she couldn't actually do anything herself, that she'd never be able to make it without the fixtures and advantages of her royal birth, and it didn't matter if she wanted to marry Raffaello or Lord Wagner or whomever else came along, because one thing was for certain, she wasn't going to be okay alone.

The stranger reached the banister and began to climb over, and finally, finally, Charli began to tear her feet from the ground where they had begun to root, and learned how to talk again, and opened her mouth to call for help —

When the stranger took off his helmet and...

"*Anthony?*"

She ran to the door, pausing only as she reached for the lock to consider the surrealness of the situation. Why on earth would her brother be here, up in the mountains of Montana, just where she happened to be hiding from the threat of her father's terrible future for her? And was he here to help or make the situation so much worse?

"Let me in, Charlotte," he said, "I'm here to help you."

She weighed her options long and hard. Raffaello was certainty, a safe, stable future, albeit one without feelings, one without freedom. Her father was...barely even worth thinking about. Perhaps, in the eleventh hour, when all seemed doomed and time had run out, a third option appeared.

Too easily. Too perfectly.

But what choice did she have? She needed to see what Anthony had to say, needed to see if there was hope to be found in a tomorrow she got to choose. Charli squared her jaw, took a deep, fortifying breath, and opened the door.

"Hi, Charlotte," Anthony said, stomping thick clouds of snow off his boots onto the mat. He placed his helmet down on the floor and went to pull her in for a hug, but he was still covered in ice and snow, and she took a step back. "Right," he laughed. "Still not used to...all this snow."

He looked around the suite, and then back at Charlotte. "So, this is where you've been hiding out."

"It was snowing," she said. "We couldn't leave."

He nodded. "Of course, I know. And I hope Rafe's been...treating you well."

Now there was a complicated question. He had given her the most important, life-changing connection she had ever experienced, had introduced her to the possibilities the world had to offer, to new friends she would always cherish, and to hope for the future. And he had asked her to marry him out of obligation and honor.

"He's been nothing but generous," she said. "Let's get him, and you can tell us both why you're here."

Anthony put his cold hand on her arm. "Not just yet, Charlotte," he said. "I... I'm here to break you out."

"What?" she let out a small laugh of disbelief. "What does that mean?"

Anthony's face took on a somber expression. "Father knows you're here. He's planning on coming to the United States as soon as he can. I overheard him talking about it, which is why I'm here. I'm going to get you to a safe place until we can figure out what to do about your contract."

"So, you didn't know?" she asked, hope springing in her chest. "You didn't know father wanted to sell me off."

Anthony grimaced. "Of course not. I would never let that happen."

"But at your apartment," she said, "I tried to go to you for help and Father was already there."

"Not my doing," Anthony replied. "I assure you. Father's choices are not my own, and I'm going to do whatever I can to take care of you, I promise."

Charli didn't care about the snow and ice still clinging to his snowsuit. She threw her arms around her brother's neck and pulled him in for a tight hug. It felt so good, so impossibly good, to know that he hadn't abandoned her, to know he was still on her side.

"This is good news," she said. "Rafe... he said you didn't know anything, but I'm so glad to hear it from you. Let's go tell him together."

"I don't think that's the best idea," Anthony said slowly.

Charli's stomach dropped a little, her nerves taking back over, the hairs on her neck standing on end.

"It's just… The Prince knows Father is coming here," he said. "Has he said anything to you?"

She shook her head. "No. How could he possibly know that?"

"He had people watching Father at the palace," Anthony said. "They were good, but I know how prepared Raffaello can be, so I kept a look out. I have no doubt they were listening to his calls. They probably followed him when he left, as well."

"You think Raffaello knows this," she said, trying to wrap her head around it. "But why wouldn't he have told me?"

"I can't even begin to imagine," Anthony said. "But it makes me wonder…"

"Wonder what?" Charli asked. "Surely you don't think he and Father…"

Her brother shook his head. "No, of course not. But I do think Rafe is a politician. He'll do what has to be done to keep the peace."

She knew he would *never* allow her to be sold off to Lord Wagner.

But on the other hand, she also thought she had known he would tell her everything, especially the details about her father that most had to do with her life and her future.

Perhaps their friendship, their intimacy and connection, perhaps it had meant much more to Charli than to Raffaello. Perhaps he would have done what needed to be done, taken her back home, given her back to her father like she was a prize to be collected.

Then why did he offer to marry you?

The voice in the back of her head was persistent and confused, looking for logic in places where she could find none. It didn't make any sense, why he would keep such an update from her, unless he had something to hide.

"What's your plan?" she asked Anthony.

"I'm going to get you out of here first," he said. "Grab your things."

Charli's mind was a jumble of uncertainty as she ran into the bedroom. She didn't have any things, not with her small bag still in the hotel in Helena, and the clothes she had been wearing for the last few days stolen from Rafe or borrowed from her new friends. She grabbed the snow suit from the day she'd had a snowball fight with the other women, and tried not to think about what she was leaving behind, tried not to think about the escape the little club in Montana had become when she had needed it most.

But she didn't have time for the details or the second guessing, not when they needed to get out before Raffaello came back.

Still…she saw the notebook she had thrown on the floor and quickly scribbled on the bottom. He deserved more of an explanation, but she couldn't give him one.

I'm sorry. Don't come looking for me.

And then she followed Anthony out onto the veranda.

Chapter Twenty-Eight

Saint settled a mug of steaming tea down in front of Rafe. They sat at a small table in the kitchen, overlooking the melting snow on the mountain, and the sun felt so much like a metaphor for his own life, the light breaking through the clouds, that he couldn't actually look at it for too long.

"I'm kind of honored you want to talk to me, Raffaello," she said quietly. "I don't know too many princes."

He had first met Saint after Dante had ended up in the emergency room when his mob boss father had paid them a call, but with his life back home in Le Isole del Contanari, Raffaello hadn't had the opportunity to get to know her as well as he would have liked.

"You know more than one?" he asked, trying to add some levity to the moment he didn't quite feel.

"Fair point." She smiled at him. She did have a lovely smile, demure and gentle, nothing like the challenging, delicious bite Charli offered every time she bared her teeth and prepared to strike. "How can I help you?"

Raffaello was so used to the professional and diplomatic conversation of courts and Lords, and in that moment, he hated all of it. He wanted to be honest, frank and unapologetic, he didn't want to skirt around the issues like he had been doing for long enough.

Maybe I just want Charli here for all this.

Maybe. Okay, definitely, but it was too late now, and walking away from Saint felt a little like running away to Rafe.

"My father is losing his memory," he said quickly, ripping the bandage off. "It's...more advanced than I wanted to admit."

"Not typical memory loss from aging then?" Saint asked kindly. "Dementia."

Rafe swallowed hard. "Yes." Such a small word. With such incredible meaning. "He's slipped in the past, missed meetings, forgotten people's names, and I've covered for him the best I can."

Not well enough, considering his father had signed a document confirming the contractual marriage of one of his royals without her consent. It made Rafe wonder about what other amendments his father had confirmed, the other things that might have slipped through the cracks.

"I'm assuming all that...covering...has something to do with why you fainted last month?" Saint asked. "Stress and exhaustion."

"Passed out," Rafe murmured. "And...maybe. I haven't wanted to *acknowledge* the situation."

She placed her hand on his, and the feeling was comforting and friendly, but nothing more. It made him feel a whole new kind of ache deep in his chest for

Charli's familiar touch. "Saying it out loud makes it too real," Saint said. "So instead, you pretend things away, forgotten details, bursts of frustration, it's easy enough to ignore the little things."

"Not when you're the prince and your father is the king," Rafe said, unable to keep the self-flagellation from his voice. "I just... I feel like I'm betraying my father for my country. And my country for my father."

"Well, that is one marked difference between you and me," Saint said. "I didn't have a country to inherit. Do you think you might be feeling a little overwhelmed by that as well?"

"Of course," Rafe admitted. "And you didn't have a country to run, but Dante said you didn't have any help, either. You took care of your grandmother all by yourself."

"For the most part," Saint acknowledged. "Our neighbor helped when I worked, but yes. I did. Because I would have done anything for my grandmother."

She looked wistful, not quite sad, just lost in memories for a long moment. "The thing is, I *did* do everything for my grandmother. And when she was gone, I had no idea who I was. I had forgotten how to live in those years, how to be anything other than a caretaker."

"The list," Rafe said, and Saint's eyes danced a little.

"She told you about that?"

Rafe remembered how Charlotte had looked, tipsy and glassy-eyed, so free from the confines of her life and expectations, funny and silly and cute, drawing him in like a moth to a flame.

"She took six tequila shots," he said. "I'm surprised she didn't tell me every secret she's ever had."

"Ah, yes," Saint laughed. "That was on my list, but I was happy to share." She squeezed Rafe's hands. "I hope you know that you're not alone. Not in any of this. You have your family here, and in that girl down the hall. And however you feel about your father's condition, it's okay. Your feelings are going to change from day to day, and that's okay too."

Guilt gnawed at Rafe's gut. "I should have done something earlier. My advisor has been trying to talk to me about this for months."

"Maybe," Saint said, shrugging her shoulders. "Maybe not. Every person's experience with this kind of thing is different. The important thing is that you can't lose yourself along the way. You can't let the what-if and could-haves destroy you, Raffaello. You have to remember to live."

It was good advice, and clearly hard-won in a woman who was quickly impressing him with her strength, resilience, and fortitude. But that didn't make it easy.

"How?" he asked. "How do I...do that?"

She smiled, as if all-too familiar with the experience herself. "You start by being honest with yourself about the situation, which you're obviously doing. You find your people, your community, the ones who are going to keep you afloat even when it all feels very, very heavy."

Saint looked around the kitchen. "I don't imagine you'll have to go too far for them."

Rafe swallowed around the thick knot in his throat. Because he did have people, brothers he could count on when things got too hard, not because he was a prince, but because he was him, and that was enough.

"And"—Saint leaned down a little conspiratorially—"you may even want to consider opening yourself up to...love."

Rafe let out a small, incredulous laugh. "What?"

She shrugged, the picture of perfect innocence, even though he knew the truth. "I'm just saying."

"What exactly are you saying?" he asked, even though he most definitely already knew.

"I'm saying you don't want to marry Charli because it'll save her from a ridiculous contract."

"Of course I do," Rafe protested. "I said I'd do what it took to keep her safe, and I meant it."

"Right," Saint said slowly, as if she were speaking to a stubborn child, "you would do anything to keep her safe because you care about her."

"I do," he said.

Saint threw her hands up in the air. "For goodness's sake, Rafe."

"Fine." He swallowed hard and looked out at the world beyond, the mountains starting the glow with sunshine, the melting snow creating a twinkling effect that turned the whole scene starry and fantastical.

Just like Charli turned my life.

Because she did, of course. She had been challenging him and pushing him, making him a better version of himself, a stronger, smarter, more capable version of himself, since the moment they had met. She had made him want to rest and recover, made him want to be a better man for his people.

Made him want to be a better man for her.

Because I love her.

"You got it," Saint teased.

"I got it," Rafe agreed.

"Because you're in love with her…"

"Yes," he said. "That is the general idea, yes."

The realization of what he had done in denial of that fact slammed into him like a truck and he stood so quickly the teacups clattered against the tabletop.

"What's wrong?" Saint asked, picking up on his sudden change of mood.

"Her father is coming here..." he explained. "And I didn't tell her."

"Why not?"

"Because you're right... I wanted her to say yes to the marriage because she wanted me. Not because she was desperate and needed a way out."

"She deserves the truth, Rafe," Saint said. "All of it."

"I know." He reached for her hand and gave it quick kiss. "Thank you."

And then he raced down the hall.

Chapter Twenty-Nine

The door to his balcony was open when Raffaello got to the room, and before he even looked around, he knew something was wrong. Breeze was blowing in from the brutally cold outdoors, scattering papers around, but it wouldn't have mattered if he were right at the center of the hurricane, because he would have known.

Charlotte was gone.

He would have known that with his eyes closed and his ears covered, because he *knew* her, knew her scent and her feel, knew what her presence felt like in the space they had shared. More importantly, he knew what her presence felt like in his life.

And he was going to do whatever it took to make sure she was okay.

He called Van, panic overtaking his body at the possibilities of what might have happened, of where she might be. Prince Johan had arrived quickly, that much was for sure, and no doubt he was a man with the means and capability to take Charlotte far away without Raffaello ever finding her.

Finally, *finally* Van picked up. Rafe didn't bother with a greeting. "She's gone," he practically shouted. "Charlotte, she's gone."

"Okay," Van said calmly. "Get dressed for the cold and meet us in the lodge as soon as you can."

Rafe dressed on autopilot, and was just about to run out of the door when he caught sight of a notepad on the bed.

I'm sorry. Don't come looking for me.

Like *hell* he wasn't going to go looking for her. Raffaello needed to see with his own two eyes that she was okay. He needed to know that she wasn't walking back into some kind of trap, locking her into a loveless marriage for the rest of her life.

Quickly flipped through the rest of the pages, his eye snagging on what had clearly been a first attempt at accepting his offer of marriage. She had crossed out half a dozen opening lines, each one more stilted and diplomatic than the last, and Rafe understood, then, exactly why she hadn't been able to accept his offer.

Because it had been just another political contract. She had no idea how he felt about her, and he hadn't given her any reason to. She had been trading in one condition for another, one type of entrapment for another. The antiquated turns of phrase showed him just she had seen the offer, one of political strategy, not care, not even friendship. Obligation and responsibility.

Raffaello swore to himself that when he found her, he would explain all of it. He wasn't going to be a coward, not again. He had waited long enough to acknowledge everything going on with his father, wasted precious time and opportunities. But he wasn't going to make the same mistake, not with Charlotte. She needed to know exactly what she meant to him, and the next time he asked her to marry him, she was going to know that it had nothing to do with politics.

Van was the first to arrive in the lodge, stomping snow from his boots. He didn't both with pleasantries. "There are snow mobile tracks going up the hill," he said. "I tried to follow them, but whoever got here was smart. They cut the lines on the other machines, so we won't be able to follow them."

"We can go on foot," Dante said, as the others quickly joined them in the lodge. "They can't have gotten that far."

"It'll take too long," Van replied, shaking his head. "We'd be better off calling in rescue."

Raffaello's panic was rising again. If he were going to be king of a nation, he was going to have to do something about that, surely. But this was Charlotte, and he found he didn't actually care about keeping his cool, not when he knew she was in trouble.

"We can't wait." He considered his options, limited as they were, and finally snagged on an idea. "I can ride."

"It's dangerous," Caleb said. "You have no idea what the conditions are like."

"I know," Rafe replied. "But I've ridden these trails so many times over the years, I know them by memory, at least enough to keep the horse safe."

"And what about yourself?" Reece asked. "We care about that too."

Raffaello caught and held Reece's eye. "If you knew Morgan was in danger, would you stop at anything to bring her home?"

Reece gave a short shake of his head, and Raffaello looked around at the rest of them. "I know how much you all love each other. You would jump in front of bullets" — he eyed Morgan — "change your entire career and life" — looked at Gabriel — "go hand-to-hand with a gun-wielding mobster" — a sharp look at Dante — "just to keep each other safe. I have to do this. I have to bring Charli home."

Saint gave him an encouraging smile, and Dante slapped Rafe on the back. "Let's get you saddled up then, Cowboy."

* * * *

The horse, a strong stallion with a black-and-white coat named Maverick, didn't actually seem to mind the cold. Of course, the horses had also been locked up for the better part of a week in the storm, and it seemed to Rafe that the stallion needed some exercise, as his muscles quivered and he expressed his distaste with their slow pace.

"We'll run soon, I promise," Rafe said. "I just need to figure out where we're going." He was following the snowmobile's parallel track through the snow, which weaved between trees and snowbanks, until it finally opened up into the open plain that spread across the mountainside, a nearly flat meadow that stretched as far as the eye could see.

He leaned down and whispered against Maverick's warm coat, "You ready, boy?"

The horse whinnied, and then a second later, Raffaello set them off like a shot, never losing sight of the trail, his face burning from the blasting cold wind, panic and fear driving him forward. Charli couldn't have gone too far, he knew, not with the conditions what they were, but his imagination ran wild with the possibilities of what he might find, and each one seemed to fuel him faster toward his destination, whatever it might be.

Finally, finally, the meadow began to narrow to smaller patches of trees and rocks, and he slowed Maverick enough to navigate them carefully without losing too much time. They cleared a small ridge, which opened to the other side of the mountain, and all at once, Rafe knew where they were headed.

A large rental home jutted out of the side of the mountain, bold and proud in shades of black and brown, and leading up to the front door was a pair of twin snow mobile tracks.

"We made it," he said to Maverick. He pulled the two-way radio Van had given him out of his pack, along with a digital compass. "I have coordinates," he said, buzzing over the line. Van quickly took them down.

"You should wait until we get there," Van told him. "Don't go in by yourself, you have no idea what you're walking into."

Raffaello squared his shoulders. "I'm sorry, but this is something I have to do."

And then he put the radio back in the bag and tied Maverick to a tree a little way away from the compound. He took the mountainside slowly, aware that there was all manner of rocks and divots hiding under the piles of snow, but it didn't take long until Raffaello was walking up the front path to the compound and pounding his fist on the front door.

"Charlotte," he shouted, "Charli, are you inside?"

Finally, the door opened, and a man Raffaello had never seen before welcomed him inside. "They're waiting for you," he said.

They. Who on earth was *they?*

The only good news was that it confirmed his suspicions that he was in the right place. It did make him wonder all the more about Charli's note. She had said not to follow her, that she was sorry. Had she somehow figured out that her father was coming for her? Had she decided to along with the original contract? It didn't make any sense, but Raffaello couldn't help feeling like he was missing some part of the story.

So, he walked into the open living room with caution, aware that any number of things could be waiting for him, including Charli with a bullet in her back...

Instead, he found her sitting on the couch with a drink in her hand. Next to her father.

"Ah." Prince Johan rose. "Our Royal Prince has arrived. Sit, sit. Can we get you a tea to warm up from the chill?"

Raffaello looked around, look at Charli to see if she bore any signs of injury or harm, but she wouldn't meet his eyes, and somehow that felt like the most unsettling part.

"What is going on?" Raffaello ground out. "Tell me now, or I swear to God, I will have you stripped of your titles and exiled."

"On what grounds?" Prince Johan asked. "We're merely enjoying all the wonderful scenery America has to offer. Not at all like home, is it? American is so much less...civilized."

He gestured to the house, and the great outdoors beyond. "There's so much empty space. Like you're all alone in the world."

When he raised his brow, the several men who had been standing by the room's exits all raised their guns at once.

And pointed them directly at Raffaello.

Chapter Thirty

Charli tried not to scream. She had told Raffaello not to come looking for her, though at the time it had been because she had been angry about what he had said and how he had treated her. And then, once her circumstances had shifted, she had hoped that maybe he had decided she wasn't worth the effort.

Except, she should have known better.

Because it was Raffaello, the Prince. The most moral and honorable man she knew.

And she knew with just as much certainty that she loved him. She had known that as Anthony had driven them away from The Ranch and it had felt like her heart was being torn in two, known that when her father's goons had found them in the snow, given Anthony a black eye and dragged them to the winter cabin, and she knew it now, as her father's soldiers pinned their guns on Raffaello, each a hair trigger away from assassinating the prince.

"What is going on?" Rafe bit out. "I demand an explanation."

Her father shrugged and indicated to two of the guards, who grabbed Raffaello around the arms, or tried to. "Very well, it's only polite. I wanted power. Wagner wanted…a wife. He agreed to support my next proposal in Lords if I provided."

Raffaello shook his head, as if trying to wrap his mind around the reality of all that her father spoke.

"You miserable, weak old man." Perhaps it wasn't wise to berate a man who directed two dozen soldiers with their guns trained on his heart. But Raffaello had been political, diplomatic, and understanding his entire life. No doubt, the reality that a prince of his nation could be so cruel, so horrid, for such a paltry cause, made his stomach sour.

Charli's father grimaced. "Hardly a surprise that you should be just like my son. Entitled, lazy, foolish. *This* is how politics works, boy. You trade and you compromise until you get what you want. Well, Anthony also turned out to be rather disappointing in that regard."

He indicated to one of the guards, and a moment later, they dragged Anthony from the other room. He had a black eye and his nose was bent at an awful angle. Blood trickled from his lip and stained the collar of his shirt. They hadn't made it far up the hill when her father's soldiers had descended, and Anthony had clearly taken the brunt of her father's anger.

Charli gasped despite herself.

Her father just patted her on the hand, and she had to summon everything in her power not to recoil at the touch. "See, daughter, this is what happens when you defy my orders."

She looked down at her feet, unable to stare at her brother a moment longer. He hadn't lied to her, not once. He had been looking for her to bring her home, to take care of her. When he had discovered the conditions her father was planning to impose, he had risked his life to try to save her.

And it had gotten him a bloody nose and black eye.

"So, what's the plan?" Raffaello demanded, straining against the guards trying to keep him pinned. "You stage some elaborate coup against the crown and, what, tell everyone I died in the mountains so you can get away with your forced marriage plan?"

Charli's heart dropped and she dug her fingers into her thighs to try to keep a sound from escaping her lips. Adrenaline had driven her this far, but she had to keep her wits about her and do whatever it took to avoid irritating her father. He had underestimated her for her entire life, and for the first time ever, it was going to work in her favor.

"That was the original plan," her father said. "It wouldn't be difficult to convince people, what with the storm and all.

"Father," Charli said quietly. "What about your... other idea?"

She knew powerful men. All her life she had known powerful men. And when it came to people like her father, Charli knew that she had to convince them an idea was their own. They would never listen otherwise.

"Ah," her father said. "That is true. See, I had originally planned to kill you. You knew too much, and you were the one person with the capacity to stop me. But with my daughter's involvement, let's just say the whole matter is...much less messy."

"What?" Rafe looked at her, and Charli quickly looked away. It only worked if her father thought she was abandoning the prince. If he saw even a hint of sympathy or intimacy in her eyes, they were both as good as dead.

He clapped his hands together, his rings loud and cold in the open space. "I learned that you intend to *wed*. Now, I can't help but think this is a better opportunity for everyone. My Charlotte becomes the Queen Consort and once she has a son, well, there will be no need for the king, will there?"

Rafe shook his head. "So all that work for the original contract..."

"This is *better*," Charli's father said. "I get what I want and there's less chance of rebellion."

He pulled a pistol from his jacket pocket and leveled it right at Charli's head.

"Now —" Her father turned back to Raffaello. "Who wants to have a wedding?"

Chapter Thirty-One

Raffaello thought he might be sick, actually. The sight of the gun trained on Charlotte's head was enough to make him see red.

But there was no respite for where Rafe could look. Anthony was bruised and battered in one corner of the room, clearly no more responsible for their father's actions than Charlotte had been. They were, once again, running low on time and options.

"If I sign this," he said, "you'll let us live. All three of us?"

Prince Johan shrugged. "I will. At least until she has the heir."

"And then?" he asked. "And then what?"

"I suppose that depends on you," Johan said.

He pointed his gun at Charlotte, and Raffaello's heart dropped. It was as if Prince Johan didn't have to pull the trigger at all, not when Raffaello felt the panic and fear like a shot to his chest.

"I'll sign," Rafe said quickly. "Give me the contract, I'll sign. Just. Put the gun away."

Prince Johan smiled. "Wagner won't be happy about this. But I say it's worth it. Brings our family up in the world, doesn't it, dear daughter?"

Charlotte didn't even look at Rafe. "Yes, Father."

Johan indicated to the table with his gun. "Go. Marriage license is on the table."

Raffaello pushed off the guards and walked over to the table. And there it was, in black and white, the marriage license. His name was written right there on the top. Charlotte's was right beside it.

"You planned for this," he said. "You double-crossed Wagner."

Johan shrugged. "He's not nearly as useful to me as you are, Prince Raffaello. Our family would be in line for the throne. The highest office in the land."

"And for that you would use your own daughter like some kind of pawn," Rafe said, the words venom on his tongue. "She's not a prize for the highest bidder."

"Charlotte knows her place," Prince Johan said. "She always has."

Raffaello wanted to rage. He wanted to scream and shout, to charge the gun in Johan Marchand's hand. But it was still trained right on Charlotte's temple, and there was no way he would be able to rescue her in time.

"But to answer your question," Johan sounded delighted that Raffaello had worked it all out, "yes, I thought we could make the most of you being locked up here in the snow. After all, Prince Raffaello is known for being a just and honorable man."

Raffaello let out a low, deep breath and tried to find his calm, but it was impossible to think straight when

Charlotte sat there in danger. "I've signed your damned license. Now let her go."

Charlotte's father lifted the gun from her temple, and indicated that she go to Raffaello's side. Out of the corner of his eye, he could see her hands shaking and her eyes downcast.

"Release the boy," Johan said, "I want him to witness the license."

The guards unlocked Anthony's cuffs and pushed him over to the table. Up close, he looked even worse for wear, and Raffaello knew they were running out of time to get Anthony to a hospital.

"He can't even hold a pen right now," Rafe said. "Have one of your men do it."

Johan shook his head. "Anthony needs to know who's in charge here."

"Father please," Charlotte said. "We did as you asked. The family will have their heir, just let us go home."

"I'm afraid I can't do that," Johan turned his gun on Anthony and cocked it.

And then all hell broke loose.

Chapter Thirty-Two

The door to the mountain house slammed open, and a dozen men ran through, boots pounding, weapons cocked, shouting loud and quickly surrounding them. Her father's guards began to respond, training guns on the intruders and throwing fists with speed and accuracy. And for a moment, it was only sound, a cacophony of noise, men shouting, boots and bodies hitting the ground, guns going off.

It felt like an eternity, but only a few minutes passed in the absolute blaze of noise and sound, and before Charli even realized what had happened, her father's guards were putting down their guns, several armed agents pushing their hands behind their backs.

It was over.

Just like that.

The guards were rounded up and dragged to a corner of the room, and then a few familiar faces walked through the door.

"They told us we had to wait outside," Reece said. "It's not like I've never been shot at before."

"You are not law enforcement," a large, red-headed man said.

"You are a *firefighter*, Sawyer," Reece shot back. "Hardly FBI."

"Hey, his girlfriend's a federal agent," Caleb said.

Reece laughed. "Yeah, FEMA. Not exactly known for taking down international royal coups."

"Can I ask...what is happening?" Charli said. Because it was all going by very fast, and she wasn't entirely sure she hadn't been knocked unconscious in the melee. Her mind was still ringing with all the implications of signing a marriage license to Prince Raffaello, not to mention her father's admission of dangerous schemes, and this was...too much.

"*Dispiace, Principessa*," Dante said. "These are our friends, Sawyer and Cade, local emergency response. Micah and Dec, Search and Rescue. They're the cavalry, so to speak."

Which meant it was over. All of it, the whole nightmare.

She turned to look at her father and Charli's stomach dropped again. Because a single bullet wound bloomed on his chest, blood creating a burst of bright color against his white shirt. She ran over to his side, confusion clouding her senses, because who would have had the opportunity to hurt him? Who had been closest in all the chaos to take her father out while no one had been looking?

"Charlotte..." His voice was thready and weak as he reached out to her, and Charli tried to resist the urge to comfort him. He had done nothing but treat her like livestock, a prize to be traded and won, and he had caged her in for most of her life, forcing her down into a box that had never fit. But there was something in his voice that made her curious, and finally she forced herself to take the step closer to his side.

"I'm not going to absolve you on your deathbed," she said, and Charli found she meant it. There was so much she could never forgive him for, so much he had stolen from her in his quest for power.

"Don't believe him," her father murmured. "Don't believe him. He's…playing the game."

"Who?" she looked around the room, which was rapidly filling with agents leading guards out of the house. "Father, *who* is playing the game?"

Her father tried to speak, but as the words got stuck, the blood flowed free, spilling over his tongue and lips, before the light left his eyes and his head fell back.

Charlotte knew she should feel some level of response, some grief or sadness, but none came.

Her father was dead.

And that meant she was finally free.

Except…

She looked back at Raffaello, who still stood by the table, watching her. Under his fingertips was the simple sheet of paper that was guaranteed to change the course of her life, her father's parting gift, one last gilded cage.

Unless…

Unless there was any possibility that Raffaello's instinct to protect her went beyond the righteous and honorable. Unless it was somehow possible that he had come to rescue her out of a sense of not duty and honor but…*love.*

She walked over to him, finding that she needed to be by his side, needed to feel his strong presence, desperate for it to hold her up, as she felt her whole world crumbling apart. Freedom was terrifying when you were used to the walls.

"The emergency team is going to take care of your brother," he said quietly. "You should be able to return home with him in just a few days."

Which meant that Raffaello had no intention of being the one to return home with her. He had no intention of confessing his undying love for her, no matter what Charli thought they had felt for each other.

Raffaello had only ever proposed to her out of his sense of responsibility, just as she had feared. Even if the marriage had gone through, they would never have been happy together, not once he started to resent her for trapping him, not once she started to feel locked into the relationship.

He looked at her, and for a second, there was the man she had shared so much with, the man who had opened the entire world for her, showed her she could be so much more than she had ever believed, challenged her and seen her in a way one else ever had.

And then in the next second, that man was gone, and the prince stood before her, diplomatic, honorable, rigid. A good man. But not her Rafe.

"And you?" she asked, even though it felt like her heart was breaking into half, caving into itself like the snow on the mountainside. "What will you do next?"

Raffaello sighed, and it sounded as though he bore the entire weight of the world on his shoulders. "The call I took was…about my father. You were right, Charlotte. I've been ignoring what's been happening in front of me for too long."

It took everything in her not to reach for him, but she held firm. She wasn't going to let him see the heartbreak, and she certainly wasn't going to add to the weight bearing down on him.

"You were scared," she said quietly. "Anyone would be."

"Perhaps," he replied. "But, as a prince, I don't have the luxury of making decisions out of fear." He indicated to the room, blood and betrayal, a fight for power and control that took so many down in it its wake. "I'll be accepting the position of Prince Regent as soon as I can. I'll be the leader you believed I could be, Charlotte."

She gave him a sad, watery smile. "Charli."

Rafe didn't return it. Instead, he looked down at the paper between them. One single page. So much damage.

Raffaello picked it up. Then he handed it to her.

"What's this?" Charli asked.

"This is me giving you a chance," he said. "Take the license. Burn it, bury it, send it out to sea. You're free now, Charlotte. The choices you make are your own now."

"It's legal," she whispered. "It's a legal document. We can't."

"I'm tired of can't," he said, and he sounded beyond tired, world-weary and lost to his path. "I'm tired of shouldn't. I'll be the highest-ranking royal in the entire country, and if that doesn't come with benefits, well..."

"Very honorable," she said.

"I can have it officially dissolved in Lords, along with the original betrothal contract to Wagner, once I'm acting Regent," he said. "Or you could take it with you and do what feels right."

What would have felt right would have been going home with Raffaello.

But Charli was done begging for scraps. She had spent so much of her life on the periphery, at her father's whim and mercy, hoping that the door would one day open to her future, to all the possibilities she had hoped of and dreamed of for herself.

And it was right there before her then, the open door.

She just hadn't realized it would hurt so much to walk through the door alone.

Chapter Thirty-Three

The palace felt different with her father gone. There was a sense of ease and lightness when she walked into a room, like more of the winter sun shone in through the open windows, no longer afraid to clear the shadows of the late Prince Johan.

Or perhaps it was simply *her*.

Because she had returned home from Montana a different version of herself.

Rather, she returned home from Montana the *true* version of herself, no more soft candy coating, no more veneers or circumstance. The trip, the decision to run away and every decision that had followed, had broken apart the mask she had been wearing for long, and underneath, Charli could see her truth staring back at her in the mirror.

She was bold now, unapologetic, no longer driven by fear. The fear was still there, under the layers of red lipstick and the thick silver rings, but it no longer controlled her, no longer contained her in a cage made up of her own worst thoughts.

And despite herself, Charli knew she had Raffaello to thank for that. The first person who had ever truly seen her without the mask, even before it turned to dust in her hands, the man who had pushed her because he believed in her, who challenged her like no one else ever had, who offered her a lifeline when she had been so certain she was about to drown.

Of course, there had been the...the rest of it. The whole world he had opened up to her, a world of possibilities she could never have dreamed of, which were now never too far from her thoughts. Perhaps one day she would consider stepping her foot back into the deep sea, but Charli could hardly imagine what it would be like without him, could hardly imagine finding someone else to meet her every spar, defend against her every attack.

The other women from the club had stayed in touch, messaging and calling often to check in on her and to see how she was settling back into life in Le Isole del Contanari. But the conversation always steered wide and far around Raffaello.

Because he hadn't reached out. Not once in the time since she and Anthony had returned. The rational, diplomatic part of Charli knew he would be settling into his role as Prince Regent soon. The week's end would mark the ceremony for the temporary transfer of power, and then it would be official, and he would be her king.

But despite how hard he worked — and Charli knew better than anyone just how hard Raffaello worked — she also knew that if he had wanted to, he would have. He would have reached out, called, sent his advisor, messaged her late in the night when they were both still up.

And he hadn't.

The weight of the marriage license was heavy on her mind, and Charli had eventually locked in the bottom drawer of her writing desk, because every time she looked at it, her feelings switched between wanting to light the damned thing on fire and wanting to march Prince Raffaello down to the courthouse for a civil ceremony.

So, she'd given up trying to decide what to do, and instead thrown herself into the proposals they had started in the snowy mountains together. Her father had never been interested in Charli taking a political position, and had rejected her proposals and suggestions so many times over the years that she had eventually stopped asking, but her father was gone, and Anthony was determined to usher in the new age, as he was so fond of saying, and Charli had spent the last three weeks polishing her latest proposals—when she hadn't been thinking about the prince—with the hope her brother would finally take her words to heart.

Laptop and notebooks in hand, she made her way to his office just in time to see a familiar official walking out. She could hardly be surprised. It had always been Anthony's way of things, shaking hands and sharing drinks. He had been charming, outgoing and easy to be around since as long as Charli could remember, and much of his style of politicking seemed to center on who came for dinner.

But it worked, and he'd been training for his role as prince since the day he was born, so Charli knew she wasn't in any position to judge.

The man before her bowed. "Princess Charlotte, I'm so pleased to see you've returned home looking so well. We were all quite worried."

Charli tried to channel some of her brother's easy charm into a smile she didn't entirely feel. There had been too many nosy reporters and the like sniffing around since she'd come back, hoping for some kind of a scandal.

A scandal like spending a week in a kink club with the Prince Regent...

Like that kind of a scandal.

"Lord Burrow," she returned the greeting. "It is good to be home. Is my brother quite finished?"

Lord Burrow nodded. "I believe so." He indicated to the laptop in her arms. "Do you have photos from your trip to share with him?"

Charli blinked, the question catching her off-guard. "Ah, no. I have some proposals I need to discuss with him."

Burrow's face took on patronizing expression, as if she was a small child who had just solved a simple puzzle. "Well, isn't that wonderful? I'm certain he'll be proud of you."

Charli removed herself from the tedious conversation with as much grace as she could muster, but the man's words lingered as she walked into Anthony's enormous office. She was smart and she wanted what was best for her country, Charli knew that much. But it still felt, somehow, like she was playing dress-up in her fitted blazer and well-tailored leather pants. She had wanted to feel confident, but at the moment, she only felt like a fraud.

The princess for the tower, never the House of Lords.

"My dear sister," Anthony's voice welcomed her into the inner sanctum of his office suite. "To what do I owe the pleasure?"

Charli squared her shoulders and took a deep breath. She could see this through. Despite how things had ended, Raffaello had taught her that, to honor her boldness and to never be afraid to announce herself to the world.

"I've finalized my suggestions for the next year's economic strategy," she said, sitting down before Anthony and opening her laptop before he could stop her. "I know you go to vote tomorrow, and I'd like for you to consider my findings."

Anthony leaned back in his chair. His black eye was nearly healed, but there remained a hint of dark green around his cheekbone that made Charli's heart surge. No matter what, he was her brother, and he had come to rescue her when she had needed him most. "I'm so pleased to hear you're finding a way to pass the time," he said. "Why don't you send me a copy, and I'll peruse?"

Charli took a deep breath. "I'd really rather spend some time with this now," she said, pleased to hear that her voice was coming out strong and steady. "You did say you were interested in hearing my thoughts."

Anthony nodded. "Of course I am. But it's just a bit busy with father's...passing. I'm about to run out for the night anyway, and I want to make sure I give your proposal the time it deserves."

Charli's gut roiled, but there wasn't much for it. She couldn't force him to sit down to a meeting with her, and the more annoyed he was at her pushing, the less likely he would be to consider her perspectives.

"Of course," she said. "I'll send you a copy."

* * * *

As it turned out, preparing to run the country in truth was easier than pretending you weren't running the country. Raffaello's decision to step into the position of Prince Regent had been all but seamless, a collectively agreed upon choice that several tittered about being *long overdue*, and Raffaello found that the weight of pretending his father was still of sound mind had been a heavy one, indeed.

But in the three weeks since his return home from Duchess, the pace of life had picked up and the intensity had slowed down. There were still a million calls and messages all day and night, the life of a ruling royal, but he had been acting in his father's stead for so long, as well as quietly putting out fires and cleaning up messes, that it felt easier and far less emotional.

Or perhaps, he had simply become numb, a kind of hazy glass distance from everything going on in his life. Because he'd glimpsed behind the velvet curtain to possibilities he could never have expected, and walked away from them.

On purpose, he reminded himself often. He'd walked away on purpose to show Charli that she had choices in her life, to avoid being yet another person who made those choices for her.

But Raffaello couldn't deny that he wished he had been her choice.

Because there were no number of calls or diplomatic meetings or confused discussions about trade imports that could distract him from the growing, impossible pain that had taken root in his belly and seemed to grow stronger every day. He thought that time away from her would soften it, but it had done nothing but remind Rafe, in full living, breathing color, of the things he had had and given up.

With no mind for business in the early morning hours, he wandered down the hallway from his office and into his mother's garden. It had been many, many years since she'd been alive to tend the blooms, but his father had insisted on curating and maintaining it just as she would have done.

In that moment, the dawn still sleeping behind the mountains, the sea fog giving the garden a silvery, dewy glow, Raffaello understood his father better than he had in a long time. If he ever lost his sense of time or self, he, too, would be wandering around, calling Charli's name.

"Your Majesty," a familiar voice called from the garden, and Rafe walked past the large, blooming bougainvillea to settle beside his father on a stone bench that overlooked the sea.

"I believe you still maintain that title, Father," he said. "And I hope you intend to for a long time."

His father chuckled. "Don't put me out to sea just yet, son. But forgive an old man his impulses. I've known since the day you were born that you were destined for greatness."

"You raised me for greatness, Father," Rafe said honestly. "You made me the man I am."

King Claudio shook his head. "No, child. You did that. I taught you what I know, to be sure, but you rose to it, each and every time. That's what true leaders do."

Raffaello remembered the last fight he'd had with Charli, about rising up and doing the difficult thing, about being a leader when his country needed him. "I've been hearing a lot about true leaders, lately," he murmured, unable to keep the thoughts of her at bay.

It was like fighting the tide in a fishing boat, and Rafe knew he would end up in splinters when the waves crashed to shore.

"That's no surprise," his father replied. "You're about to become one." He turned to look at Rafe. "I understand you've been one for some time."

Rafe put his hand on his father's back. "It was a pleasure and an honor to help you serve the nation, Father."

Claudio wrapped his arm around Rafe, pulling him close. "You are a good man, my boy. Perhaps the greatness comes from me, born or raised to it. But the goodness, that was your mother. My Avelina."

He looked around the garden, and his gaze grew distant, seeing things that weren't there. "It matters who you surround yourself with, Raffaello. Who has your back on the difficult days, and I promise there will be a great many difficult days. When the day comes to pick your queen, pick the one you know will always challenge you and always make you better."

It had been many years since Raffaello had leaned his head on his father's shoulder, but he did it then, letting his father's heartbeat provide a strong, comforting rhythm to the turmoil in his heart and soul. Great men, as it turned out, were made in the difficult moments, when choices were narrow and undesirable, when sacrifices had to be made and options weighed for the sake of their souls.

But he reached not for greatness then, but the goodness his father had spoken of. Goodness could be found in the smallest moments, in the in-betweens, in the simple actions that would last for a long time to come.

And Raffaello knew exactly what he needed to do next.

Chapter Thirty-Four

Charli had the television on as she packed her bags. The time had come to leave the palace — and without a plan to return. Because Anthony had never looked at her suggestions. He had gone out for drinks or diplomatic dancing or some celebration or gala or festivity and let the project she had spent weeks perfecting linger in his inbox, never introducing it into the next day's sessions.

And it had made her realize that nothing much had changed at all with her father's death. She had more freedom, that was for certain, as Anthony spent most of his days off and gone, but he had been blowing off her ideas and suggestions nearly since they had returned and, if Charli were being honest with herself, for much, much longer than that.

She had her freedom.

But she still had no power.

And she was sick and damned tired of feeling powerless.

So she was leaving. She had messaged the program directors for her Servizio, and they had welcomed her back with open arms. They had completed work on the school she had helped to build, but there were always others in need, and they could have her placed in only a few days.

And with that response, Charli had pulled out her suitcase for the second time in a month and begun packing without much of a plan.

She was barely paying attention to the news broadcast, until a familiar voice snagged her attention. When Charli turned to the television, there he stood at the podium addressing the press.

His hair was slightly longer, curling at the nape, and he wore the same small glasses he had worn the night they had played at professor and honor student. Despite herself, Charli's stomach warmed.

And lower.

Because weeks had passed, longer than the amount of time they had spent together in the mountains, and still she couldn't shake off the immediate, aching need he inspired within her, still she couldn't ignore how the very sight of the prince turned her body to fire, ready to fight. Ready to fuck. Ready for whatever happened when they came together.

And came together.

Charli turned up the volume before she could stop herself, just in time to see the prince holding up a large document.

A familiar-looking document.

"Some articles are controversial," Raffaello was saying. "And some just make sense. This new bill has my full support, and I hope to bring it to life by early next year. The Continuation to Honor Academics: Right to

Learn Inclusive bill," he said. "Or as I prefer to call it, the Charli Bill, for the woman who both inspired and designed what I believe will be one of the most important pieces of legislation this country has seen for a long time."

He looked at the camera, but it was as if he was looking right at her in that moment. "Charli believes that everyone in the nation is deserving of the tools and resources needed for a strong, foundation education. And I agree. So, I plan to sponsor this bill at our next session, and I want Charli and the nation to know that as your prince, I will continue to fight what is right, what is just, and what is fair. Because I believe everyone deserves a chance to live the life of their choosing."

He was bombarded with questions after that, about his Prince Regent confirmation the following day, about where he had been after his spell in Lords, about the contents of the bill.

But Charli knew the contents of the bill.

Because she had crafted it.

And unlike her brother, who had found a dozen different ways to reject her and push her away, Raffaello had listened. He had heard her, respected her insight, and given her a chance.

He was the first person who had ever seen her.

And in that moment, she saw him, too. In the proposal of marriage, in the gesture of giving her back the license.

In the words he shared with the whole nation.

Because I believe everyone deserves a chance to live the life of their choosing.

He had let her go free because he cared. He had given her the license so she could make a choice, rather than making the choice for her, as everyone in her life had done before. He had shown her that the decision to move forward would be her own, not one born out of desperation or old traditions, but one of respect and equality and trust.

Because you didn't get on your knees and crawl for someone unless you trusted them. And time and again, Raffaello had earned her submission.

Charli slammed her suitcase shut and reached for her bottom desk drawer. But she paused before she could free the marriage license.

Because there was one thing she needed to do first. For both of them.

She practically ran to her brother's office, the office he had taken over from their father almost immediately after their return home, grateful to find that no one was around.

Without grace or calm, Charli tore through the drawers, looking for the last piece, the final thread she had to cut before she could tell Raffaello the truth – that she was choosing him.

She pulled drawers free, tried dozens of combinations on the lock box in the cabinet, and was just about to finally give up the ghost when she tugged on one final drawer in the desk and it stuck.

She climbed under the desk, only to find that there was something lodged between the wood and the rolling mechanism. Something in a plain envelope.

Charli's heart sped up at the possibility that it was what she had been looking for, and she grabbed for it with shaky fingers. Without bothering to climb out from under the desk, she tore past her father's official seal and unfolded the pages below.

And there it was. The amended copy of her betrothal contract to Lord Wagner, signed and dated the year prior with the ailing king's approval.

Charli's heart studded to a stop, and all at once, it felt impossible to breathe, golden stars circling around her head, sounds, lights, bright and loud and making it difficult to concentrate, because surely, surely she wasn't seeing what she thought she was seeing on the document that had very nearly ruined her life.

But then she blinked her eyes again to push away the tears — when had she started crying? — and there it was in black and white on the final line of the marriage contract he had sworn he knew nothing about.

Witnessed by Anthony Marchand, Prince of Fontaine.

Her brother.

Chapter Thirty-Five

For a moment, Charli simply sat under the desk in her brother's new office, her heart pounding her chest as loud as rocks falling from the mountain into the sea and nearly as uneven, *pound, beat, pound, pound, pound, beat.*

She had come looking for the contract to tear it up, a clear, fresh start when she finally told Raffaello the truth of how she felt about him. Nothing standing in their way, and especially not a single damned contract.

It had been a symbolic gesture, in Charli's own mind, a way of clearing the path for a future of support and happiness…and love.

But instead of relief and peace of mind, instead of the great catharsis she had been aching for and needing the best way, Charli had only fallen further down the rabbit hole, finding evidence of betrayal that went so much deeper than she could have ever expected.

Anthony.

But he saved me. He found me in the mountains, and he saved me.

He had. But then again, how had he been able to find her? And why was he so against her ideas and recommendations, and…and what had her father meant when in his dying breath he had said, *don't trust him, he's only playing the game?*

She had never thought she would trust her father's word over Anthony's after all they had been through, but she had never thought he would be such a practiced liar, telling both her and Rafe again and again that he had no idea about the contract, the same contract which had his signature on it.

She couldn't quite figure out what it meant. Charli read the name on the page, familiar and somehow all at once foreign and indecipherable. Because there truly was only one explanation, and it crashed a fiery hole into everything she had believed and known for so long. Because if Anthony had known about the betrothal, not just the first one, but the new one that linked her to the violent Lord Wagner, then that meant he had been lying from the start.

To what end?

Charli shook her head, trying to clear some of the racing thoughts. She could talk to Anthony. Surely, surely, he would have some kind of explanation, some good reason for why his name was on a document he swore he had never seen or heard of before.

She just had to ask him.

She went to climb out from under the desk, when she heard the door to his office open, and then Anthony walked in, speaking to someone.

When there was no response to his words, Charli realized he was speaking on the phone, and she sent up a silent hope that he wouldn't choose to sit at his formal desk, the one she was currently hiding under.

She hadn't *meant* to hide under it. But she found that her plan and reasoning were flying out the door when she heard her brother's voice. Something in his tone, in the dripping charm that was there and then gone, it made her nervous, as if the revelations in the envelope shaded him in an entirely new light, and not even something as simple and innocuous as a phone call could be entirely innocent.

Except, as she listened to the words he spoke and the tone he used, Charli had to wondered if the call truly was as innocent as she believed. Perhaps she simply needed him to be guilty of something, to better understand all that had come to light in the last moment, but he spoke with an intensity she had rarely ever heard from him before, and despite her shaking fingers and pounding heart, she finally focused on the words he was saying.

"They were married," he said. "I'll find the license eventually. Besides, it's too late now."

Too late for what?

"I am telling you, this is our only option. Once he becomes Prince Regent, it's all over. He's already suspicious about the trade route numbers I sent to him." Anthony paused. "Yes, I am *aware* the ceremony is tomorrow. That's why I'm telling you this." He muttered something Charli couldn't hear, and then his voice grew louder and more irritated. "My father was a fool. He couldn't see past his nose, but I have vision. And it does not include Raffaello Chiaramonte sitting on the throne, even temporarily."

He went quiet again, and Charli could almost picture him pinching the bridge of his nose, as if this was some kind of trade dispute, and not a discussion of treason.

"Yes," Anthony said finally. "That's exactly what I'm saying."

The pause seemed to last years, weighty and heavy, thick with betrayal and the fear that flooded Charli's own body, fear that made her limbs too heavy to move and her chest too tight to breathe.

Because in the next moment, Anthony said the words that confirmed everything Charli had feared, that he was no longer her loving brother, that he never had been. That she didn't even know him at all.

"At tomorrow's confirmation, we need to kill the prince."

Chapter Thirty-Six

Charli didn't know how long she had been hiding under the desk by the time Anthony finally left the office. It might have been minutes, it might have been years. But no amount of time would have been enough to change what she had heard or all that it had meant.

Her brother was a traitor.

And, more importantly, Raffaello was in danger. The man she loved, whom she had never gotten to tell, whom she had left because he hadn't said the words when he had been saying them over and over again, was going to be killed.

And she was the only one who could stop it.

Which required her legs and arms to work, first.

Charli pushed out of the cramped space under the desk, the intense pounding in her heart subsiding just a little when she saw that the office was empty. Only a little, though.

Because her phone and laptop were back in her bedroom, and somehow the idea of traversing the palace, now knowing all that she did about her brother, felt like crossing a minefield.

Not that she had any choice.

She peered down the hall and quickly slipped out of the office, trying to keep her pace as steady and calm as she could, but it was difficult when her head was swimming and her survival instincts were kicking in to get out of the house, to get as far out of the house as she could.

She took the long way back to her rooms, because it felt like the house was busier than usual, filled with strong, silent looking men that seemed to be standing near every door. And with the weight in her feet and her heart, it took what could have been years to make her way back to her room.

And then Charli was yanking open the door to her bedroom, nearly overcome with relief at being back in her own safe space, when she froze.

Because Anthony sat there on her bed, flipping through a magazine as if he didn't have a care in the world. Maybe his expression was different, or maybe she just finally saw through the façade he had been putting on for so long, because when she looked at him, she saw a predator, a deep unyielding in his eyes, as if he would stop at nothing to achieve his goals—including taking her down.

Just as he was willing to take down the prince.

"Sister," he said, with such a saccharine-sweet tone that Charli almost gagged. "I haven't seen you all day, and here I come in to find your bags packed."

Charli moved around the room, giving Anthony as wide a berth as she would have given a wild animal. "I was going back on Servizio," she explained. "To build more schools."

Anthony smiled with all his teeth. "Well, that is noble of you. Always thinking of others, aren't you, Charlotte?"

She squared her jaw, rage filling her, all the revelations and intensity of the day bubbling to the surface. "It's *Charli*."

Anthony stood. He was so much taller than her, and now that she knew exactly what he was capable of, he seemed bigger still. "No. It's Charlotte, a name befitting a princess of Fontaine. And if you know what's good for you, you will act in a way befitting the country."

She shook her head. "I don't know what you're talking about."

Anthony took a step forward. Charli took a step back, hating how she still felt so small in her own room in her own home, how her father dying had done nothing but change the face on the monster in the closet.

"I think you do, Charlotte," he said. "You didn't do a very good job of cleaning up after yourself in my office. I needed to find something, so I went back… after you left, of course."

She winced. She had been so determined to find the contract and go to Raffaello that she hadn't put everything back the way she had found it.

"I was only looking for the original contract," she said. Panic made her brain slow, and it took a second for Charli to remember that it was just as damning as the phone call. "I didn't find it. I just… I just looked."

"I think we're done with you looking for now, Charlotte," he said, holding up the white envelope she had torn into under the desk. She must have tossed it to the floor by the chair, rather than into the trash, when she had been distracted with the contents — with her brother's signature.

"Fine," Charli managed. "Yes, I found it. And I have questions."

Anthony got into her face, fury in his eyes like she had never seen before. No, she had seen it before, in her father's eyes, every time she had pushed for something more. "You don't get to have questions, Charlotte. That's not your role in this family."

Charli reared back, as if struck. "My *role*. Anthony, I am a princess of Fontaine and I am deserving of respect."

Anthony moved so quickly Charli didn't have time to brace before his hand was colliding with her face in a horrifying, ringing slap. It made the room shake around her. It made the very foundation shake under her. "*Deserving*." His voice was cold and harsh. "You deserve nothing, Charlotte."

She resisted the urge to spit at him, but only barely. She needed him to leave so she could find her phone, could call Rafe, could do *something*. The intense, sharp pain in her skin was fading to a dull, pulsing throb, and it was making it difficult for Charli to think.

"Why, Anthony?" she asked finally. "Why sign? Why *any* of it?"

He shook his head. "You wouldn't understand."

"But we had plans," Charli's voice broke on the last. "We were going to help the country."

When Anthony laughed, it was brutal and ice cold, and she realized she had never truly known her brother at all, not the man beneath the mask, the charm, the society veneer. She had never had an ally in him, let alone a friend.

"This *is* me helping the country, *sister,*" he bit out. "And I can't have you getting in my way."

"I won't," Charli tried. "I'll leave. I'll go build schools and I won't come back."

"And then I'll be left with the question of a missing princess," Anthony replied, as if she was stupid for even suggesting such a thing. "No, I need you close by."

He walked over to her drawer and pulled out her phone. Then he tossed it to the ground and stomped hard on the screen with his heel. Finally, he grabbed her laptop from the desk and tucked it under his arm. "I have some business to attend to. I'll figure out what to do with you when I return."

And with that, he walked out, slamming and locking the door behind him.

In the sudden and unsettling silence, Charli took a deep breath, but it quickly turned into a shuddering sob. It was clear that Anthony didn't know she had overheard his call, which was a good thing. But he had taken her phone and computer and locked her in, leaving her with no way to communicate with the outside world.

No way to tell Raffaello what was coming.

She was, in every sense of the story, the princess locked in the tower.

And no one was coming to rescue her.

* * * *

It took Charli the better part of an hour to recycle her panic and despair into determination and fearlessness.

No one was coming to rescue her.

No one was coming to rescue her.

Which meant the time had come to rescue herself.

She had done it before, the night she had packed a bag and run for her brother's apartments, then caught the first flight out when she had seen her father. She had done it before, fleeing to the United States to escape yet again.

And this time, nothing was going to stop her. Because Charli knew she wasn't alone. She knew that Raffaello cared for her, knew that from every gesture, from every offer of marriage, from the gift of her contract back.

He was in her blood and bones, the confidence he had in her, the respect he gave her with every sparring match, the gift he had introduced her to in the club, in the world and lifestyle. She wasn't running scared anymore, away from the monsters that threatened and loomed.

She wasn't running away at all.

For the first time in her life, she was running *toward*. She was running toward Raffaello, to save him, to tell him the truth about Anthony and more importantly, about how she felt for him, how she had been feeling for him for far longer than was wise, how she had only rejected his offer of marriage because he had made it out of obligation and honor.

How she wanted to spend the rest of their lives in intense, heated battles of wills and pleasures.

But first, she was going to have to save his life.

Charli glanced out of the peephole to see two enormous bodyguards standing watch in her hallway. Which meant the front door was out.

But she did have a terrace. And bedsheets.

One afternoon, Morgan had taught her how to tie climbing knots, which she had explained were very different from Shibari knots. It had made the girls all laugh at the time, but Charli reached for the memory now, and for the feeling of excitement and freedom she had enjoyed in those stolen moments with her new friends.

She pulled sheets free and tied them the way Morgan had taught, albeit without the grace or elegance, but they would be capable of holding her weight as she climbed down from the terrace and into the garden below.

Charli hoped.

She stepped out onto the balcony, which overlooked the enormous garden to the back of the palace property. It would be difficult to make her way down to the water, but not impossible. First, she just had to get out of a third-story window without being seen. With that thought in mind, she tied the sheets even more securely around the headboard, finding only the smallest amount of irony in the act. The last time she had been tied to the headboard, Raffaello had been pushing her to the edge of pleasure and desire and holding her there, a far more preferable memory to attempting a haphazard escape.

But the knots held, and she climbed the terrace ledge, testing her weight against the straining sheets. Voices carried up from the garden and she made herself small, pressing against the cold stone of the palace wall until the voices passed, and then she put one foot in front of the other, one foot in front of the other, slowly and unsteadily making her way down the side of the palace wall until her feet brushed the top of the shrubbery and she was finally able to jump the last meter.

She was down from the tower, but not out of the woods. Because the problem now would be getting to the mainland, and the ports and docks were busy this time of day. Someone was sure to recognize her if she tried to board a commercial ship, and no doubt her brother would shoot the jet out of the sky if he knew she was trying to make it to Raffaello.

Panic beginning to take over, Charli finally remembered a small cove where she and Anthony had swum in the summers when they had been growing up. It hurt to think of, the way their lives had been, how different from the truth her memories really were, but Charli knew she didn't have time for the pain and grief of never really knowing her brother, not then, when everything was on the line.

Instead, she focused, looked all around the garden, and broke into a run, cutting through the maze and flower gardens. The cove was a' short walk down crumbling stone stairs and, heart pounding, breathing coming in tight, short bursts as she rounded the corner.

No one was there.

Charli let out a long, exasperated breath. She had been hoping for a boat of any kind, a canoe would have done the trick. It was a day's paddle from Fontaine to Cielo, but if she kept up her pace and remembered her goal, she could make it. She would have to make it.

But it was a moot point and that meant she was going to have to come up with another idea, turning around, losing precious time, and the tears threatened, her eyes going hot and her vision cloudy.

It was that cloudiness in her vision and her thoughts, that had Charli thinking she imaged the sound of an approaching motor. Right until she saw a small fishing boat approach, the two men aboard looking at her as if she were completely insane.

No doubt she looked it, after her climb down the terrace and near fall into the garden. But it didn't matter. All that mattered in that moment was getting to Raffaello.

"I'm the Princess of Fontaine," she managed to call out. "And I'm going to have to commandeer this vessel."

Chapter Thirty-Seven

Raffaello sat in his office with Madison before the ceremony. It was a strange thing, to be rising to the position of Prince Regent. His father was still alive, still lucid and understanding most days, but the decision was inarguably the right one. They needed to know that every decision the nation made was sound, and they could no longer rely on the action of King Claudio to offer such reassurances.

But, despite knowing the rationality and logic behind the choice, Raffaello still felt the weight of it on his heart. He had been denying the truth about his father for a long time, and everything that implied with it, the responsibility that Raffaello would have to rise to in ruling his nation, the ailing of the man who had raised and loved him, the possibility that such declines ran in the family, putting him at risk. And now that he had opened himself to the possibility of them all, they were strong presences in the back of his mind.

Not the only presence, of course. A day had passed since his press briefing, his opportunity to show Charli off to the country and the world. He had expected — naively hoped, perhaps — that she would call him, that she would arrive on his doorstep and…

Well, the *and* didn't matter. Because he hadn't heard from her since the briefing, and he needed to be all the way focused on the upcoming ceremony, not pining for a woman who was clearly aching for freedom he couldn't give her.

"You're distracted," Madison said.

Rafe snorted a laugh. "And that's why you have the reputation you do."

Madison gave Rafe the approximation of the smile he gave, because he didn't exactly *smile*. "No, I have the reputation I do because I know *why* you're distracted."

Despite himself, Raffaello rubbed his hands over his face, only just resisting the urge to scream into them. They didn't need the news circulating about two mad men of the throne. "She needs to live her own life. I'm not going to take that away from her."

"And what about you, Raffaello?" Madison asked. "What do you deserve?"

Rafe didn't know the answer to that question. He was an hour away from being sworn in as the most powerful man in the nation. Surely, he didn't deserve any more than that.

But he knew what he wanted. He knew he wanted Charli in his space again, tied to the bed, pressed against the desk, curled into his arms as they woke together in the soft light of the snowstorm. He knew he wanted her challenging words and the way she forced him to be better, the way they seemed so much better together, pushing to grow and learn and build. The bill had been proof of that, of the good they could accomplish when they put their heads together.

"Your Highness" — a man stepped into the room — "it's time."

Raffaello stood, doing his damnedest to push away all thoughts of Charli from his mind. It was a fool's errand, however. Because, as he stepped out into the ceremonial hall, all he could think about were his father's words, about finding the right person to serve by your side, about how he knew that right person was Charli.

But he was a prince, and duty had been instilled in him from the very day he was born, so he climbed the dais and followed the directions of the deacon, moving his gaze between his father's kind and supportive one and the faces in the crowd, his representatives, his royals, his people.

It was on this tracking, perhaps a habit he had picked up from Madison over the years, perhaps simply instinct to connect with as many of his constituents as possible, that had Raffaello glancing at the rafters of the long hall, only for a second, only for the time it took to catch sight of a man in all black, black gloves, black shirt, black mask…

Black sniper rifle.

Everything slowed, time, movement, the sound of the words from the deacon's mouth, and Raffaello had to push against gravity, against force, against the weight of his own body to jump out of his throne seat and over his father's body, crashing them both to the ground in the same second a single gunshot rang out in the long and open space.

Silence, the delay of shock, and then complete pandemonium, people racing and rushing all around the hall, his security jumping into action, Madison guiding Raffaello to his offices as another service member took his father away, separating the Royal Family for safety as they raced to find the threat.

Madison practically had to pull Rafe from the melee, his instinct to stay, to fight, to help, but finally Madison got him from the room and shoved him into the office…

Where someone was already waiting.

Chapter Thirty-Eight

The palace was in a state of absolute madness by the time Charli ran the steps from the docks to the front gate. The fishermen who had found her, Emilio and Gianni, had thankfully believed her story, and they had raced the current, breaking every law and record to get Charli to the capital in time for the ceremony.

In time to stop an assassination.

Neither of them had cell phones, claiming that the technology interrupted the calm of the workday, but it would hardly have mattered if they had. The service was spotty on the water and Charli had worried about getting through to the right people, about who they could trust in Rafe's inner circle.

Which meant she'd run all the way from the docks, up the ancient stone steps Cielo was known from, around the enormous perimeter of the gate to the entrance for diplomats and representatives. The gates had been locked and closed off, but she'd become an expert at getting into and out of gardens in the last day, and Charli practically threw herself over the hedge, landing unceremoniously in a rose bush, the thorns stinging her skin.

But she barely noticed, yanking open the veranda doors and racing into the palace, only to find complete chaos beyond…

As if…

No. She couldn't be too late. She refused to believe she was too late. Raffaello was a smart, capable man — and he was still alive, damn it. Something in her gut, in the heart and soul he had claimed sometime between the first spanking and the dark promises that told her he was okay, that there was still time to reach him.

She ran against the tide, regretting her heavy leather boots for the first time as they dragged her and slowed her down, but finally she found the royal wing, pushing against the crowds to sneak down the hall, trying to keep her wits about her as the sounds and sights overwhelmed her already exhausted system.

And then, finally, finally, she caught sight of Madison standing outside a closed door, and she willed her legs faster, pushing herself harder than she had ever pushed before, her lungs practically screaming for air by the time she pulled up before him.

"Please tell me he's inside," she panted, the words like fire in her chest. "Please tell me he's okay."

Madison nodded. "He's inside, Princess. And he's okay."

He stepped back from the door to let Charli inside, and it only took a second for her to realize that while Rafe might have been inside the room, he was most certainly *not* okay.

"Close the door." The voice was that of a ghost, familiar and yet so distant, so far away from the man she knew, the man she had loved her whole life.

Anthony stood in the center of the room, a gun trained at Raffaello's head.

Charli didn't move. She didn't breathe.

"I said" — Anthony gestured with the gun — "*close the door*."

Charli slowly reached behind herself, shutting the door to any help from Madison or anyone else. It was just the three of them in the room now, and Anthony was the one with the gun.

"What are you doing?" she asked, trying to keep her voice level and calm. In a different life on a different day, she would have claimed to know his tells and his signs, but as it turned out, she didn't know any damn thing about her brother at all. "You can't kill him."

"Can't or won't?" Anthony asked. "Father was very much in the *won't* category. But then again, he never had the vision I do."

"And what vision is that?" Raffaello asked. Only then did Charli realize how scuffed the normally pristine and tailored prince looked. His tie was askew, hair mussed and messy, his jacket tossed to the floor and several buttons of his shirt open, revealing the familiar skin below.

Despite the very intense moment, Charli ached for him, like a planet yearning for the sun. It had been too many weeks without the touch she had grown so accustomed to, too many lonely, sleepless nights, where she'd needed nothing more than his touch.

"You know, I'm glad you asked," Anthony replied. "It's very clever, truth be told."

Charli's pulse raced, but it was out of not fear but anger, fury, red hot and racing through her veins like lava spilling down the mountainside, growing faster with every inch it stole. "There's nothing clever about you. You're a bully and a fool."

Anthony turned the gun on her. "And you are in my way, *sister*." He looked back at Rafe. "See, my father was going to use Charlotte for personal gain. Strengthen the connections among the families, you know. But that's just so short-sighted. I thought Fontaine could do so much better."

And then it fell into place, every decision Anthony made, all the connections he forged over dinners and galas, the way his numbers had never matched up with the ones she had calculated herself, how he always seemed to have his eye on the horizon. "You wanted to be king."

Anthony turned to her, a look of surprise on his face. "Very good, Charlotte. Perhaps you're smarter than I've been giving you credit for. Yes. I want to be king. I *deserve* to be king."

"And why is that?" Rafe asked. "Prince isn't enough for you?"

Anthony tapped the gun against his lip, as if deep in thought. "It might have been, if your father had stayed in command. Much, much easier to get things past a man who is slowly going mad... But then it became clear that you were going to take over, and I knew you'd figure out the truth sooner rather than later."

Charli gasped. "The numbers weren't a mistake. You've been creating unauthorized trade routes."

Anthony nodded. "Among other things. But the trades were my favorite. Much more money. Anyway..."

He paced, waving the gun around wildly, and Charli had the brief thought that maybe none of them were going to get out of the room alive. "Anyway, Father thought the idea to force a marriage between you two was his brilliant plan. Like I had nothing to do with you playing her white knight…

"You wanted me to chase after Charlotte," Rafe said quietly. "You wanted us to get married."

"It was a much better idea than some simple contract between the houses," Anthony agreed. "There's no heir to Chiaramonte name. If something were to happen to the Prince Regent and his Royal wife…as the brother-in-law, I would be the nearest thing to it. Father never considered the possibilities."

"You killed him." That wasn't a question at all. The pieces were in place now, and Charli knew, the foundation crumbling under her feet, that her brother was in every way capable of cold-blooded murder."

He grinned. "He didn't leave me much of a choice. Those bruises weren't faked. I think he started to realize that our goals were…no longer aligned."

"So what?" Raffaello asked. "You shove your sister toward me and hope we get married. And then you kill me."

"So close," Anthony replied. "And then I kill you *both*. I was thinking boating accident. Just like Mother."

And that was the last shattered piece of Charli's heart cracking apart. Because Anthony had never cared, likely *couldn't* care. Because he spoke of her as if she were a problem to be dealt with, so much trash to be disposed of. And because he mentioned their mother's death in passing with such simply cruelty, it felt as though he were confessing…

"Oh, you didn't know…" Anthony laughed, a cool, cruel laugh. "Mother was starting to ask…too many questions. So Father took care of it."

"Like father like son," Rafe spit out. "You would never be the prince this country deserves, let alone its king."

"Deserves, deserves, deserves," Anthony sing-songed. "It's never been about the people, *prince*. It's always been about the power. You should know that better than anyone."

"Shut up." Charli stepped forward, even as Rafe protested. Anthony opened his mouth, but Charli got even closer. She was so damned tired of being afraid, of being hurt by the people who were supposed to love her the most. Anthony and her father had taught her the wrong way to be leaders, the wrong way to care for their position and country.

It was Raffaello and his father who were the true leaders, who did what was hard, who stood up for what was right, and Raffaello was the only man who had ever seen her for *her*, who had appreciated and respected her, who made her feel like she mattered. She would pick his brand of leadership each and every time.

"You forget, *brother*," Charli said. "You may be your father's son. But I am his daughter."

And she lunged for the gun.

Chapter Thirty-Nine

"Good morning, Princess," Rafe murmured, as Charli's eyes began to flutter open. "How are you feeling?"

"Sore," she managed, her voice hoarse and dry. "Oh, *ow*. Was I hit by a truck?"

"A bullet," Raffaello replied. "In the shoulder."

"Nice," she whispered. "Morgan and I will match now."

He tried to keep his cool, but the dominant, claiming side in Rafe's blood had been sitting in the private hospital wing for two days, needing nothing more than to shake Charli awake, to make sure she was okay, to hold her tight and never let her go again.

"Not nice," he practically growled. "You could have been *killed*, Charli. You could have died."

"Protecting my prince," she whispered. "I think they give out medals for that."

"No." His tone was panicked, none of the control he so prided himself on, just pure fear about all the things that could have gone wrong, all that could have been taken from him. "I can't, Charli, I can't think about it. I can't picture it. I would be the worst prince this country has ever seen because I would be lost to the grief of you."

She reached out her hand, grabbing him, and it was like a balm to his heated soul, the connection all he had been needing and craving for what felt like a lifetime. "I'm here," she whispered.

That sparked a curiosity in him. "How exactly *are* you here?"

Chari smiled and struggled to push up, accepting the water he held for her with a grateful sip. "I saw your broadcast," she admitted, "and then I understand, Rafe, all of it, why you pushed me away, why you proposed in the first place, what it all meant. And I decided I was ready, because I knew you were no longer acting out of honor or obligation."

Rafe swallowed. "I was a coward."

Charli shook her head. "I didn't make it easy for you."

He leaned into her touch. "You make everything easy for me. So let me say it now, no contracts, no games. I love you, Charli. I think I have since the day I found you dancing in that club. And I was too scared to say it for so long, too scared to face the possibility of you needing to leave despite it."

"You have a lifetime to make it up to me," she whispered. "Because I love you too, Rafe. You were the first person to see me, the first person to believe in me, because you're brilliant and kind, because you care so much about what's right. For all those reasons and so many more."

Rafe kissed her hand. "A lifetime, you say?"

She nodded. "I still have our license. And you are a man of honor."

Rafe licked his lips. "Maybe not that much honor, Princess."

It made her whole body light up, bursting to flame and need at the very possibility of all that Rafe had in store for her that night and for many, many more nights to come.

There were just a few things they need to get out of the way first. "What happened to Anthony?"

"Madison heard the shot," Rafe explained. "Anthony survived, but he's going away for a long time. He'll lose his position and his titles."

"Good," she said. "He's not deserving of his titles."

"Nope," Rafe's voice got very low. "But you know who is, Little Brat?"

Charli was saved from a very uncomfortable conversation with a nurse about her blood pressure when the door opened, and a flood of people spilled in. Morgan, Rhylee, Saint, Emerson, Skylar—and the Sinclair Seven.

"Brothers are way overrated," Emerson said, placing flowers on Charli's bedside. "How do you feel about some sisters, instead?"

"Look—" Morgan pointed at her upper arm, the same spot where Charli wore a bandage. "We're already twins!"

And that was how it went, the lot of them, cooing over her, sharing the love and friendship Charli had always craved but never wanted to admit to, making her feel as if she were part of a family who truly wanted her, rather than a family who saw her only as a pawn in a grand game of power and deceit.

And right at the center of it all was Rafe, never taking his eyes off her for long, never leaving her side, showing her, as he had done so many times before, that she was his, just as he was hers.

And that together, they could do anything.

Epilogue

One year later

"Total punk princess, I *love* it."

Charli grinned at Rhylee in the mirror. "The Princess of Comtois *did not*."

One look at Charli's piercings and new tattoos, visible below the lace sleeves of her designer wedding dress, the princess had turned her nose up and made a distinct sniffing sound. She hadn't been the only one to voice their concerns about Princess *Charli* running the country, and Charli was certain she would spend more of her life in the tabloids than not, but only one person's opinion had mattered to her on her wedding day.

And Raffaello *loved* her tattoos. And her piercings — *all* of them.

It really was a boon to have friends who owned a tattoo shop, especially when those friends shared the same…interests.

It was why they were back in Duchess now, the first stop on their honeymoon after a wedding to end all weddings.

And why Charli was back in a wedding dress.

Or something close to it.

The dress *was* white. But this one had a low hem, enough to show off the dark ink she had been collecting over the year, and she had earrings in every hole along the conch of her ear. Her septum piercing was matching silver, with glistening pearl inlays. Instead of the demure pink lipstick she had conceded to for the Royal Wedding, she wore the same bold red color she had worn the night she'd gone dancing in Helena, a night that had changed her life forever.

"Those old biddies need a little excitement in their lives," Rhylee said. "And with you as the Royal Princess, they will *get it!*"

Charli grinned at Rhylee in the reflection. The dresses Charli had picked for her friends to wear were black, elegant and lacy, and with her hair and makeup done up, Rhylee looked like a movie star.

Perhaps it wasn't traditional to have a second wedding. But Charli and Rafe had wanted something for themselves, without the press and the pomp and circumstance, just something with them and their closest friends, in the place where they had found each other.

And hell, Charli had never been one for tradition, anyway.

Rhylee pulled Charli in close. "You look beautiful. Happy."

Charli leaned her head on Rhylee's shoulder. "I am."

It was the truth.

Before either of them could cry off their makeup, there was a knock on the door, and Saint popped her head in. "We're almost ready."

Rhylee gestured for her to come in, and a moment later she was followed by Skylar, Morgan, and Emerson, all looking pretty as pictures in their bridesmaids' dresses.

Charli did almost cry then.

Because she had never believed, never hoped, that she would find friends like them, vivacious, passionate, kind, caring women who lifted each other up every chance they got.

"Oh, Raffaello is going to *lose it* when he sees you," Morgan said. "Hell, if you weren't already married, I'd sweep you away myself."

"Pretty sure I laid claim first," Rhylee teased.

In the year since Charli had learned of The Ranch and its devilish secrets, her world had opened. Raffaello had introduced her to a million sensual pleasures, and she had helped him discover several, as well. They sometimes played with the others, inviting Rhylee or Dante and Saint into Rafe's steam room, and Charli had come to appreciate the hot houses of home in a whole new light.

"There's enough of me to go around," she teased, kissing Rhylee on the cheek and then Morgan. "But I think my husband gets first taste."

"Oh, *first* taste," Emerson joked. "Do we need to tell you about what happens on the wedding night."

That made them all laugh, and Charli just watched in the mirror as her friends stood at her side and brightened her day, her life. It had taken so much to get to this point, where she could put her burden down and live her life authentically, free from the strictures and rules that had confined her for so long.

And all that work had been worth it.

With one final group hug, they all made their way out of the room and toward the lodge. And then, one by one, they walked out of the back door and up the small mountain path, disappearing out of sight.

And then it was Charli's turn.

The first time she had walked the aisle to Raffaello, it had been on his father's arm. Now, as she stood in the mountains, surrounded by the bright colors of the fading trees, bursts of fiery orange and yellow, a clear blue sky overhead, Charli took the steps alone.

She had started her journey to Rafe, to her new life, alone, as well. But that had all changed, and Charli knew, without a shadow of a doubt, that she would never be alone again.

She took a deep breath, and then crested the small mountain to the clearing they had picked for their private ceremony. A wooden altar stood in the center of the clearing, covered in Montana wildflowers, and opening to a wide, wild view of the mountain beyond. To one side stood her friends, each looking beautiful in their black gowns. To the other side, Raffaello's friends, Charli's friends, in sharp suits, topped with matching cowboy hats.

And right there in the middle was Raffaello.

Charli caught and held his gaze as she walked the final steps, never breaking eye contact as she handed her bouquet to Saint and then took Rafe's hand.

Dante slipped out of the line and came to stand before them. "Now, I did go through the *whole* process of getting my online minister's license, but since you two are already married we can skip all that. I believe you've both prepared your own vows."

They nodded.

Dante grinned. "Princess, would you like to begin?"

Charli looked deep into Raffaello's eyes, blue as the sea they loved, bright and filled with passion and joy, her intense, controlled Rafe, who had welcomed her into a whole new path, who had supported and loved her every step of the way.

"Rafe," she murmured. She glanced at her friends, then gave Rafe a wicked grin, "Master Raffaello..."

Rafe pressed his thumb against the sensitive part of her wrist. "Cheeky..."

Charli couldn't help but smile. "As a princess, I grew up hearing all about the happily ever after. Every princess got her storybook ending, her prince and palace, her big white dress. But I never believed, never dared to hope, that life would be for me. When you live in the shadows of expectation and self-doubt for so long, you start to believe what others think of you."

She took a deep breath. "And then I met *my* prince. And you were the first person to see me for *me*, to have faith, to help me step out of the box that had been built around me. You opened up my world, Rafe, and with it, you opened my heart to possibilities — the possibility of a shared life. I had written off my happy ending because I didn't dare hope. But as I stand here with you now, I have nothing but hope, hope and love. Because *you* are my happily ever after."

Rafe's smile deepened, the soft crinkles around his eyes making him look boyish and beautiful. Her prince.

"Charlotte," he started.

Her mouth dropped open. "Now who's being cheeky?"

He just gave her a dangerous grin. "You came into my life like a hurricane, at a time when I already felt like I was losing control. You were wild and passionate and beautiful, and I was terrified you were going to turn my life completely upside down."

That got a few laughs from his friends.

"You did," Rafe continued. "You broke down my barriers and pushed me to the limit. You *challenged* me, Charli, and with that challenge you have and continue each and every day to make me a better man. With you at my side, I know I have the space to breathe, to grow, to evolve, because you are the kind of woman who never backs down, who never gives up, and who lives each day as if it were the greatest gift. Charli, you are *my* gift. And I promise to cherish you for the rest of our lives."

In the distance, Charli heard Dante telling them to kiss, but she was already reaching for Rafe, pulling him in, finding the connection they both craved. They kissed on the mountaintop, surrounded by their closest friends, and Charli knew that her whole new life was about to begin.

* * * *

Later that night, after champagne and dancing and toasts and cake, the party she hadn't been able to enjoy at the Royal Wedding, Rafe carried Charli across the threshold. It wasn't a typical bridal scene, to be brought to a room filled with kink toys and restraints, but it was perfect for them.

"Wife," Rafe said, sitting on the bed with Charli in his lap.

"Husband," she responded.

"Was it terrible of me to expect sass from you up at the altar?" he teased, brushing a loose curl behind her ear. "I thought Dante was going to say *kiss* and you were going to put your hands on your hips and ask why."

"That's only for you," she replied, kissing his throat and anything else she could reach. "I would never be bratty for Dante."

Rafe chuckled. "Lucky me." He pulled her face close to hold her gaze. "I mean it, Charli. Lucky me."

She nodded. "Lucky me, too." Charli pushed up to stand. "I have a wedding day present for you."

Rafe grinned. "Great minds think alike. I have one for you too."

"Mine first," Charli said. "But you have to come get it."

She pointed to the zipper of her dress, and Rafe came up behind her, dragging one hand across her waist and using the other to slowly pull the zipper down. And then he stopped, the zipper just at her waist. "Do you like it?"

It was a large tattoo of a lion on her shoulder, an illustration she had worked with Saint on until it was completely perfect. Because Rafe was her lion, her prince, her ruler, and because she was proud to stand by his side each and every day,

"I love it, Charli," he murmured, his voice full of awe. "It's incredible."

Charli turned. "You're incredible, Raffaello. And now you're mine. Forever."

Rafe kissed Charli's forehead. "It seems we might have had similar thoughts," he said. He walked over to the nightstand and pulled out a large velvet box.

"We're already married," Charli teased.

Rafe shook his head. "This is just for us."

He opened the box. Inside was an elegant choker. It looked like a tiara, with peaks and points, and was made of glistening diamonds. "Be mine, Charli. Forever. Wear my collar, and be mine."

Charli's eyes welled with tears, and she choked them back. Because they had been playing for nearly a year, and each night in their shared intimacy and kink only brought them closer, only connected them on a deeper, more carnal level, a level of trust and respect that would never be broken.

To be his was like nothing else in the world.

"Raffaello," Charli choked out.

Rafe gave a good-natured shake of his head. "Try again, Princess."

Charli grinned despite herself. "*Master* Raffaello."

"Not anymore, Princess. From the moment you put this on, it's simply Master. Your Master, only yours."

She wanted him to collar her like she wanted air to breathe. Charli stepped out of her wedding dress, and because she knew it would push her husband to the limit, because she knew what a picture it would paint with her wedding lingerie and heels and red lipstick, she dropped to her knees.

"That's right, Little Brat," Rafe said, his voice dark and straining, her Rafe, right at the edge of his control. "I said you'd crawl to me."

"You say a lot of things," Charli teased. "It's hard to keep track."

Rafe gazed down at her. Dark. Commanding. "Then let me remind me you... I said you would crawl to me, dripping wet, a plug in your tight little ass and a gag in your mouth so you couldn't talk back." He eyed her.

"Do you know what color goes so well with white, Little Brat? Pink…"

Charli whimpered because, even after all this time, she still craved the filthy, dark words Rafe tormented her with, craved his demands and domination, enough that instead of teasing back, she stretched forward.

And then she began to crawl.

She had crawled to him before, stuffed and plugged and dripping wet, but there was something altogether different about crawling for her collar, for her *Master*, and soon Charli's body was aching with need, desperation coiling in her belly, want and need making her nipples tight and her pussy clench and her patience disappear.

"The sight of you on your knees is…delicious," Rafe murmured. "So, I ask again, Princess, would you do me the greatest honor in the world. Would you wear my collar?"

Charli swallowed hard. "It would be my honor…Master."

Rafe's eyes blazed at that. Charli kneeled before him, hot and needy and aching as Rafe lifted the beautiful tiara collar from the box and locked it. It placed delicious pressure on her throat, and when Charli swallowed, it felt that much more intense, a throbbing building from deep within her. One she knew only Rafe could tame.

"Such a pretty word on your pretty lips, Little Brat," Rafe said, dragging his hand up her throat, and pressing his thumb to her lower lip. "You know how I like seeing you tied up."

"Devil," Charli whispered, unable to keep from responding to him, even now after all this time.

"And here's the deal you just made," Rafe replied. "I'm going to fill you up like you're *aching* for, and then I'm going to tie you down to the bench and pleasure you until you forget your name. And then again."

"Cocky," Charli teased, loving how the word made her throat bob against the collar.

Rafe grinned. "That's very much the point, Princess," he said. "Now, stand for me. I want to see all this beautiful white lace before it gets dirty…"

Charli took his hand and stood, then turned in a circle to show off the wedding lingerie and the large tattoo on her shoulder.

"Beautiful," Rafe whispered, his voice reverent. He leaned down and placed a kiss on the curve of her ass. "Bend over, Charli, I want to see what's mine."

She shot him a glare, but bent over, only gasping a little as Rafe pushed the string of her thong to one side and exposed her ass and pussy to the cool room.

"Tell me, Princess, do you feel…empty?"

Charli shook her head. "Not a bit."

He slapped her ass, just enough to send a bolt of desire and pleasure racing up her spine. "Try again, Little Brat."

"Fine," Charli bit out. "Yes…I'm…*empty.*"

"Where?" Rafe teased.

"My pussy," Charli responded, knowing it wasn't the answer he was looking for. It earned her another slap.

"Please…" She bucked against Rafe's hold.

"You don't get to beg if you don't follow the rules, Charli. So, I'll ask again. Do you feel empty?"

Charli tore the words off with her teeth. "Yes…I need…I need the plug in my ass…"

"Better," Rafe said. "But I know you have more you want to say. So stop playing games and be a good girl for once."

Charli's glare darkened. "Please...Daddy...please plug up my tight little asshole..."

"Since you asked so nicely..."

A second later, Charli felt the cool press of the lubed plug at her entrance, and she gripped Rafe's strong thigh as he pushed the toy in, filling her, stretching her.

"So pretty," he said. "So pretty stretched around the plug." He tapped the tip and it sent a powerful wash of pleasure bursting through her sensitized nerves. Then he stood, his powerful body looming and intense over her, and she felt its absence the second Master Rafe walked away.

Not Master Rafe.

Just Master. Her Master.

So when he spoke from the other side of the room, his dark tone so familiar in its need and aching, burning desire to lose control, she listened. Because she wanted to. Because they had *earned* this.

"Crawl to me, Princess..."

Charli did, the action so humiliating and base, so incredibly hot and intense, her entire body on fire, burning up, making her pussy wetter and her nipples harder, and she watched him as she crawled, loving the harsh desire in her husband's eyes, sliced through with white-hot need that mirrored her own.

"I will never get tired of seeing you on your knees, Little Brat," he whispered. "But right now, I think I'd prefer to see you all tied up."

It was the work of a moment for him to lift her and lock her into the bench, the same kind of bench that had first caught her attention a year before, and each click of the lock and tie of the restraint made Charli's own restraint fly out of the window, because *fuck,* she needed this man like she needed to breathe, and he was touching her in all the ways he knew would drive her crazy, all the ways that would push her right up to the very edge. Control and power, that was Rafe.

And she loved him for it.

Loved, even more, when she could be the one to push him to the edge.

Charli wiggled as best she could in her restrained position. "Are you done playing with your toys?"

That earned her a swat on the ass. "If you keep acting like a little brat, I'm never going to be done playing with you," Rafe said. "Is that what you want to be, Charli, my toy?"

She choked on the word, instinct telling her to rebel, desire telling her to submit, the war as vicious and passionate as the line between pain and pleasure. "No."

Another swat. "And here I thought we were doing so well."

Behind her, Charli could hear the sound of Rafe undressing, carefully placing his jacket on the bed, then removing his shoes, his cufflinks, undoing the buttons of his shirt. Each sound was as loud as gunfire, with how tuned into him she was.

"*We...*" Charli choked out a laugh. "Like you're the one with the plug in your ass..."

"I could take it out," he threatened.

Her brat broke. "No...please... Keep it in, Sir."

Rafe's voice was positively lethal. "And is there anything else you want...in?"

Charli grinned. "Only you, Sir. Please..."

"Please, Master."

"Please..." She reveled in the silence, even as her need overwhelmed her, a hot, living thing that stole her breath and made her beg. "Master."

In the next second, Rafe pressed his cock against her slick entrance, and then he was pushing inside, stretching her full around the plug and making Charli whimper. She was locked and tied in place, entirely at Rafe's mercy, and that was how they both wanted it...how they both needed it.

And then Rafe was sliding in and out, his thrusts hard and slow, as if doing his very best to push her to the very edge, and each one did, again and again, Charli locked in place, only able to take what he gave her.

"So fucking perfect," Rafe muttered, as if the words had been stolen from his lips. "Even when you open your bratty little mouth."

"You love it..." she taunted, sucking in a harsh breath when he gripped her chin and turned her head toward his for a brutal kiss.

"I do," Rafe admitted. "And I'm especially going to love seeing you wear my collar in front of the whole country, just like you wear my ring. Because you're mine, Charli."

"I'm yours..." she whispered, and in the spiral of emotion and desire and friction and fight, they broke together, a single new thrust, a stolen kiss, a white-hot barb that took them both spiraling into the abyss, shaking, coming, thrusting, falling hard and fast in each other's arms until they were both hoarse and wracked with pleasure.

* * * *

It turned out, in some fairy tales, the princess didn't just save herself, she saved the prince as well, a fishing boat for a white steed, a corrupt brother for a fire-breathing dragon, beautiful new friends for magical godmothers.

And if it turned out that some happy endings were...well, a little kinkier than most, that was part of what made them so happy, right? The rest, well, the rest was the love they shared, the country they stewarded, and a lifetime of chapters they were going to write together.

Charli had never believed in fairy tales. Until she met her prince.

And they rode off into the Montana sunset together...and lived, truly and without reservation, *happily ever after*.

Sign up for our newsletter and find out about all our romance book releases, eBook sales and promotions, sneak peeks and FREE romance books!

Want to see more from this author?
Here's a taster for you to enjoy!

Triple Diamond:
The Lovin' is Easy
Gemma Snow

Excerpt

"A *what?*"

Against the din of the ancient window air conditioner chugging into the room, Madison's voice had a tinny, almost petulant sound. But of all the things she had expected from the impromptu meeting with some family estate lawyer she'd never heard of, *this* wasn't it.

"A *ranch*, Ms. Hollis," Mr. Sidney replied, the tone of his voice indicating that he'd picked up on her confusion and ensuing frustration with the afternoon's events and that, frankly, he didn't care. "The Triple Diamond Ranch in Wolf Creek, Montana, to be exact."

Madison rubbed her hands over her face and tried to make sense of everything. Mr. Sidney had contacted her a week prior about a will left to her by some uncle on her mother's side, an uncle she'd never heard of, from a mother who'd been gone some eighteen years now. She took a deep breath, trying a different tack.

"Are you certain this is my uncle" — she glanced at the stack of legal documents two inches thick on the desk before her — "Mason?"

Mr. Sidney peered down at her over the wire rim of his thin glasses — a remarkable feat, given that she had at least two inches on the man, who sat short and boney in the chair across the desk.

"Mr. Mason Westerly King first arranged this inheritance with Sidney and Sidney nearly two decades ago," he replied. "We've had ample time to determine and confirm your identity, Ms. Hollis."

Madison resisted the urge to roll her eyes, but only just. Mr. Sidney's attitude came on the tail of what had already been the week from hell. She sighed, her heavy breath spilling out of her mouth like a deflating hot air balloon. *It's only Wednesday.*

"Mr. Sidney, I'm afraid I still don't quite understand. What am I supposed to do with a ranch" — she gestured with her hand — "I don't know, eight, ten hours away from here?"

He gave a slow blink. "My advice, Ms. Hollis, is to go inspect the ranch yourself. You have all the information on the mineral rights and past financial records. Once you get the lay of the land, you can determine whether you wish to sell or keep the property. But otherwise, after I get your signature on these forms, I'm afraid there's not much else I can help you with."

Madison did scowl that time, but with her head bent over the stack of papers while signing the requisite lines, he couldn't see it. She was perfectly pleased to be done with Mr. Sidney for good, but he was wrong about one major thing. She wasn't going to decide whether or not to keep the ranch — she had decided the very first time he had mentioned the word *inheritance*. No, the second she got out to Montana, she would sell the damn thing and be done with it. Maybe then everything would go back to normal. *Ha. Yeah, right.*

About the Author

Gemma Snow loves high heat, high adventures and high expectations for her heroes! Her stories are set in the past and present, from the glittering streets of Paris to cowboy-rich Triple Diamond Ranch in Wolf Creek, Montana.

In her free time, she loves to travel, and spent several months living in a fourteenth-century castle in the Netherlands. When not exploring the world, she likes dreaming up stories, eating spicy food, driving fast cars and talking to strangers. She recently moved to Nashville with a cute redheaded cat and a cute redheaded boy.

Gemma loves to hear from readers. You can find her contact information, website details and author profile page at https://www.firstforromance.com

ENTWINED PUBLISHING

www.ingramcontent.com/pod-product-compliance
Lightning Source LLC
Chambersburg PA
CBHW032238010726
47494CB00002B/538